Praise for *Never In Ink*

"In *Never in Ink*, Jax gives the reader yet another can't-put-down mystery. The storyline pits one man's desire to hide his secret against the private investigators' hunger to uncover it. This battle of wills will keep you reading through the night. Five-star read!"

—Jordana Green, host of *The Jordana Green Show*, WCCO Radio

"With mystery novels, nothing is ever as it seems, nor should it be—and *Never in Ink* has a never-ending well of surprises. Well-developed characters and a fast-paced, suspenseful plot will keep the reader itching for more."

—*US Review of Books*

Praise for *Sapphire Trails*

"Delightfully suspenseful story. *Sapphire Trails* by Marilyn Jax is one of those books that readers will speed through yet wish for more after the ending. All the scenes are active, and there are enough sequels between the scenes to (barely) give readers a chance to catch their breath before diving into another nail-biting scene."

—Judge, Writer's Digest Book Awards

"A truly riveting read that captures the reader's total attention from beginning to end. *Sapphire Trails* clearly identifies Marilyn Jax as an experienced and singularly gifted novelist who will leave her readers eagerly looking toward her next literary effort. A solid entertainment from first page to last, *Sapphire Trails* is highly recommended for personal reading lists and community library collections."

—*Midwest Book Review*

Praise for *Road to Omalos*

"Jax expertly weaves this gripping narrative from the opening paragraph. Meticulously drawn details entice and enthrall, consistently employing the five senses to bring her literary vision vividly to life. Vibrantly depicted characters often struggle with conscience as they vacillate between virtue and obligation, in an array of interlacing subplots that serve to enhance this spellbinding tale."

—*US Review of Books*

"Marilyn Jax has done it again! The suspense, interplay, and conflict between the characters will keep the reader on edge right up to the brilliant, unexpected, and explosive ending. A Greek thriller!"

—**Dr. Thomas Rumreich, forensic odontologist**

Praise for *The Find*

"*The Find* is a gripping, suspenseful murder mystery from beginning to end. Modern criminology is joined with Aztec history to solve a murder decades old and to give flesh and narrative to a skeleton found beneath the rubble. Throughout the novel, there is much to uncover. Written in a crisp style, *The Find* is quite a find!"

—**Michael Berenbaum, author, lecturer**

"From the Caribbean to Miami to London and back, the plot has more twists than even the most addicted mystery buff can handle. Just when you think you've solved the case, a new suspect takes you in another direction. Marilyn Jax has written a thriller that will keep you guessing to the very end."

—**Ron Meshbesher, past president of the National Association of Criminal Defense Lawyers**

ALSO BY MARILYN JAX

The Find

Road to Omalos

Sapphire Trails

Never In Ink

. . . and watch for *I Heard Everything*

THE PLOY

a novel

For Jackie,
Enjoy!

THE PLOY

a novel

MARILYN JAX

INTERNATIONAL AWARD-WINNING AUTHOR

BEAVER'S
POND
PRESS

This book is a work of fiction. Names, characters, places, and incidents either are
products of the author's imagination or are used fictitiously. Any resemblance to
actual events or locales or persons, living or dead, is entirely coincidental.

ISBN 13: 978-1-59298-752-8

Library of Congress Catalog Number: 2017910639

Printed in Canada

First Printing: 2017

21 20 19 18 17   5 4 3 2 1

Also available electronically.

Author photograph by Patrick Broderick.
Cover and interior design by James Monroe Design, LLC.

Beaver's Pond Press, Inc.
7108 Ohms Lane
Edina, MN 55439-2129
(952) 829-8818
www.BeaversPondPress.com

BEAVER'S
POND
PRESS

To order, visit www.BeaversPondBooks.com or call (800) 901-3480.
Reseller discounts available.

Dedicated to my beloved, Daniel,

Who shares the roller coaster of life with me.

The ups. The downs. The rounds and rounds.

The turns. Steep slopes. The ever-changing panorama.

My love for you is without end.

ACKNOWLEDGMENTS

To my loyal reader base and to my new readers, I thank you. Your insatiable thirst for more Caswell & Lombard mysteries is the inspiration for my creativity.

Daniel, *The Ploy* is dedicated to you. You've been by my side through thick and thin during the writing of each book in the series. Thank you for your ever-present support, encouragement, and love.

To my amazing family of relatives and friends, your cheering on is a constant shot in my arm stimulating vision and inventiveness within me to create each next installment. Thank you.

Also, I wish to extend a heartfelt thank-you to my simply amazing managing editor and friend, Hanna Kjeldbjerg, for her ever-present source of belief in me and for her invaluable guidance; James Monroe, my master designer, for his incredible gift of creativity that he shares with me when he designs the covers and interiors of my books; my skilled editors and proofreaders, Angela Wiechmann, Erik Hane, and Sara and Chris Ensey; and the staff at

Beaver's Pond Press.

Finally, *The Ploy* reminds me of my endless days in Miami Beach—"The Beach" to those who live there—a place of everlasting sunshine, azure skies, turquoise waters, graceful palm trees, and breathtaking fuchsia bougainvillea hedges; a place of hot and muggy weather, people-watching, congested traffic, and high crime. Thank you, Miami Beach, for your flair, neon lights, and inspiration.

PROLOGUE

CLAIRE CASWELL COLLAPSED into the arms of a padded brocade chair, pulled her legs onto the nearby ottoman, and vigorously kicked off her blush-pink satin heels. She sank back into the cushy seating and exhaled loudly. She closed her eyes, blissfully.

She slowly blinked them open, focusing on the ceiling of the opulent hotel room.

Guy could tell she was deep in thought. He walked over and gently kissed her on the forehead. "Are you okay?"

"I'm okay," she said. "Just a little overwhelmed." She took in a deep breath and released it slowly. "Did we just *get married*?"

Her gaze fell to the wedding dress cloaking her body. Her hands gripped its lace and satin overlay. A look of astonishment pranced across her face. Then alarm.

Guy stooped down and watched her closely. "You're kidding, right?"

Claire turned her head and looked him squarely in his eyes. "Yes, of course I'm kidding, you silly thing. *We're married! We finally did it!*"

1

Office of Caswell & Lombard, Private Investigation
Miami Beach, Florida

CLAIRE CASWELL LIFTED the steaming peppermint tea to her lips. She had filled the flamingo mug to its very brim, and she cautiously took a short sip. It was too hot, and it burned her mouth. She nearly dropped it to her desk attempting to set it down.

"Ouch!" she pronounced loudly. "My mind is somewhere else today. I should have waited 'til it cooled a bit."

"Are you all right?" Jin asked.

"Yeah, I think so. Very preoccupied, though."

Every time she was overly absorbed in her thoughts, it usually preceded something major. She reminded herself to be vigilant.

Remaining seated, she turned her office chair around and set her attention on the student. She disappeared in thought and momentarily reflected back to the day she and Guy Lombard had hired Jin Ikeda as an intern at their private investigation firm. Jin was currently a third-year law student at the University of Miami School of Law, and when he wasn't attending classes or studying, he was working at the Caswell & Lombard firm. In a short time, he had become an invaluable part of the business. It had been close to a year already. How time had flown.

Claire let her mind drift. Gaston "Guy" Lombard, her business and life partner, and now husband, was out on a case interviewing a prospective client, and that provided her some time to catch up on the never-ending stacks of paperwork cluttering her desk.

The phone rang.

"For you, Ms. Caswell," Jin announced.

Claire picked up the phone.

"Yes? Claire Caswell here."

She listened.

"*What? . . . How? . . . When? . . .*" she asked.

Her eyes jolted wide open, and her voice trembled with shock and horror. She listened carefully as the caller continued.

"But I saw her yesterday. *Yesterday!*" Claire protested. "It's not possible. She's . . . my friend." She hesitated, her voice breaking up. "Yes. I'll be there Friday. Yes, I'll say a few words."

Claire hung up and let her head fall down to her desk, catching her forehead in her hands. She closed her eyes. She stayed in this position for a time, permitting her mind to reminisce.

Fun times she'd spent in her college days with Charlotte Truman frolicked through her head. She had so many memories. The two had been kindred spirits from the first time they'd met—similar personalities, interests, and even likes and dislikes. How could her friend be gone? Tears began to well in her eyes. Claire would never again be able to spend time with Charlotte. There would be no more lunches, shopping sprees, or talking on the phone for hours. The loss was immeasurable.

Charlotte had been killed instantly in a fatal car accident, and all the treasured things the two shared had been taken away forever in the blink of an eye. Without warning. Without so much as a chance to say good-bye.

Time blurred.

She felt a soft touch on her left shoulder. She lifted her head and opened her eyes.

"Ms. Caswell, is there anything I can do?" Jin asked.

"No, Jin. Please hold my calls for the rest of the day."

Claire's face looked as white as a cloud, and her expression was one of disturbed surprise.

"Are you okay, Ms. Caswell?" Jin persisted. "You don't look well. Maybe I should contact Mr. Lombard?"

"No, thank you, Jin. He's busy with an interview. It won't change a thing if you interrupt him now. I'll tell him when he returns." She hesitated. "I'm going out for a walk. Please hold down the fort." The sadness in her voice was unmistakable.

As Claire walked she thought about the day before.

CHARLOTTE TRUMAN had bulldozed her way into the office of Caswell & Lombard, Private Investigation. It was ten minutes to noon.

"Thank goodness you're here—we're going to lunch!" Charlotte announced. She walked over to her friend, leaned down, and gave Claire a quick hug.

"Now?" Claire asked.

"Yes. Right now! I have something to show you."

There was a sense of playful mystery in Charlotte's voice. Her eyes sparkled with vivaciousness.

Claire closed the file she was working on and stood up. "Okay. Let's go."

"I'm celebrating! And I'm treating!" Charlotte announced.

"Guy, I'm having lunch with Charlotte," Claire called out. "I'll be back soon."

Guy looked up from his work. "Enjoy yourselves." He flashed his famous grin. "I know you will."

"And I'm driving too!" Charlotte said.

The two walked from the office. Before long, Claire saw the source of Charlotte's exuberance.

"It's a beauty!" Claire said, staring at the latest model of a Porsche Cayenne SUV—white with black wheels. She peeked inside the sparkling-clean vehicle. The interior was white leather piped in black. "Did you have to mortgage your home to buy this?"

"No, not quite." She giggled. "I've wanted it for a long time. And I figured if not now . . . when? Life is short." She beamed from ear to ear. "I walked into the dealership two weeks ago and bought it on the spot."

"Well, if anyone deserves it, you do. I don't know anyone who works harder than you."

"Jump in!" Charlotte said. "Wait 'til you see how it rides. Pure luxury!"

Claire was clearly impressed. "How much does a stockbroker get paid these days?" She smiled.

Charlotte smiled back. "I admit I've had a good year." She chuckled. "In fact, I've had a *great* year. Single women are buying luxury cars more and more, you know. They've captured a huge percentage of the sales. And why not?"

Soon the two arrived at an open-air restaurant located on The

Beach. The hostess led them to a table under a large umbrella, affording the friends a magnificent view of the water. It was a typical sun-drenched Miami day, and the shade was welcomed.

They ordered beverages and lobster salads tossed in a light orange dressing.

Minutes later, Charlotte looked like she was about to burst. "I can't hold it in a second longer, Claire. There's something else," she said. "I met a man. We're dating, and I've never been happier."

"Charlotte, that's wonderful," Claire said. "Who is he? Where did you meet?"

"You won't believe it. He works at the car dealership where I bought my SUV. He's the finance manager. Brilliant when it comes to numbers. And he's also a salesman there. He's quite nice to look at, too, although he's a bit older than I am." She hesitated. "I haven't felt this way in a long time, Claire. We've been together every minute the two of us have had free time over the past two weeks."

"A new car? And a new man? This is big news! We do have a lot to celebrate!"

The two friends clicked their iced teas together.

"To happiness," Claire said.

"To happiness!" Charlotte repeated.

"What's his name?" Claire asked.

"Stephen—with a *ph*, not a *v*—Fox." Charlotte's eyes looked amorous as she spoke of him. "I think I . . . love him, Claire. I've waited so long and then it happened so quickly."

CLAIRE JOLTED back to reality. How could life be this cruel? How could Charlotte have been so blissfully happy one day and wind up dead the next? It wasn't fair.

Claire returned to the office and was pleased to see Guy had returned.

"What happened, Claire?" Guy asked. "I just got back and Jin told me you received a terribly upsetting call."

"Guy, Charlotte is dead. She died in a car accident."

He rushed over and cradled her in his arms.

"*What?* We saw her yesterday!" A look of utter disbelief appeared on Guy's face.

Claire broke into tears. "I'll miss her, Guy. We've been good friends a long time."

"This doesn't seem right," he said. "It can't be right."

"It *can't* be," Claire echoed. She forced back the tears and gently broke away from Guy's embrace. She walked to her desk and called the Miami-Dade County Police Department.

"Captain Massey, please. It's Claire Caswell. He'll take my call."

She tapped her foot impatiently.

"Ms. Caswell. They pulled me out of a meeting. I know this must be important," the often-irritable captain said. He cracked his knuckles.

"I wouldn't interrupt you if it wasn't," Claire shot back. "I need some information, and I need it fast. A longtime friend, Charlotte Truman, was killed this morning in a car accident. I'd like to learn the specifics. Will you find out everything there is to know about the incident? I'll be forever grateful. It's a tough pill to swallow, and I want to make sure no stone is left unturned. This one hits close to home. Thank you, Captain Massey. I owe you yet another one."

"Yes, you will. And I do keep track," he said in his gravelly voice. He asked Claire for the accurate spelling of the victim's first and last name and the specifics of her vehicle. "I'll get right on it. And, Ms. Caswell—my condolences about your friend."

Guy observed Claire. It was clear her spirit was broken by the loss of her friend. And it was also clear that Claire was driven to find out exactly what had happened.

"If I can do *anything*, Claire, you know I'm here. Maybe you should take the rest of the day off. There's nothing Jin and I can't handle. Take some time to deal with your loss."

Claire mustered a forced smile. "I'd rather be here with you. Work keeps my mind busy. I have to stay busy."

Guy walked over and kissed her on her forehead. "I'm sorry, Claire. So sorry."

Jin sat at his desk in the back of the office, observing the interaction of the two investigators. He remained silent, but his mind went into overdrive. The sense of loss of someone close was always hard hitting and often unexpected. In this case, it was a permanent end to something Claire Caswell thought would always be a part of her life. He felt her pain.

While Jin's demeanor portrayed a stoic soon-to-be attorney on the outside—always immaculately dressed in gray or black slacks, a crisp pastel cotton shirt, and coordinating tie—his emotions, although tucked securely within, ran deep. He removed his round, rimless glasses and wiped his dark eyes. Over the months he had worked at Caswell & Lombard, Private Investigation, he had come to highly respect and like both Claire Caswell and Gaston Lombard. They had taught him more than any textbook ever could, and he owed them everything. He knew that once he graduated from law school, his experience working at the firm would provide him an invaluable step up in the competitive job market. And he would forever be grateful. He looked over at Claire. She appeared devastated.

He walked to her desk. "Ms. Caswell, if there is anything you need—"

"Thank you, Jin. You're the best." She squeezed his hand.

CAPTAIN MASSEY telephoned Claire the following morning.

"I have that info you requested, Ms. Caswell," he said.

"Please give me everything."

"Here you go," he continued. "Charlotte Truman's car lost control at a high speed and plowed directly into the front glass of a restaurant. Her head went through the windshield, and the glass severed her jugular vein. She died instantly."

Silence followed as Claire absorbed his words.

"What about her seat belt? The airbag?" she asked.

"It looks like she was out of the cross strap of the belt at the time of impact, so only the lower horizontal strap was in place. And the airbag? It's impossible to determine what happened with that now." He hesitated. "Ms. Caswell, your friend never knew what hit her, if that gives you any solace. It happened in a flash."

"She was always an excellent driver. I don't get it. Did something mechanical go wrong with her new car? Did the accelerator stick? The brakes not work? What?"

"What was left of the car was towed to a station yesterday and thoroughly examined. The reports are clear. No mechanical reason for the accident was found, so a determination has been reached that the accident was a tragic case of driver error. No one else was in the car with her and fortunately no one in the restaurant was hurt."

"So . . . that's it?" Claire asked. "Is an autopsy going to be conducted?"

"Yes. Probably tomorrow."

"You said Charlotte was driving 'at a high speed.' At what speed was she traveling?"

"At least seventy."

"What is the speed limit in the area where the restaurant is located?"

"That's the funny part. Thirty-five."

Claire took a moment to process what she was hearing. "Oh, no, no, no!" She shook her head. "Charlotte was an extremely attentive driver. Something is not right with this."

"Was she going through any problems you were aware of?" Captain Massey asked. "A breakup? Work problems? Anything else? Perhaps something distracting her concentration? It happens."

"Not to her." Claire was definitive and couldn't be budged. "She was the happiest I've seen her in years. She just bought a new car, and she just met a man she was crazy about. No, I do not think she may have been distracted to that degree. Not a chance." She paused. "Can you give me the name of the station and mechanic who looked over her car?"

She jotted down the information as he spoke.

"The car is still there," the captain said. "In fact, if you'd feel better giving it your once-over—"

"You know I would," Claire interrupted. "Thanks for the information. I'll get back to you if I find anything."

"No problem, Ms. Caswell. Good luck on your quest."

"I won't stop until I know what happened. No matter how long it takes."

"That I know," he said. Cracking knuckles echoed in the background.

Claire thanked him, hung up, and turned to face Guy and Jin.

"I'm going out for a while," she said.

The female investigator stepped outside. She felt anger pulsing through her veins. She took a few breaths, and suddenly crumpled into tears.

2

CLAIRE DROVE TO the station and caught sight of Charlotte's wrecked vehicle. She felt a constriction tightening in her throat. The female investigator struggled to breathe as powerful choking emotions overtook her. She parked her car and forced herself to take deep breaths, each time exhaling slowly.

No one could have survived this accident, she thought. She wept. The SUV looked as if it had slammed into a brick wall traveling one hundred miles per hour. The rear half was basically all that remained.

Claire hesitated as she listened to the myriad of thoughts competing for attention in her mind. What had Charlotte's final thoughts been just before impact? Did she suffer horrific pain for a fleeting moment? How could she have possibly been so distracted that she'd plow into the front glass of a building at any speed, let alone seventy miles an hour? Charlotte was one who never exceeded the posted speed limit. Ever.

"No!" Claire shouted. She refused to accept or believe the crash was Charlotte's fault. Nothing added up. Nothing.

Claire gulped in another deep breath and stepped from her car. She placed one foot in front of the other as she made her way toward the remains of her friend's damaged vehicle. All at once the surroundings soared into a field of surreal images, and she felt as if she were gliding on air. Each footstep seemed lighter than the last. Progress was slow. Only feet to walk; and yet, it seemed like a mile. All instincts within her pushed her backward as she struggled forward.

"Can I help you, ma'am?"

The stifled sound of a male voice echoed through her head. She kept walking.

"Ma'am, can I be of any assistance?"

There was that voice again. Still muted.

It annoyed her.

Befogged, she trekked on.

Suddenly, the person belonging to the voice was standing directly in front of her, blocking her way. "No one goes near that vehicle! Understand?" His growl fractured her self-imposed cloud of protection.

Reality snarled at her, and with difficulty she fought back, trying to focus. Words poured out as if she automatically switched back into the *on* position.

"My name is Claire Caswell. I was a friend of the driver of this vehicle. The Miami-Dade Police captain, Captain Massey, gave me permission to take a look at it—inside and out. Call him to verify if you'd like."

"Hold tight, lady. Stop in your tracks. Don't take another step."

The serviceman yanked a piece of scratch paper from his shirt pocket, turned halfway around, and made a call on his cell phone. "Captain Massey, please."

The serviceman began to explain that a Claire Caswell was there, trying to approach and examine the crashed Cayenne, but he was cut short before he could complete his sentence.

"Of course she can have access!" the captain barked. "She's a top private investigator in Miami Beach, and she has the department's unbridled permission. Give her whatever she needs. Full and unlimited access. Any other questions?"

"No, sir."

The serviceman turned back to face Claire. He looked rattled. "Go ahead, ma'am. Take as much time as you need. Rear doors are open. Let me know if I can help."

She snapped back to full alertness.

"Who examined this vehicle when it was towed to the station?" Claire asked.

"That would be me. My name is Mick Allen. Oh, and a couple of members of Miami-Dade Police Department's forensics team. They were here too. I looked for any mechanical problems. And they searched for clues of foul play left behind—you know, evidence."

"And? And what did you all find?"

"Nothing. On all counts," Mick said. "Not a thing. And they talked about thoroughly investigating the crash site too. It was such an unusual accident that they had to explore all possibilities."

"Thank you, Mick. Now I'd like to take a look around. If I need anything, I'll let you know."

Claire pulled a pair of latex gloves from the stash she carried in her bag and stretched them onto her hands. She reached for the back door handle and felt Mick's breath on her back.

She turned and looked him directly in the face. "I'll need some time *alone* to process this, if you don't mind."

"Say no more, lady. I get it," the serviceman stuttered. His body started to shake. "The whole thing makes me kind of edgy. I think it's that smell inside."

He walked away.

Claire carefully pulled open the rear door and poked her head and upper body inside. She was immediately overtaken by the strong scent of Charlotte's favorite perfume. But there was something else. That pleasant fragrance was mixed with the distinctively pungent and sickeningly fruity odor of death. Claire choked back her raw emotions and briskly backed out of the car. She closed the door and drew in deep and prolonged breaths of fresh air.

Minutes passed. She pressed tissues over her nose and mouth and prepared to give it a second try. This had to be done, and she had to do it. She knew it wouldn't be easy. She reopened the door of the vehicle and pushed her head back inside. Even with the front of the car almost totally demolished and outside air pouring into the back, the smell was overwhelmingly rank. She sat down on the rear seat of the vehicle and closed her eyes. She relived the disastrous accident in her mind. She only hoped that Charlotte had not been conscious at the time of impact.

With her free hand Claire pulled a small LED flashlight from her pocket. She began to examine every remaining inch of the vehicle. The job would be grueling. But nothing could be overlooked. Nothing.

She spoke quietly to Charlotte. "I miss you, Charlotte! It's difficult to understand why you left. I have to talk to you, so I will." She whimpered. "I'm here, sitting in the back seat of your new car. There's not much remaining of the front end. I'm looking for clues to figure out what caused the crash. I have to know. Your driving skills were top notch, and this would never have happened without either mechanical error or foul play. Forensic investigators and a trained mechanic have searched and come up with nothing. Now it's my turn."

Talking to Charlotte gave Claire fleeting comfort.

She worked orderly and systematically in qualmish silence, searching everything remaining inside the back of the SUV. The investigator moved slowly and proceeded with caution. She covered the back seats, the floor mats, the carpet, the rear doors and handles, the remaining windows, the console, down the sides of the back seats, the space under the headrests, and anything and everything in between. Then she examined the seat belts. Nearly two hours passed.

She stepped outside to take a rest. She dialed Captain Massey.

"Any word on the autopsy yet, Captain?"

"I'll let you know as soon as I get the results," he said. His voice dropped, and suddenly he seemed uncharacteristically reflective. "In a split second your friend lost her life. It makes us all think, doesn't it?" He paused. "We believe we'll live forever, and then something like this happens to show us how wrong we are."

"I know." She paused. "I've had similar thoughts." She inhaled and exhaled completely. "I've been examining what's left of Charlotte's vehicle for the past couple of hours. You said your forensic workers were thorough and found no clues, including fingerprints, but a total absence of fingerprints in those back seats strikes me as odd. There must be some somewhere. I'd like another favor, Captain."

"Yes, Ms. Caswell?"

"I'll be here a while longer. Would you please send over one of your top forensics investigators with a fingerprinting kit? I'd like to hone in on a couple of areas in the back seat. I need to do this to satisfy something nagging at me. I've been wearing gloves, of course, so none of my prints will be present." She paused to catch her breath. "I'll owe you two favors now."

"Yes, you will. At least." He cracked his knuckles. "And, yes, I'll ask one of my brightest to meet you at the station. He was there for the first round also. Hold tight. I, too, am hopeful something will turn up to tell us what the hell happened."

"Thank you, Captain. I'll keep you posted. Oh, and one more thing."

"Yes?" he grunted.

"Was Charlotte's purse found in the wreckage?"

"Hold on a minute," he said. The sound of crumpling paperwork could be heard in the background. "Yes. But it was smashed almost beyond recognition. I'm looking at the accident report now."

Claire continued her sweeping examination of the car. Her inner voice—the one she never ignored—kept telling her there was more to the story, and it nudged her to concentrate on the seat belts. She changed her focus and began to eyeball every part of the seat belts: the lap straps, the diagonal sashes, the retractors used to hold the straps when not in use, and the buckles.

The forensics expert, Stanley O'Leary, arrived and, at Claire's insistence, went over the seat belts and buckles for a second time.

"I've already done this, miss," he insisted. "I carefully went over everything left of this car."

"Just humor me, please," Claire said.

Time passed.

As before, Stanley found nothing of interest when he reexamined the rear seat belts. But when he looked again at where the driver's seat had once been, he noticed something. He scrutinized the buckle that served to secure the tongue of the driver's seat belt. It was still intact, close to the foot area of the backseat passenger space. Something caught his eye. He could see a problem.

"Ah, what's *this*?" Stanley asked.

"What is it? What did you find?" Claire asked.

"Not sure how I missed this before," he muttered under his breath as he continued his routine.

"What?" Claire persisted.

The forensic expert continued working as if he had not heard Claire's questions. Minutes passed in silence. Claire knew not to speak again until Stanley did.

Finally, he spoke. His voice was serious and hushed, and he seemed genuinely disturbed. "Someone monkeyed around with the driver's seat belt. It was tinkered with."

Claire stared at him. "Meaning exactly *what*?"

"Meaning once your friend locked the seat belt around her, she could never have released it without cutting her way out. She was trapped."

The color drained from Claire's face.

Stanley stared at the remains of the vehicle, clearly stunned by the revelation.

Claire called out to Mick. "Mick, we need you. Come here, please."

Mick rushed over. "What is it? Did you find something?"

"Yeah, we did," Claire said. "The driver's seat belt was fiddled with. The driver couldn't have released it if she had wanted to."

"I missed it," Mick said. He swallowed with difficulty. "If someone messed with the seat belt, are you thinking this crash was intentional? Or could the impact of the accident have caused the seat belt to lock in place?" He looked to Stanley for an answer.

"I'd normally say yes to your second question, but in this case there is definite evidence of tampering. There are peculiar impressions visible right here—definite scrape marks caused by a clamp. Look." Stanley pointed them out. "So my answer to your first question is yes. This crash most likely was intentional."

"*Shit!*" Mick said.

"Is there any way to check the accelerator at this point?" Stanley asked.

"In a word, no," Mick said. "There's nothing left to check."

Claire stared straight ahead. "Except for the tampering marks of the jammed seat belt, this might have been the perfect crime."

"Captain Massey mentioned the victim was your friend. Who would have wanted to hurt her?" Stanley asked.

"That's the question," Claire said.

"Well, I must say you have your work cut out for you," Stanley said. "There are no fingerprints on the seat belt buckle, so whoever did this wore gloves. My guess is the person or persons responsible for this may have also interfered with the accelerator so it would have stuck when depressed. The driver would not have been able to stop or slow down. We'll never know for sure, but considering the speed at which your friend barreled into that restaurant window, it's about the only thing that makes any sense. It's clear she lost all control of the vehicle." He paused, obviously deep in thought. "It was a death drive. She had no way out."

Claire steadied herself. "It was premeditated," she declared. "*Charlotte was murdered.*"

3

THE FUNERAL SERVICE for Charlotte was rapidly approaching, and Claire had agreed to say a few words. Captain Massey had instructed her not to mention the tampering of Charlotte's vehicle, as he wanted to keep it under wraps for a time as the investigation ensued. She started to write down words she would say, but with each attempt she found herself crumpling up the paper and throwing it away. She laid her pen on the desk until she could put her anger on a shelf.

After a time, she picked up her pen to let words pour from her heart. How could she say good-bye to her kindred spirit? Her confidante? Her defender? Her trusted friend? Teardrops fell from her eyes. She decided to talk about the many things they'd shared over the years—the fellowship and harmony, baking and decorating gingerbread cookies for the holidays, trading stories, and listening to one another vent through difficult moments in life. She would speak about Charlotte's unique qualities. About her willingness to help anyone in need, and the many times she witnessed her friend walk up to a stranger to hand the person a few dollars. Charlotte would always smile and say, "Hope this helps a little." In a word, she was selfless. And she was filled with energy. Always looking for the best in people. It's what made her special. Also vulnerable.

Claire choked back her feelings as she scribbled notes for her talk. As hard as she tried, she couldn't halt the many questions plaguing her. How could anyone have wanted to harm Charlotte? To kill her? How could she have had such a fierce enemy that Claire was not aware of? Claire's thoughts fell on Charlotte's new friend, Stephen. Was it sympathy she was feeling for him? Or suspicion? She couldn't be sure.

The questions drained Claire's energy, and she had to take a nap. In her sleep she envisioned the crash. She woke with a start and a throbbing headache.

THE FUNERAL service was standing room only. Relatives, friends, neighbors, and work associates poured into the chapel. Claire was not the only friend to say moving words. There were several others too. Even Charlotte's new male friend got up and introduced himself to the crowd as Stephen Fox. He expressed a few warmhearted thoughts.

Singing, necessary tears, and even laughter filled the air. Despite the fact that Charlotte died way too young—and in a perfect world, that none of the attendees should have been there to memorialize her passing—the service was life affirming and a celebration of Charlotte's days on earth.

Guy sat by Claire's side, his hand gripping hers tightly. The day was difficult for her, and his touch meant everything. He leaned over and kissed her on the cheek.

Claire leaned in closer and whispered in his ear, "I'm glad her parents went before her. They couldn't have taken it."

He gave her a knowing nod.

"Did she have any siblings?" Guy asked softly. "I guess I never heard you mention any."

"No. She was an only child," Claire said. "She always told me that I was her family. That she thought of me as her sister." She brushed away a tear. "It hurts so much."

She moved even closer to Guy so that she could feel his body next to hers. It made her feel better.

The service ended, and attendees moved into a different room for a light buffet lunch. They mulled around to chat with one another, expressing sympathy and exchanging stories about Charlotte.

Claire spotted Stephen. He was standing alone looking over the crowd. Stephen was a man people noticed. He had an air of sophistication about him. The female investigator watched him with interest. He appeared totally unruffled and virtually unfazed by Charlotte's death. She saw no evidence of emotion in the man. He glanced at his watch every couple of minutes.

"I'm going over to introduce myself and extend my condolences," Claire said to Guy. "I'll be right back." She headed for Stephen.

"Your words were powerful," Stephen said to Claire after she introduced herself.

"Thank you. Yours too," she said.

"It's hard to believe," he said. "Of all things. A fatal accident in the car I sold Charlotte. But then, these things happen."

"I'm sorry for your loss," Claire said. "Did you see her on the day of the crash?"

"Um. Let me think," Stephen said. "I really don't remember." He shuffled his feet and darted his gaze all around.

"Really?" She shifted into investigator mode. "How can you not remember?"

"Perhaps we should continue this conversation another time," he said. He directed his eyes squarely on hers and didn't blink. He handed Claire a business card.

"Perhaps we should," Claire said.

She turned and walked back to where Guy was standing in a far corner of the room. She filled him in on the conversation.

"I don't like him," she said.

"Maybe he's just upset," Guy said.

"I don't like him," Claire repeated.

She watched Stephen from afar and observed him approaching one woman after another in the crowd, handing each a business card.

"Probably trying to sell every one of them a new car," Claire said. "He's actually doing business at Charlotte's funeral. Can you believe it?"

"Not a class act, that's for sure," Guy said. "But maybe it's how he's handling his grief. Pushing onward. You never know."

"Perhaps," Claire said. Her tone sent the clear message that she didn't agree with Guy's hypothesis.

THE NEXT day Claire decided to pay a visit to Stephen Fox at his place of business.

She walked into the high-end car dealership and asked to see Stephen. Minutes later, he appeared. All smiles.

"Ms. Caswell. What a pleasure to see you again. And so soon. Please come to my office."

Claire followed him as he led the way.

"Have a seat," he instructed. "Now, what brings you here today?"

Before she could respond, he asked another question. "Can I get you a coffee? We also have delicious smoothies. I could have my associate, Jim, make one fresh for you. They're a hit with all our clients."

"No, thank you. I'm here to discuss Charlotte with you," Claire said. She was annoyed Stephen seemed to have zero clue about why she would be there. "You didn't answer my question at her funeral service."

"What question was that?" he asked.

"Did you see Charlotte on the day of the accident?"

"I'm not sure. As I told you, I really don't remember."

Claire stared at him without blinking.

"Could you check your calendar to refresh your memory?"

"I could," he said nonchalantly. He paged back on his desk calendar to the date Charlotte was killed. "I do recall talking with her on the phone that morning. And, yes, I guess she was here. I made a notation on that date."

"I know she was quite taken with you, and as her good friend, I'd like to know your thoughts about the crash. She loved her new car and—" Claire stumbled over her words as an image of Charlotte appeared in her mind.

"Ms. Caswell, I'm sorry for your loss, in case I failed to say that before. I truly am." He handed her a box of tissues. "No one can predict when these unfortunate things will happen in life. Sometimes they just do. And we must deal with them. We can't understand why. But life is for the living. It goes on."

"You two were close lately," Claire continued, ignoring his philosophical comments on life. "Was Charlotte upset about anything on the day of the crash?"

"Not to my knowledge," he fired out his answer without hesitation. "Actually, she seemed quite happy; content, really."

"Did she seem distracted by anything?" Claire asked.

"Again, not that I was aware of," he said. "Did *you* talk to her that morning?" His tone suddenly turned chilly.

"No, but I saw her the day before," Claire said. "We had lunch."

Claire stared at Stephen. She didn't like him turning the question around on her. After all, she was there to ask him the questions. And she also didn't appreciate his apparent insensitivity to Charlotte's death. He displayed no emotion whatsoever.

Claire took a bold step. "Did you love her?"

For once Stephen seemed at a loss for words. Her question clearly took him by surprise. He stumbled to respond. "Right to the point, aren't you?"

"It's an honest question," she said. "Were you?"

"Well, now that's a deep subject matter," he said. "How does one define *love*?"

Claire had heard enough.

"I will take that as a no," she said. "I wonder if Charlotte knew your true feelings? She was head over heels in love with you."

He smiled peculiarly.

"I keep my emotions and feelings close to the vest," he said. "It's safer that way."

Claire stood to leave.

"Maybe we can talk further another time," she said.

"I'd like that," he said.

"If any additional questions arise regarding the crash, I'll contact you again."

"What possible questions would you have for me regarding the accident? I only sell cars. I don't assemble them. If the car had a problem, that would have nothing to do with me."

Claire stopped in her tracks.

"What makes you think her brand-new car might have had a problem?"

"I meant nothing by that comment." His face and body stiffened.

At that moment, the young lady from the reception desk rushed into Stephen's office. Her skirt was short, her neckline low, and her expectations high. "Ready for lunch, Foxy?" she asked. She immediately noticed Claire standing there and said, "Oh, excuse me, miss. I assumed you had left by now."

"I am leaving," Claire said. She nodded to Stephen and walked out.

Back at the office, she told Guy about her encounter with Stephen.

"Wonder what Charlotte saw in him?" Guy asked.

"I can't imagine," she said. "His looks, probably. Aside from that, I'm not sure what else there is. Charlotte was a quality person. Maybe she was lonely for male companionship? We'll probably never know."

"Let's have Jin do a workup on him—a full background check. We'll see if anything shows up in his history," Guy said.

"My thoughts exactly," Claire said. She looked up as her mother, Abbey, walked into the office.

"Mom!" Claire said. "What brings you here?" She walked over and embraced her in a bear hug.

"Can we grab a cup of coffee?" her mom asked. "I need to talk to you." Her tone was serious.

Claire glanced at her watch. "Of course." She grabbed her purse, let Guy and Jin know her plans, and left with her mom.

Seated at a nearby café, Abbey expressed her condolences to Claire over the premature death of Charlotte.

"You two were always such good friends," she said. "I can't imagine what it feels like to lose her." She paused. "Honey, do you remember our next-door neighbor, Ester Rollings? Everyone calls her Estee?"

"I do," Claire said. "I've met her several times over the years."

Abbey took a deep breath. "Well, we don't want to seem nosy, but she has taken up with a man. She's been somewhat depressed since her husband died a year ago, and then suddenly this man enters her life and, poof, everything changes. We try to look out for her, and we're not sure what to do about this. Estee's husband was a top corporate executive, and he left her a very wealthy widow. I guess your dad and I are questioning the motives of this man."

"Have you asked Estee about him?" Claire asked.

"I've tried. But each time she changes the subject. She claims they are merely friends, yet he monopolizes her time. She used to come to our home for dinner once a week, but since she met this man those occasions have come to a screeching halt. The only time I talk to her now is when I initiate the contact. It's just strange. Something does not seem right to us."

"What are you afraid of?" Claire asked. "That he's after her money?"

"I guess so. Yes. He seemed to appear out of the blue."

"It does sound a bit strange, I agree. Would you like me to talk to her?"

"Would you, Claire?"

"Of course, if it will put your mind at ease. When is the best time to find her home?"

"Most mornings, I would say. Before eleven."

"I'll try tomorrow, Mom."

"Thank you, Claire. I'll feel better hearing your take on the situation."

After her mom left, Claire's mind went into overdrive. She wanted to pour every ounce of her time and energy into Charlotte's case; yet she also wanted to help her mom. She felt torn. Overburdened. But she could handle both situations—especially with the help of Guy and Jin. She couldn't ask for a better partner and intern. It would take the three of them to sufficiently handle both cases.

THE FOLLOWING morning Claire drove to her parents' home. She parked curbside and walked up to Estee's door.

Estee, a well-put-together woman in her early sixties, answered the door.

"Estee, it's Claire Caswell—the daughter of your neighbors Abbey and Don."

"Oh, Claire. It's been a while. What a nice surprise! Please come in. Will you stay for a cup of tea?"

"That would be lovely, thank you," Claire said.

Minutes later, the two sat at Estee's dining room table sipping the hot beverages.

"What brings you here?" Estee asked.

"Well, I guess I never offered you condolences on the death of your husband, William. So I'm here to extend my belated sympathy. It must be difficult."

"How sweet of you," Estee said. "His death took me by surprise, and quite frankly, for a time I didn't know how I would go on. But then—"

"But then, *what*?"

"Well, then I met a very nice gentleman, and everything changed." She smiled timidly.

"How did you meet?" Claire asked.

"That's the funny part of the story," Estee said. "He knocked on my door one day and introduced himself as Charlie McDermott. He said he worked with my husband and he wanted to check on me, to see if he could help with anything. Well, one thing led to another, and before I knew it, we were . . . seeing each other on a regular basis. Now he helps me with my finances and other things—things I never tended to on my own. Things that William always took care of. I'd be absolutely lost without Charlie. I see him almost every day. We do something fun most afternoons."

All sorts of warning bells were going off for Claire.

"Did your husband ever talk about Charlie, Estee?"

"Actually, no. I had never heard his name before, not that I remember anyway, but he said he knew William. He said William always talked about me and how much he loved me."

"Fascinating," Claire said. "Well, I wish you the very best, Estee." She smiled kindly.

After finishing her tea, she departed.

She stopped to say hello to her parents and fill them in on what she had learned.

"What was the name of the corporation William worked for?" Claire asked.

"It was Donegale Inc. on Biscayne," Don said.

"I'll check it out," Claire said.

She returned to her office and opened a file on Charlie McDermott.

Claire allowed herself a few minutes of solitude to digest the situation with Estee. She really wanted to help this woman. If Charlie had a plan to take advantage of Estee, Claire needed to stop him in his tracks. Again, her investigative energy felt split. Charlotte's case remained at the forefront. Soon Jin would have valuable information on Stephen, allowing them to proceed on that investigation. Her firm would have to balance the investigation of both cases.

THE FEMALE investigator looked up the number for Donegale Inc. and called the company. A receptionist answered, and Claire asked to speak to Charlie McDermott.

"We have no one here by that name," the friendly voice responded.

"Has a Charlie McDermott ever worked there?" Claire asked.

"I've been here eight years, and he hasn't worked here during my time. Hold on. I'll ask a coworker who has been here close to twenty."

Three minutes later, the woman returned to the phone. "No one by that name has worked here in the last twenty years. What department are you looking for? Can I connect you to someone else?"

"Oh, no, thank you. My mistake," Claire said. "Thank you for your time."

She hung up.

She dialed her parents. Abbey answered.

"Your instincts are correct. This Charlie character is not who he claims to be. At least he didn't work with Estee's husband as he told her."

Her mom let out a long sigh. "We'll have to handle this with care. She really likes this man, and I'm afraid she'll not take in anything we say about him that she doesn't want to hear. Verbalizing our concerns may even push her closer to him."

"Well, keep me posted," Claire said. "In the meantime, we'll do a background check on this Charlie McDermott, assuming that's his real name, and see what we can come up with." She paused. "Keep your eye on Estee. She could be in danger."

4

"JIN, I'VE GOT another name for you. Charlie McDermott."
Claire scratched his name down on a notepad and passed it to Jin.
"Find out everything you can on him, will you?" She thought for a
moment. "In fact, let's all three of us do some background work on
Charlie McDermott as well as Stephen Fox," she said. "Great minds
together should make great progress. Keeping my fingers crossed."

The day quickly became hectic with each of the three banging
away on their computers and making phone calls.

When the workday was coming to a close, Claire called an
impromptu meeting at her desk.

"Let's share whatever information we've each discovered on the
two subjects in question. Jin, would you like to begin?"

"Sure," Jin said. "As far as Stephen Fox goes, he appears to be
squeaky clean. No criminal record. Just a couple of traffic tickets
years ago. He's a numbers man. He's been at the car dealership

where Charlotte purchased her car for several years. Climbed to the top fast. Never a complaint. He's probably making around a quarter of a million dollars annually between his salary and investments. He owns a house with a sizable mortgage in a nice area of Miami Beach." Jin stated the house address, and the investigators made a note.

"Records show he was married twice," Claire said. "First to a Christine, who died five years ago. That union produced one child—a son named Eric. And more recently, he was married to a Carli. That was a short marriage that ended in divorce."

"He handles all the financial business at the dealership," Guy said. "A real brain when it comes to numbers, as Jin indicated. He's a wheeler-dealer and able to arrange financing for just about anyone who walks through the door and wants to purchase a Porsche. He makes a lot of buyers really happy. There is no one he can't work out financing for—regardless of his or her situation. Oh, and he attended AA after his wife died."

"Interesting," Claire said. "And, Jin, what about Charlie McDermott?"

"Well, now McDermott is a different story altogether," he began. "He doesn't exist—in records, anyway. I was unable to find a Charlie McDermott anywhere in the Miami area or, for that matter, in the state of Florida. As hard as I looked, I couldn't find anything. It's like he's a ghost."

Guy chimed in, "And here I thought I had lost my touch. Same exact findings for me. The man is off the grid. There is no such person as Charlie McDermott."

"It's looking like Charlie McDermott might be an alias," Claire said. "We need to find out his real name." She looked at the law student. "Jin, consider yourself assigned to the Charlie McDermott case. You'll need to do some surveillance on him. Locate someone who knows him and his real name. See where the man goes on a typical day. How does he spend his time? Where does he live? Where does he take Estee? What kind of a car does he drive? Try to get the license plate number and check it out."

"Claire and I will take on the Stephen Fox file," Guy said. "We need to determine who might have wanted Charlotte dead. And right now, he's the only person of interest in the case."

Claire jotted down Estee's address and the address of her parents and handed the paper to Jin. "My parents live right next door—in the one-story bungalow-style house—so if you should need anything, please knock on their door. I'll let them know you're putting Estee under surveillance."

She paused to gather her thoughts.

"Sounds like McDermott visits Estee pretty much on a daily basis—in the afternoons—and then the two of them 'do something fun,' according to Estee," Claire continued. "Since he sees her most every day, this should work well with your schedule, as most of your classes are in the morning. Keep your distance, Jin, but follow them. See where he takes her. And follow Charlie when he drops her off. See where he goes on his own. Take notes. We need to know all his movements." Claire stared directly into Jin's eyes. "Consider nothing he does irrelevant. Write down every detail. Just don't get caught."

"Time is of the essence, Jin," Guy said. "There's no telling when this man intends to make a move if he has a plan to harm Estee in some way. She's vulnerable after losing her husband and will probably turn a blind eye to any red flags that arise where he's concerned. Remember, he's her hero now. She thinks he's her rescuer. We need to tread softly until we find evidence to the contrary."

"Got it," Jin said. "I'll be an invisible shadow. And I'll stick to it for days if I have to. I'll report in periodically to let you know what

I'm finding."

"Great," Guy said. "And, Claire, I'm warning you about this Stephen character. I'd be extremely careful. If he is involved in this incident with Charlotte, he could be dangerous if he thinks you're onto him."

"I realize that," the female investigator said. "You don't have to warn me. I'm always careful. And I think I'll use your car, Guy, when I conduct some surveillance of my own, just in case Stephen saw my car when I visited him at the dealership."

"I insist," Guy said. "And let's all check in with each other on a regular basis. We're working straight through the weekends, Jin, as time is of the essence on both of these cases."

BRIGHT AND early the next morning, Claire drove to the dealership and parked across from the entrance and down the street. Several other vehicles parked in that location provided sufficient cover for her to keep an eye on Stephen's comings and goings without being observed. She'd packed a lunch the night before, knowing it could be a long day.

Most employees of the dealership strolled in just before 9:00 a.m., but Stephen did not arrive until 10:00 a.m. He drove a used black Range Rover. Claire assumed it was probably a trade-in on a new Porsche.

Stephen radiated self-assurance in his stride. He held his head high. He dressed in a dark suit and a grape-and-white-checkered shirt. Slicked-back ebony hair ended in a jumble of natural curls at the nape of his neck. His eyes were a velvety brown and intense. But to Claire, they exuded no warmth. The man's ego could fill a large room. He overflowed with exaggerated self-importance.

This was not the type of man Charlotte had dated in the past, and Claire again wondered what the attraction had been to Stephen.

Shortly after Stephen arrived, another car pulled into the lot near the front door of the dealership. Out stepped the receptionist Claire had seen the day she'd visited Stephen. The young woman looked exhausted and somewhat disheveled, like she had overslept and rushed to get into work. She scurried through the front double doors. Since the building was encased in glass windows from top to bottom, Claire could easily see inside.

She watched as the receptionist hurried to her post and plopped down in the chair behind the lobby desk. She pulled a mirror from a drawer and proceeded to apply makeup before she brushed her hair.

I wonder what she knows? Claire asked herself. *I'd love to talk with her.*

Hours dragged on, cars drove into and out of the dealership lot, and soon the lunch hour approached. Claire pulled a tuna salad sandwich from her lunch bag and devoured it. She poured a cup of hot coffee from her thermos and sipped as she continued to watch. Various employees left for a lunch break at irregular times. Then, quite late, after most employees had returned to their desks for the afternoon, Claire observed the receptionist walk to her car and drive off. Not ten minutes later, Stephen walked out and drove off in the same direction.

She pulled on a cap and sunglasses and followed a comfortable distance behind. Fifteen minutes later, he pulled into an apartment building parking lot. Claire observed the receptionist's car parked nearby. He walked to the building, waited to be let into the security door, and entered.

Claire glanced at her watch. Exactly thirty minutes later, to the minute, the two walked out. Each got into their respective cars and zoomed back to work.

Okay. The two clearly had some connection. Having a fling was an obvious option, but Claire had to be sure. *Never assume anything*, she reminded herself. One thing was certain, however: Stephen and the receptionist had something going on. And Claire needed to find out what that something was.

She retraced her drive back to the dealership in time to see Stephen entering through its front doors. The receptionist was already seated behind her desk and talking on the phone.

The remaining afternoon hours passed. Some workers left, and others came in for the later shift. The dealership remained open until 8:00 p.m. The receptionist left around 5:00 p.m., and Stephen stayed until closing time. Claire followed him as he drove off. He stopped at a tavern and went inside. Claire followed him in, making certain to keep a low profile. She stood at the back of the establishment in a dark corner and observed Stephen sitting on a stool in front of the extended bar. He was sitting next to a woman, and the two were talking like old friends.

Claire returned to her car and waited.

Two hours passed. Stephen walked out, got in his car, and drove away. Claire followed him to his home address. He went in, turned on the lights, and minutes later turned them off. He was in for the night.

The female sleuth called Guy.

"I'm on my way home. It's been a long day," she said. "I'll tell you everything I learned when I see you."

THE FOLLOWING morning Claire was back at it—sitting outside the auto dealership, watching for movements of Stephen, the receptionist, or both.

At noon, the receptionist walked to her car and drove off. Claire decided to trail her. The young woman pulled into a spot directly in front of a Pilates studio and walked in.

Claire tucked her shoulder-length strawberry-blonde hair under a short, feathery dark wig, put on a pair of bold red glasses, and followed her inside.

"I'm interested in possibly joining," she told the instructor.

"You're in comfortable clothes, so why not sit in this hour and see what you think. You can use this exercise mat." She smiled and handed Claire a folded mat.

Inconspicuously, the investigator eyed the room and located the receptionist.

She placed her mat on the floor next to hers.

The exercises were done in a specific order, and one followed directly after the other. The instructor called out names like the Elephant, Criss-Cross, the Swan, and the 100. All students knew exactly what she was referring to, and although the moves looked simple, they required control and precision. The trainer repeatedly emphasized technique. Forty-five minutes later, the class ended.

Claire was exhausted. She sighed loudly.

The receptionist chuckled. "It'll get easier. I promise. You'll get stronger and stronger, and you'll notice your muscles becoming more sculpted. You'll even feel more flexible than ever before. And your outlook on life will be better."

"Wow. That's quite a lot of promises. Have you been at this a long time?" Claire asked.

"Oh, yes. And I'm thoroughly addicted." She grinned. "You do have to add cardio to your workout plan, too, you realize."

"Sure. I understand. I'm intrigued," Claire said. "Any chance we could grab a quick snack and talk more about this?"

"Well, I do need to get back to work, but a *quick* snack? Sure, why not? There's a place right next door that actually serves healthy food. Great salads!"

"Just what I'm craving," Claire said. She walked out with the receptionist and over to the restaurant.

"Oh, by the way, my name is Ellen," Claire lied. She made sure to talk in a tone lower than her normal voice.

"I'm Natalie," the receptionist said. "Pleased to meet you."

"Likewise," Claire said.

They ordered salads and iced teas.

"Tell me about yourself," Claire said. "Are you from this area?"

"Yes. How about you?"

"Me too," Claire said. "Do you work nearby?"

"I work at a car dealership," Natalie said. "I've been there a handful of years and hope to one day actually become a salesperson. I'm in training now."

"Interesting," Claire said.

Natalie ate only a bit of salad before pushing the plate away. She looked a little uncomfortable.

Claire wondered if the receptionist was ill.

"Can I interest you in buying a Porsche? Perhaps a Cayenne?" Natalie asked. "Women are buying luxury cars more than ever before. Historically, women were considered the practical car buyers, but not anymore." She laughed. "We even host art exhibits, fashion shows, and other events specifically tailored to bring potential women customers in to view our inventory."

"I can't swing it now, but possibly in the future," Claire said.

"Well, let me know." She handed Claire her business card.

"I just had a random thought," the investigator said. She took a couple of small bites of her salad. "I heard on the news not long ago that a woman was killed when her new Porsche Cayenne crashed into a restaurant. Did you hear about that?"

"Of course. It was very sad," Natalie said.

Claire watched the receptionist and tried to assess her sincerity.

Was Natalie kind? Sympathetic? Or shady? She wished she knew.

"And my friend at the dealership did the financial closing for her on that car," Natalie said.

"You're kidding," Claire said. "Small world. Do you think the car had a mechanical problem?"

"No way! It was brand new! They never have problems. It had to be driver error."

"What did your friend at the dealership think?" Claire asked.

"He really didn't have much to say about it," Natalie said. "I was horrified. I had talked to the woman—the driver—many times when she'd stopped into the dealership. Her name was Charlotte. She was always nice to me. I liked her."

"I wonder why your friend wouldn't have felt horrified too?" Claire asked.

"Between you and me, I couldn't understand it." She wiggled restlessly in her seat. "And I believe the two of them had been seeing quite a bit of each other after the car transaction closed. I think Charlotte really liked him. It didn't make sense."

5

JIN FOLLOWED CHARLIE McDermott for close to three days—whenever his class schedule allowed.

Charlie did not follow a regular routine. Each day was different. He never arrived at Estee's house at the same time and never left at the same time. He was a medium-framed man who dressed in Bermuda shorts and an array of short-sleeved Hawaiian-print shirts—all featuring either palm trees, parrots, or flowers. On his feet, he wore boat shoes and no socks. His disheveled hair was a dark shade of dishwater blond, and he sported a tan. He appeared to be in his midfifties. He drove a fully restored Volkswagen Karmann Ghia, Irish green in color, with what appeared to be the original tan convertible top. Jin guessed the model year to be 1974.

Jin recorded detailed notes in his daily record of the subject's schedule. And the intern snapped many photos of the subject on his smartphone each day.

On the second day of surveillance, Jin had trailed behind Charlie and observed him driving into the underground parking area of a pricy, twenty-four-story, luxury oceanfront condominium in Bal Harbour—a village on The Beach in Miami-Dade County. He did not come out again. Jin jotted down the address and noted he assumed this to be where Charlie lived.

Based upon early observations, the student wrote in his journal that Charlie appeared to be a regular kind of guy in many respects—*excessively casual*, if Jin had to choose adjectives to describe the man. He didn't appear to care much about his physical appearance.

Jin wondered whether Charlie had a job. He also pondered where the money came from to purchase a condominium unit of this nature. While there was always the possibility of inheritance, his gut feeling told him to look further.

Claire Caswell continually trained Jin to trust and consider his instincts—his internal impressions and inclinations—and not always wait for cold, hard facts to line up before setting out in one direction or another in an investigation. "Rely on your hunches," she had told him so often. And Jin was slowly learning to do so.

The law student studied Charlie and his movements. He noted the man seemed ill at ease walking from the lobby of the elegant building adorned with a doorman, full-time concierge, and parking valet. There was something about how he walked, how he held his head, and how he looked downward when entering or exiting the building that brought Jin to this conclusion.

When Charlie arrived at Estee's front door each afternoon, he was smiling. And so was Estee whenever she opened the door and invited him in. The two stayed inside her house for a period of time, and later they always left together in his car. Jin made a notation of the Karmann Ghia's license plate number. He would check out the ownership.

Jin trailed far behind the pair each day, always making sure to keep them within his view. On the first two days, the couple went out for late leisurely lunches. On the third afternoon, Jin followed them to a marina located along the Intracoastal Waterway. He parked in a nearby lot and observed.

The intern soon discovered that Charlie either owned, leased, or borrowed a boat. And not just any boat. The two boarded an iconic Hinckley MKIII Picnic Boat. Living on The Beach, Jin had become a bit of an aficionado when it came to boats, and a Hinckley was nothing less than a work of art. Coming in around $750,000, it was not a boat that just any boat lover could own. And again Jin wondered how the heck Charlie afforded such a luxury, if he was the owner.

The boat was named *Black Pearl*. Jin jotted down the name and snapped photos of the magnificent vessel. He would also check out its ownership when he returned to the office.

Jin watched Charlie and Estee disappear into the boat's lower cabin and soon reappear wearing swimming attire. Estee had slipped on a wide-brimmed straw hat and a pair of dark sunglasses, and Charlie wore a cap and classic Ray-Ban Wayfarer tinted glasses. The pair hugged and kissed before pulling out for a cruise, Charlie behind the wheel at the helm. Seeing the Hinckley, a boat generally spotted in the waters off the northeastern coast of the United States, was candy to Jin's eyes.

He let his mind wander. As a youngster, he had refused to play with toy trucks like the other boys. Instead, he had badgered his parents for toy boats. He recalled a high-speed remote-control racing boat, a ferryboat with cars, and a pirate battleship as being among his favorites. But his most-loved possession was his hand-made hardwood Hinckley.

Jin never tired of playing with the variety of boats he collected over his childhood years, and he fondly remembered whiling away the hours pretending to be captain of a large vessel on the South Seas. Over the years, he added docks, ramps, and a wide collection of other toy vessels to his elaborate collection. Having no siblings, Jin remembered feeling lonely and friendless in his youth. He had had to learn to come up with creative ways to keep his mind entertained.

On weekends his parents would bring him to the beach to play, handing him a shovel to dig in the sand, while they sat nearby on lounge chairs talking and enjoying the day.

And when they would take him to the Intracoastal Waterway, he would watch the boats and yachts travel up and down the canal, memorizing the makes and models of each. Soon he knew them all. Each one had been given a name by its owner. And the names the owners attached to their prized possessions intrigued Jin to no end. Some were serious, many humorous, and others clever.

In his wildest imaginations, he'd envision maneuvering in and around high tides and whopping waves, having full responsibility for saving himself, the crew, and the ship from certain peril. He smiled, remembering. These were some of his best recollections of being a child. "The captain goes down with the ship!" he would declare time and time again. And if the ship should be struck by an enemy and begin to sink, he would be the last one off. He snickered. When his mom called him for lunch, he'd answer, "Aye, aye, matey!" And for Halloween each year he'd always dressed as a pirate.

These fond memories would forever be a part of him. They helped him survive a somewhat isolated childhood—despite constant efforts of his doctor parents to reassure him he was their pride and joy.

His mind jumped to present day—attending law school and working at the prestigious private investigation firm. He was doing exactly what he wanted to do at this point in his life. But he yearned to put law school behind him and venture out into the real world—a place where he alone could make a difference. Being an intern at Caswell & Lombard, Private Investigation afforded him an incredible break. The experience provided him an insider's look into the world of business and investigation, and it imparted invaluable experience that he would always draw from in his career. But to be a real lawyer, out on his own, able to make decisions that affected people's lives—now that was the carrot that kept him going. He had always wanted to be a lawyer, and nothing else would ever do.

BLACK PEARL had been out for two hours, and Jin fought the urge to nap. He poured a cup of strong hot coffee from the double-walled insulated container he toted along and sipped it slowly. Surveillance could be fraught with risk and danger—expected and unexpected— that was often unforeseeable and uncontrollable. Being ready for anything that might crop up was the name of the game. A caffeine-induced adrenaline rush suddenly heightened his level of awareness.

Claire and Guy had carefully schooled Jin in undercover surveillance, and he had been a good student. He knew to always stay alert. He knew to use an overabundance of caution at all times. And he also knew never to doze on the job.

After a time he again felt fatigued. This time he kicked into plan B. He got out of his car, stretched vigorously, and took in giant quantities of fresh air. Then he jogged a short distance before he returned to his post, at all times keeping his eye on the water and watching for the return of the Hinckley. Endless waiting was a huge part of surveillance and was something he did not savor.

Before too much longer, Jin caught sight of the watercraft returning to the dock. He watched with interest as it came in closer and closer and finally anchored in its usual spot at the marina. The intern lifted his binoculars from the passenger seat and pulled them close to his eyes, playing with the dial until the parties came into perfect focus.

Charlie set up a plastic table and two chairs in the rear section of the boat and insisted Estee take a seat. He vanished into the cabin below and minutes later appeared with a tray holding a bottle of wine, two goblets, and a plate of what appeared to be grapes, cheeses, and crackers. The two sat for a long stretch, together downing the entire bottle. They laughed, kissed, and gazed into each other's eyes.

To any outsider, the pair looked like a perfect match. But, as Jin had learned from his limited experience, looks could be deceiving, and things were not always as they seemed. He left his car and stealthily walked closer to the dock area where many other vessels were moored. He took up a position near the Hinckley, but behind a trash dumpster where he could not be observed. He crouched low and peered around the receptacle. He watched and listened.

Charlie spewed lungfuls of sugary compliments upon Estee. His words, although sickeningly sweet to Jin, appeared to please Estee to no end. The expression in her eyes signaled she craved and devoured the praise and obsequious flattery like food to a hungry child.

Charlie deposited his arms firmly around Estee's waist, pulled her close, and firmly pressed his lips to hers. The couple disappeared into the boat's cabin.

Deep in thought, Jin returned to his car where he could still keep an eye on *Black Pearl*.

Estee is in love with this man, the law student told himself. He shook his head.

A good hour passed before the pair resurfaced. They gathered their personal belongings and walked toward Charlie's car. Jin scrunched low in his vehicle in order not to be seen. When Charlie's car left the lot, Jin trailed behind.

JIN RETURNED to the marina the following day after class and hunted down the on-site manager. Rick Alfaro had held the position for ten years and would most assuredly know a lot about the boat owners. Jin began with small talk and then decided to take a courageous leap.

"I'm interested in learning about the boat named *Black Pearl*."

"Ah, you have good taste, sir," Rick said. "She's a beauty. Are you interested in buying one like that?"

"I'm definitely interested, but . . ." Jin said.

"Oh, I understand." Rick nodded. "Money could be an issue, right? They cost a small fortune."

"It could be," Jin said.

"Maybe you should talk to the owner of *Black Pearl*," Rick said. "He might even take you out for a ride so you can see how she handles on the water." He smiled. "Many of the owners buy boats just for the prestige of having one. They use them 'bout once a year, I swear. A real waste, if you ask me. But *Black Pearl* gets used more than all the rest."

"Good idea, Rick," Jin said. "What's the owner's name? And do you have a contact number?"

"Well, now that's a good question," Rick said. "The owner? Or the one who takes her out several times a week? They are not one and the same."

"Either. Or both," Jin said.

"Well, the owner is anonymous. Many of them are. They want their ownership to remain hidden from the public. But Charlie McDermott is the one who uses the boat. Not sure what his arrangement is with the actual owner. I don't have Charlie's number, but I would talk to his friend Hugo. Hugo Bello. He's Charlie's emergency contact and also the person I call if I need to reach Charlie for any reason. Hugo cleans the boat for Charlie, stocks it with food and drinks, and takes care of anything else Charlie needs."

"You have a number for this Hugo?" Jin asked.

"Yeah." He reached for his Rolodex, pulled it close, and scrolled through the cards. "Here it is." He gave Jin the number.

Jin thanked Rick and walked from the office. When he reached his car, he pulled out his cell phone and called Hugo. Jin said he was considering the purchase of a Hinckley. "Rick Alfaro recommended I contact you to see if you would show me around *Black Pearl*." As luck would have it, Hugo bought into it.

"You talked to Rick?" Hugo asked. "No problem. Of course I'll show you around."

"Do you need to check with Charlie first?" Jin asked. "Rick told me you work for a Charlie McDermott."

"Nah. I'm cleaning the boat today, so Charlie won't be around. I'm on my way to the marina now and will be there in a few minutes. Are you anywhere close?"

"As a matter of fact, I'm at the marina now," Jin said. "I'll wait for you."

Hugo arrived within the half hour. The men shook hands, and Hugo invited Jin aboard. Hugo offered Jin a cold beer, and Jin accepted. The two drank from the cold bottles and shot the breeze for the first several minutes. Hugo showed Jin around the Picnic Boat and pointed out all its features.

"Yeah, life doesn't get much better than this. Wish she were mine," Hugo said. "But life isn't always fair, is it? Some seem to have an easy ride while others hit every fricking bump on the road." He exhaled loudly. "Now Charlie, for example, he gets all the breaks."

Jin reached into his pocket and pulled out a twenty. He handed it to Hugo.

"I really appreciate you showing me the Hinckley," Jin said. "And on such short notice. I've always wanted to step aboard one of these beauties."

"Oh, no problem." He stuffed the bill into his shirt pocket. "Thanks."

"Why do you think this Charlie gets all the breaks?" Jin asked. "Just dealt the right cards?"

"Charlie knows the right people. That's all I can say." He paused and quickly changed the subject. "You'd think this boat was *his* baby the way he tends to it. He has me wash it once a week, whether it needs it or not." He chuckled. "It's how he takes care of everything."

"Everything?"

"Yeah. *Black Pearl*. His vintage Hawaiian shirts. His car. Everything he has or uses is well maintained."

"What kind of work does he do?" Jin asked.

"Work? Are you kidding? He just plays, far as I know."

"Okay. Okay. I get the picture. Do you know the actual owner of *Black Pearl*?"

Hugo eyed Jin with curiosity. "Why do you ask?"

6

CLAIRE GLANCED DOWN at the simple platinum wedding band adorning her left ring finger. She had finally said *yes*! And truthfully, she felt no different from before. Not really. Why had she fought it for such a long time? The unembellished circular symbol of eternal love, loyalty, and commitment sat alongside the diamond eternity band Guy had given her years before. She touched the new ring and rolled it around on her finger. *She was married.* Her heart pounded. It had been just a few months. She'd been committed to Guy for many years, so for her the ceremony had been nothing more than a legal formality. But he had wanted it, and at long last she had given in at a weak moment.

She closed her eyes and relived the simple but elegant church ceremony. It had been everything they both wanted: a sophisticated blush-pink gown of satin and lace for her; a black tuxedo with tails for Guy; a small group of their families and closest friends present, including Charlotte; and an almond paste–infused tiered cake iced with almond-flavored frosting and decorated with the palest of pink roses. And, of course, chilled champagne. The betrothed had each written their respective vows and delivered them in a touching manner. Those present broke into applause when Guy and Claire sealed their promises with a kiss, and voices in the group shouted, *"Finally!"*

Claire beamed as a surprising feeling of contentment washed over her. She was actually beginning to like the idea. Yet, a myriad of troubling thoughts jumped in to compete with her pleasant thoughts.

Her marriage to Guy was still new. And the tragedy of losing Charlotte now tainted everything. An olio of sweet and bitter thoughts and memories pummeled Claire's psyche. Her mind raced between thoughts of Guy and thoughts of Charlotte. Thoughts of her parents. And thoughts of her friends. Of the hills. And valleys. The good. The bad. The ups. The downs. The easy. The difficult. The mundane. The happy. The glorious. The sad. The devastating. Never had Claire been more aware of the extremes the jumbled medley of life proffered than now.

She wiped a lone tear from her cheek as she thought about Charlotte. When you're young and the whole of life lies before you, you never allow yourself as much as a thought that the people and things you care about most can leave you in an instant. But then it happens and you are forever changed and reminded of the fragility of life.

JUST THEN, Guy walked through the office door holding a large pizza box.

"Hungry?" he asked.

"No. I'm not hungry. I'm *starving.* How did you know?" Claire asked. This was a happy distraction.

"Well, it's lunchtime, and you've been working hard. I picked this up at that new place that opened a couple of blocks from here. I heard it's great. Can't wait for us to try it."

He placed the box on her desk and pulled open the cover. The mélange of fresh mushrooms, onions, black olives, and extra mozzarella wafted through the air. "It's your favorite."

"Yum," Claire said. She pulled napkins from a desk drawer, and the two dug in without delay.

Between the first couple of bites, Guy called out to Jin. "Come join us. Better hurry!"

The law student appeared in a flash, carrying three ice-cold sodas from the back cooler.

The trio quickly devoured the amazing pie, never stopping even once to comment or talk.

When the box sat empty, words erupted.

"Too good," Jin said. "Just plain too good."

"The *best!*" Claire said. "It's like New York pizza!"

"You'll get no disagreement from me," Guy chimed in. "Unbelievable. And they deliver."

Jin carted away the box and empty cans.

"What a nice surprise, Guy," Claire said. "Thank you for being so thoughtful. Really. It was just what I needed."

His look was one of concern. "What is it, Claire? What's wrong?"

"Why?"

"Because I know that look. Your eyebrows are furrowing despite your great attempts to hide it. That means something's on your mind. Don't deny it."

"Okay. Okay," Claire said slowly. "You're right." She inhaled deeply. "I'm thrilled that we're married. I'm excited about our big step, but . . ."

"But *what*? You regret it?"

"No, of course not! But I feel guilty being so happy when Charlotte's life was snatched away just like that." She snapped her fingers. A look of sadness penetrated her emerald eyes. "It could happen to any of us."

Guy pulled Claire from her chair and held her close. "Let it out, my beauty. It's okay. Time will heal, but never completely. None of us are guaranteed another day. That's why we must make the most of the time we have together and be thankful for each day."

Claire sobbed until her tears ran dry.

"I want the truth," she declared with a renewed boldness. "I need to know how it happened and who did it."

Claire was determined to find the reason for the crash, to identify who orchestrated it, and to make certain the perpetrator went to prison. Her instincts told her Charlotte's new boyfriend might be involved, but she couldn't be sure. She'd go visit him again. That little voice within her, the one she unfailingly listened to, kept telling her to do so. She would obey.

THE FEMALE investigator glanced at her watch. There was still time that day. She announced she'd be gone for a while and drove to the car dealership. As she pulled into the parking area, she observed Stephen entering through the front door. When she entered the lobby, Natalie was manning the information desk. It was clear she didn't recognize her as "Ellen" from the Pilates studio.

"What can I help you with today?" she inquired.

"I'd like to see Stephen Fox again," Claire said.

"Concerning?" Her voice had a distinctly unpleasant edge.

"Oh, I would like to talk to Stephen directly," Claire said.

"Concerning?" Natalie repeated.

"Concerning a matter I will discuss with him in person," Claire bantered back.

"I'll see if he's available. Please have a seat." Natalie motioned toward the chairs in a nearby seating area.

Claire didn't move. "I'll stand. Thank you."

"Whatever," the receptionist said. She sauntered off.

Her attitude bothered Claire, but she shrugged it off. Natalie seemed like a nicer person at the Pilates studio.

Minutes later, she reappeared. "I'm afraid he's left for the day."

"When did he leave?" Claire challenged.

"Early this afternoon," Natalie replied. She sat down in the chair behind the information desk and attempted to look busy. "Now if there's nothing further . . ."

Claire looked at her without responding.

The woman readjusted herself in the chair, avoiding Claire's eyes.

"Actually, I just saw him walk in as I was driving up a couple of minutes ago," Claire said. "So you're not being honest."

"It must have been someone else," the woman said, flustered. "Someone who looks like him."

"It was Stephen. I have no doubt," Claire said. She walked confidently past the impertinent receptionist and in the direction of Stephen's office.

"You can't go in there!" the woman wailed. "Wait!"

Claire ignored the pleas. When she arrived at the office, the door was closed. She grabbed the knob, turned it, and pushed the door open.

There sat Stephen, playing chess with another salesman.

Stephen looked up, a look of utter incredulity pasted on his face.

Natalie followed directly behind, throwing her arms in the air. "I tried—"

He waved her off.

"So, you *are* here," Claire said.

"The question is, what are *you* doing here again?" he asked. "I thought I had answered all your questions the last time you stopped by."

"We need to talk," Claire said. "And I will not be put off. Why was I told you were not in?"

He threw a pen across the room, clearly unhinged by her nerve.

"Get out, Jim," Stephen said to the salesman.

Claire did not let her displeasure with Stephen's attitude show.

He walked over to shut the door. As he did, she quickly stooped down to pick up the pen he had thrown. She placed it on his desk.

She remained standing.

"What's going on, Stephen?" Claire asked. Her eyes took on a steely professional appearance. She did not blink.

She wanted to make one thing abundantly clear: this friend of Charlotte's was not to be deterred, discouraged, intimidated, repelled, or diverted. Or befriended. She was going nowhere until he talked to her.

"What it is then?" he asked, sitting back down in his chair.

"I have some additional questions," the investigator said.

"Of course you do. Ask away," he replied. "But please consider this your final interrogation, Ms. Caswell. If not, I will consider it harassment."

"We'll see," she said. His threat did not faze her in the least. "How are things going for you since Charlotte died in the car crash?"

"Okay. Why?" He looked puzzled by the question.

"I'm personally having a lot of difficulty dealing with her passing," Claire said. "And I'm wondering. Are you too?" Her eyes did not leave him.

"Of course," he said. He cleared his throat. "Of course."

"What do you think happened to make her car crash into that

wall of glass?" Claire asked.

"You've asked me that before. Maybe you should ask the car manufacturer. I just sell them. Remember?"

Claire observed his behavior. He seemed detached and unsympathetic.

"Perhaps I will," she said.

"Is there anything else?" he asked.

Her eyes dropped to the fingers on both of his hands—tapping away on the desktop.

"You seem edgy. Are you?"

He stood up. "I guess I am. I guess it's that I don't relish being questioned."

"Well, you were in Charlotte's life for her final days. Naturally, we all want to know just what was going on that might have contributed to the horrific car crash. What can you tell me that might be helpful?"

"Zip. Nada. Squat. Zilch. Nothing. Not a thing. Did I answer your question thoroughly enough?" His eyes looked cold.

Claire's dislike for the man was growing by the minute. He seemed despicable and totally unworthy of Charlotte's affection.

His eyes shot to the glass panel adjacent to the office door. Claire couldn't be sure, but it seemed he gave a quick wink in that direction. She spun around just in time to see the receptionist turning on her heels to patter down the hallway.

"Am I keeping you from something?" Claire asked. "Or someone?" She suddenly felt great pleasure in knowing she was disrupting the schedule of this egotistical human being.

"I have work to do, Ms. Caswell. I'm a busy man. Now, enough is enough."

"Well, I must thank you very much for cooperating so fully in this murder investigation." Sarcasm dripped from her lips like honey poured over an apple.

He perked up. "Did you say *murder* investigation?"

"I did," Claire said.

"Oh, and am I to believe that I'm a *suspect*?" he asked.

"You said it. Not me," she snapped back.

"Get out!" he bellowed. "I mean it!"

Claire had pushed his buttons.

"I am leaving. But I will not promise I won't return."

"Next time, if there is a next time, you'll talk to my lawyer," he belted out. "I'm through talking to you."

"Are you at all surprised that I said *murder* investigation?" she persisted.

The investigator couldn't help asking that final question.

"Get out!" he barked.

She left his office, analyzing how to interpret his anger. Everyone had triggers, as she was well aware. *In this case, did he feel threatened? Attacked? Powerless? Frustrated? Guilty? Or was it a reasonable response from a man who thought he was being treated unfairly?* She continued to mull these thoughts over in her mind as she drove off in the direction of her office.

Suddenly, she made a turn and headed to the scene of Charlotte's car crash.

Something told her to take a good look at the place where the incident had occurred. When she arrived, she noted the yellow *Crime Scene Do Not Cross* tape was still in place. No one was visible in the immediate area, and seeing a large board nailed in place where the plate glass window had stood prior to the crash made her swallow hard. She parked nearby. Once again, emotions got the best of her, and she hung her head.

After several minutes, she walked toward the building. She knew police investigators had already attempted to reconstruct facts surrounding the accident. And she also knew they had photographed the scene and inspected the wreckage. She stood and accessed the adjacent surroundings and the actual crash site. No skid marks were visible. There was no evidence that Charlotte had attempted to stop or break her speed in any way. The remains of her automobile had been towed away for final examination, so there wasn't much to look at. But her eyes dropped to the ground where the SUV had impacted with the large window, and she searched frantically for a clue—for anything the police may have overlooked.

At first, she saw nothing.

Then, she saw something.

7

CLAIRE GRABBED A pair of latex gloves from her tote and pulled them on. She yanked a fresh plastic bag from a container in her car and wiggled a pair of sterilized tongs from its sealed holder. She walked back to the crash scene and stooped low under the tape. Scattered pieces of glass still peppered the sidewalk running along the front of the restaurant. Ever so carefully, she lifted a dark bit from the fragments. Then she spotted another. And another. Altogether, she found three. They would have been so easy to miss among the shards. What were they? She was sure the police forensics lab would be able to tell her. Had they been thrown from the car upon impact? She had to know.

Deep in thought, she headed toward the Miami-Dade Police Department. Upon arrival, she informed Captain Massey of her find. She dropped the specimens off at the police lab. Perhaps it would turn out to be nothing. But then, what if it was overlooked evidence?

As she drove, she touched the single white baroque pearl necklace Guy had given her as a wedding gift. She adored it. She never took it off, except to shower or swim. Knowing it was there somehow provided a sense of closeness to him even when they were apart.

JIN LOOKED at his wristwatch. It was time to play spy, to watch from afar, to view Charlie in his daily activities. He was handling this case to give Claire and Guy the time they needed to put together the pieces of Charlotte's demise. The intern's surveillance and research had to be flawless. If there was something amiss with Charlie, Jin had to find it. There was no room for mistakes, getting caught, or flubbing up. He felt internal pressure building within his lanky frame. Although neither Claire nor Guy had said anything to make him feel this strain, there had been a palpable unspoken tension in the office since Charlotte's death—a solemn, ever-present seriousness hanging in the air. Jin knew Claire would never be okay until the matter involving Charlotte was resolved to her satisfaction.

He would not let the investigators down on the Charlie McDermott case.

Jin drove to Charlie's condo. He parked down the street from its entrance and waited. He thought about the case. He knew he needed to clarify certain things the next time he was in the office: ownership of the condo, ownership of the Karmann Ghia, and ownership of *Black Pearl*. He also needed to determine Charlie's real name.

For the most part, the subject portrayed a meek and mild demeanor. In an odd way, he almost seemed to be floating through life clouded in absent-mindedness. Jin often felt as if he were watching a silent film as he studied the man—his gestures and overtures were like those of an old-time actor playing a role on the big screen. In fact, to add some comic relief to the otherwise mundane hours of observation, Jin found himself, on more than one occasion, searching his car radio for the perfect music to accompany Charlie's movements.

Most of the time, Charlie played out each day like an on-screen Hollywood legend. His actions went from overly emotive and dramatic to almost lamblike—whichever his life script seemed to demand.

Jin found Charlie the most unusual man he had ever come across.

But there was something else. There was something about his behavior that niggled Jin. What was it? What was he hiding? At a deep level, Jin sensed a secret hovering within the man. Perhaps something he kept hidden for fear exposure would damage or ruin him.

Jin vowed to uncover it.

He waited until Charlie drove away from the condo building. The student intern trailed behind the subject at an unobservable distance. Charlie's first stop was at a French bakery. He parked around the corner in the alleyway and entered through the business's front street door. Jin parked his car. There were no spots in the shade that day, and hot sunlight poured in.

All at once, Jin sneezed an enormous sneeze. Then several other sneezes followed in rapid succession. The sudden involuntary expulsions of air forced themselves from his nose despite his effort to stop them. The bout was deep and obviously a photic sneeze reflex to sunlight—something Jin had lived with from an early age. Each sneeze compelled him to close his eyes for nanoseconds at a time. When the spurt finally ended, Jin's eyes were watering and red. He grabbed for a tissue from the box he kept on the passenger seat. His gaze returned to the bakery's front entrance. He waited. Minutes passed. Had he missed Charlie leaving?

More time passed. Jin exited his car and strolled toward the shop.

He entered and was at once hit by the delicious mélange of aromas wafting through the air. Fresh-baked croissants, muffins, quiche, pies, colorful pastel macarons, and other savories lined the shelves under glass on one entire side of the shop. A few small circular tables with chairs scattered the open area. Most of the seating held singles or couples enjoying cafés or lattes and sweet pastries. His eyes quickly scanned the room. There was no sight of Charlie.

Jin made his way to the men's room. He found no one inside.

He spotted a back door abutting the entrance to the kitchen and walked toward it.

An employee yelled at him. "Hey! This door is not for customers. Use the front door like everybody else!" He walked over and stood between Jin and the exit.

"I'm looking for my friend. I was to meet him here. I saw him walk in, but I don't see him anywhere inside. He must have left through this back door," Jin said. "Did you stop *him*?" Jin's voice cradled a defiant tone.

"I don't have to answer your questions," the employee said. "But you need to obey our rules. Customers come and go through the front door *only*." He now stood with feet apart and his arms folded across his chest. It was clear he had no intention of budging.

"Okay, okay," Jin said. "Cool down, buddy. Hey, did you see my friend leave? He said he'd wait for me." He described Charlie and what he was wearing.

"Oh, you mean *Richard*? You're Richard's friend? Why didn't you say so?" The employee chortled, and his voice became some-what friendlier. "He came to collect his final paycheck. He only worked here a couple of days a week, but he up and quit. Did some of the baking here. And today he left with a bag of fresh-out-of-the-oven chocolate croissants. They're our *heavenly* croissants. Said he had to meet someone special. She must be a real *angel*. Said he was running late."

"Dang it!" Jin said. "He must have forgotten our meeting. And I drove all the way over here." He acted miffed. "How long did he work here, anyway?" Jin asked.

"Couple of years, I guess." The employee eyed him. "You don't know that?"

"I couldn't remember," Jin said.

The employee shot a quizzical look Jin's way.

"Is that 'someone special' his wife, you think?" Jin persisted. "He doesn't tell me much about himself."

This was a tactic he had learned from Claire Caswell. Keep the questions rolling. One after another. The student was throwing out anything he could to get more information about Charlie.

"His wife died. Probably why he won't talk about it."

"I didn't know. What did she die from?" Jin asked.

"A simple surgery gone bad," the employee said. "An appendectomy, I think." He paused. "Boy, you ask a lot of questions."

"Just curious," Jin said. "Always have been." He took a brazen step. "By the way, what is Richard's *last* name?"

Now the employee leveled his eyes on Jin and kept them there. "You don't know your *friend's* last name?"

"Believe it or not, he's never told me," Jin said. He chuckled. "Funny, isn't it? I don't even know his last name. I told you he doesn't tell me much!"

"Connors. Richard Connors. Now I'm all out of answers, and I hope you're all out of questions." The employee turned on his heels and walked into the kitchen, shaking his head and muttering under his breath.

Jin exited through the front door, a bag of chocolate croissants hanging from his hand. He called the office on his cell phone to report in.

"I lost him," he said. "But I think I know where he's going. And I've got his real name. It's Richard Connors. I'll get back to you."

CLAIRE SAT at her desk reviewing the information she had gathered so far on Charlotte's death. There wasn't much. A horrific vehicle crash—initially ruled fatal error on the part of the driver and later deemed to be a homicide. A new boyfriend who appeared unaffected by her loss. And the strange items she had located on the ground at the crash site. The investigator gazed through the front window of the office, and her eyes settled on a nearby palm tree, its fronds blowing ever so gently in the almost undetectable afternoon breeze. She and Charlotte had often talked about their love of palm trees—their majesty, serenity, and elegance. Claire smiled as she remembered Charlotte.

Claire picked up the phone and dialed the police crime lab.

"Have you had a chance to look at the specimens I dropped off?" she asked.

"Ms. Caswell, we really just got them. You'll have to be patient. We analyze items in the order we receive them," the head of the lab explained. "You know that."

"Of course," she replied. "I do. It's just . . . it's just that I'm very anxious to get the results."

"I understand. Everyone is always anxious to get the results. And we'll get those to you as quickly as possible."

"Okay. You'll call me when you have something?"

"Yes, Ms. Caswell. You have my word."

"Thank you." She realized she was expecting unrealistically fast results, and she told herself to take a deep breath.

The phone rang.

"Ms. Caswell, it's Captain Massey. The autopsy on your friend is completed. I asked them to put a rush on it. Because of the condition of her body, it was a difficult autopsy. She died of both head and chest injuries from the impact. Nothing else remarkable was detected. I'm looking over the report now."

"Thank you, Captain. I might want to look at that report at some time." She hung up.

Just then, Guy walked in. He walked over to Claire, leaned down, and kissed her on the cheek.

"How goes it, my love?" he asked.

She explained her discovery at the site of Charlotte's crash and informed him she was waiting for the test results from the crime lab.

"Interesting," Guy said. "What's your best guess on what you found?"

"I have no idea. They were partially round. Darkish in color."

"Hmm. Let me know what the lab has to say when you hear back," Guy said.

"And Charlotte's autopsy was completed. Nothing worthy to note. She died of both head and chest injuries."

"What can I do to spur the investigation forward?" Guy asked.

Claire thought a moment. "I'd like you to buy a car. Well, not exactly *buy* a car, but go to the Porsche dealership and act like you might be interested in buying a car. I want you to wear your curly wig and that fake mustache of yours and maybe throw on a pair of round horn-rimmed glasses. Use a false name, of course. I need you to seek out Stephen Fox to help you."

"I saw him at Charlotte's funeral, Claire. He might have seen me too. What if he recognizes me?"

"He won't. Not wearing the wig, mustache, and glasses. Especially since he barely gave me the time of day when I tried to talk to him. And you never did actually meet him. I think you can easily pull this off. Try to get him into his office to talk. See what you can find out. Something seems off with him, but I don't know what it is. Charlotte said she was in love with the man, and I have yet to find anything appealing about him. He shows absolutely no sadness about her passing. Maybe I'm missing something. Try to shoot the breeze a bit with Stephen. Perhaps you'll pick up on a clue to follow."

"I'll go tomorrow morning. No problem," Guy said. "By the way, and on another subject, how is Jin handling the surveillance of Charlie—or whatever his name really is? Has he found out anything interesting?"

"He actually lost him today. The man went into the front door of a bakery and out the back. But Jin thought he knew where the man was going with his purchase of French pastries, so he planned to check it out. He did get his real name, though. It's Richard Connors. I'm waiting to hear back from Jin."

"Good," Guy said. "He's really turning out to be quite an asset to our firm."

"I agree," Claire said. "Not sure what we'd do without him."

JIN TRAVELED to Estee's house and arrived just in time to see Charlie's car pulling away from the curb. The two were on their way to some destination. Jin followed. Soon they arrived at the pier. Hand in hand, the couple paced to *Black Pearl*, the subject toting the bag of chocolate croissants in his free hand. They boarded and disappeared below deck.

Jin knew the exquisite Hinckley Picnic Boat like the back of his hand. He imagined Charlie was turning on the electric coffeemaker in the galley at that moment to brew a pot of aromatic coffee to accompany the fresh croissants. Jin fixed his gaze on the US flag, prominently attached to the boat's stern. From his position in the nearby lot, and with the help of high-powered binoculars, he was able to see the navy, gray, and white-striped fabric covering the cushioned seating. Also, the magnificent gloss of the Burmese teak emblazoning the deck and giving the boat its stunning design lines. He knew the amount of sanding and multiple layers of varnishing it took to create this masterpiece, a boat that could travel at close to forty miles per hour. *No other boat looks like a Hinckley*, Jin thought. It had the ideal layout between interior and exterior space.

The intern closed his eyes and let his mind imagine. Soon he pictured himself at the helm of his own Hinckley Picnic Boat. He felt the connection to the water, to its look and smell. He inhaled deeply. *One day*, he told himself as he opened his eyes to continue his surveillance, *one day, I will own a Hinckley.*

Soon the couple appeared on deck. The two wore swimwear and carried beach towels. Charlie drove the boat slowly out into the open water. He dropped anchor. Jin's binoculars afforded him the opportunity to continue observing them at close range from a distance.

Before long, Charlie pulled Estee into his arms and held her close. He leaned in and kissed her slowly. Then he grabbed her by the hand, and together they jumped off the back of the boat into the waiting water. It was obvious the two delighted in their frolic. They laughed and romped in flirtatious ways, Charlie often pulling Estee close for yet another spell of amorous kissing.

For a fleeting moment, Jin wondered if perhaps this was a real romance. But then he reminded himself the man might have a different motivation altogether. He had to find out.

He waited patiently until *Black Pearl* returned to shore and the couple left to drive back to Estee's place.

His next stop was the office.

First Jin tried to check out the name *Richard Connors*. He located only one in the immediate area that matched the man's approximate age. He delved further. Richard Connors had a criminal record. And when Jin investigated the reason for the record, he discovered a multitude of drunk driving charges. Other than that, he found nothing. So was Richard Connors going by the name Charlie McDermott simply to avoid people knowing about his felony convictions for driving under the influence? Or was there another reason?

Jin knew the Hinckley was a semi-custom boat. Anyone ordering one was assigned a project manager to work with throughout its creation. He decided to call the company, pose as a potential buyer, say he saw and really liked the boat named *Black Pearl*, and see if he could garner further information, including the name of the person who ordered the boat. He searched for the sales office's contact number.

8

A FIGURE WALKED surreptitiously to the fenced area in one corner of the backyard, unlocked the padlock on the gate with the key he kept so finely polished, walked in, and quietly closed the gate behind him. The old wooden fence was tall and coated with peeling green paint. But it was solidly built, and it hid his prized possessions. He pulled on a pair of gardening gloves. He was prepared for the task ahead. He looked up. The moonlight was sufficient to illuminate the area. Carefully, oh so carefully, he tended to each plant and shrub. These were his babies. He treated them like royalty, seeing to their every need. He stepped back, ogled his secret world, and smiled curiously. Oh, what a wonderful creation he had forged—not unlike a fine tapestry of interlacing threads crafted on a weaver's loom. The whole was magnificent; each part extraordinary.

Moisture appeared on his brow, despite the breezes of the evening.

"I'll see you soon, my pretties." He exited and closed the door to his private sphere behind him, relocking the padlock firmly in place.

GUY ARRIVED at the dealership the following morning in disguise. He took off his wedding band and slid it into his pocket. He walked inside and mulled around the showroom. Before long, an overbearing salesman approached to offer him assistance. The man had a voice larger than his size.

"I'm Jim Kesson," he said. "Or Jimmy, if you prefer. And you are?"

"And I am *just looking*," Guy said. He chuckled slightly.

"Go ahead. Look all you want," the salesman said. "Let me know if you need anything or have any questions. My office is down the hall and around the corner." He passed Guy his card. "Make sure to ask for me—Jimmy Kesson."

Claire had indicated to Guy just where Stephen's office was located, and on the spot Guy calculated that he would have to walk right past Stephen's office to get to Jimmy's. It would work perfectly.

After a few minutes, Guy made his way down the hallway. When he reached Stephen's office, he observed that the door was open partway. He pushed it fully open and stepped in. Stephen looked up.

"Oh, sorry, I was looking for Jimmy's office," Guy said. "I just had a couple of questions about a Cayenne."

"Maybe I can help you," Stephen said. "I just saw a client of Jim's pass by my office, so I'm guessing he's busy right now. Come in. Have a seat."

Guy strode to the chair in front of Stephen's desk and sat down.

So far so good, Guy thought.

Stephen closed the office door.

"Now, what can I help you with?" he asked.

"Well, I might be interested in a Porsche SUV. Convince me why

I should buy one." Guy exuded a persona of ultimate confidence.

"Where do I start?" Stephen said. He forced a laugh. "How does one describe the best of the best?"

Guy grinned. "I hear you, but I need more than that. Why do people like these vehicles so much?"

"Okay. Can I get you a cup of coffee? A smoothie?" Stephen asked.

"Why not?" Guy said. "Coffee sounds good."

"Sugar? Cream?"

"Just black. Thank you."

Stephen left the room to brew capsules of coffee. Seconds later, Jimmy poked his head into the room.

"There you are," he said. "I was looking everywhere for you."

"Oh, no problem," Guy said. "I'm just talking with . . ." He overtly glanced at the nameplate on the desk. "With Stephen Fox about these cars in general. You were busy."

"Uh-huh," Jimmy said.

His tone sent the instant message that he was not happy about losing a potential customer. Guy assumed it was a cutthroat business.

Stephen reappeared holding a cup of steaming coffee in each hand. He strolled right past Jimmy still standing in the doorway and offered a cup to Guy.

"Jim, is there something I can help you with?" Stephen asked, sending the clear message that the salesman should vanish.

"I talked to this customer earlier. He's actually my—"

Stephen glared at the salesman. If looks could kill, Jimmy would be a dead man.

"If there's nothing further, Jim," Stephen said.

Reluctantly, Jimmy walked from the office.

"Touchy, touchy, touchy," Stephen said. "Working on commissions makes some of the salespeople a bit tetchy. I apologize for his behavior. Now, where were we?" He took a sip of the hot beverage.

"You were about to tell me why I should give some serious thought to purchasing a Porsche Cayenne," Guy said. He sipped his coffee. "Hope I didn't cause friction between the two of you."

"Oh, no worries. Jim easily becomes irascible. He's been here longer than I have, he trained me a bit when I first started, and he thinks he owns the place. I'm sure you know the type. Fact is you can work with whomever you want to." He paused and sipped. "Well, first things first. My name is Stephen Fox. Your name is?"

Guy thought fast. He needed to come up with a name common enough that there would be plenty around to research, should Stephen decide to find out more about him. "John Williams."

Stephen jotted down his name. "Okay, Mr. Williams. Let me tell you about these fabulous cars. They perform like a sports car, and they're a fancy ride. They also give you off-road ability. It's basically a five-star-rated-across-the-board vehicle." He stopped. "Do you need to hear more?"

Guy chuckled. "Of course."

"Okay. All kidding aside, this is a German-made midsize SUV that has been sold in the United States since 2003—"

Guy glanced at his watch. "I don't have a ton of time today. What is the price?"

"I'm getting there," Stephen said. He continued, prattling on about the Cayenne's other features.

"Sounds like a great vehicle. Really," Guy said. "What is the price?" His face revealed he was becoming somewhat annoyed.

"Before I tell you the price, I think we should take it on a test drive," Stephen said. "Oh, and one more thing: the ladies like it." He winked.

Guy realized he'd hit gold. He forced a smile. "Okay, I will take time to hear about that."

"Well, women come in to buy these cars quite often. And when they do, I get to meet a lot of high-buck females." He stared at Guy. "The ones making the big salaries. And they're usually single. It's an added benefit. They also like men who drive them."

"Now you're getting me more interested," Guy said. "Go on."

Stephen lowered his voice to a whisper. "I've helped many women over the years who have come in to buy a Porsche. I've ended up in bed with most of them." He smiled wolfishly.

Guy's thoughts went to Charlotte. The woman thought this Casanova was actually in love with her. He was nothing more than an egomaniacal braggart. It sickened him.

Guy forced himself to speak. "No wife? Longtime girlfriend?"

"Not for me," Stephen crowed. "I like variety. I'm easily bored."

Guy again glanced at his wristwatch. "I need to leave. I have to get to a meeting. If I decide to take the plunge, I'll contact you."

"Can I get a phone number for you, John?" Stephen asked.

"I'll contact you if I'm interested," Guy repeated.

Handshakes were exchanged.

As Guy walked toward the dealership's front doors, he noticed Jimmy off to one side, standing by a desk and glaring at him. He nodded good-bye to the man.

Guy walked to his car that he had thoughtfully parked a block away. That way curious eyes could not see his vehicle. He slipped his wedding band back on his finger.

JIN WAS on the phone with a Hinckley dealer in the Miami area. He had first blocked the caller ID. He talked for a time to the store manager as though he may be interested in purchasing one. Then he popped the question.

"A friend of mine owns a Hinckley Picnic Boat named *Black Pearl*. Do you know it?"

"As a matter of fact, I do. I sold him the boat," the manager said.

A pleased expression appeared on Jin's face.

"I do like his boat," Jin said. "Is it pretty standard as far as custom features?"

"Not at all," the dealer said. "He spared no expense whatsoever. Said he'd always wanted a Hinckley and the sky was the limit. He selected all the top options across the board. No wonder you like Roise's boat. She's a stunner."

"Can I ask you what Roise paid for the boat?" Jin asked.

"You can ask. But I won't tell. That's confidential."

"Of course," Jin said. "Well, let me ponder this a bit. If I decide to take a serious look at a Hinckley, I'll call you back."

"Okay. Can I get your name and number?" the dealer asked.

Jin hung up.

BACK AT the office, Claire, Guy, and Jin sat in chairs around the conference table. Claire had picked up a large platter of sushi, and they indulged.

"Let's see what we've all discovered up to this point," Claire said.

Guy went first, filling the others in on his experience at the Porsche dealership. "My opinion? This Stephen Fox, who Charlotte thought she was in love with, is an arrogant, slithery toad. He's as transparent as glass. I detest the man."

"My readings exactly," Claire said. "Other than that he's a sleazebag, do you think there's more to his story?"

"That remains to be seen," Guy said. "I think we need to check him out further."

"I agree," Claire said. "His apparent total lack of feelings about Charlotte's death tells me there is more to learn."

Jin was up next.

"As you know, I've had Charlie McDermott under surveillance for a few days now. He's an interesting man. Strange, really. He moves and acts like he's auditioning for a movie part. Overly dramatic, to be sure. And there's an issue with his name, as we suspected. I followed him to a bakery where he used to work a couple of days a week until recently when he quit. They knew him at the bakery as *Richard Connors.* And I've followed Charlie and Estee to a Hinckley Picnic Boat. The two are clearly lovey-dovey. Can't keep their hands off each other. She's obviously older, but it doesn't seem to bother either one. And . . ."

"And what, Jin?" Claire asked.

"Well, if I just looked at their relationship from afar, I would say I've seen no red flags. Not yet, anyway. They go boating, go swimming, dance on deck, and disappear below to eat chocolate croissants and do whatever else they do. They just seem to be having a good time. But the issue with the names he uses is problematic. Not sure what that's all about."

"It doesn't pass the smell test, does it? Why the different names? What is he hiding?" Claire asked. She looked concerned.

"There's more," Jin said. "I spoke to the Hinckley dealer where the boat was ordered, and the manager referred to the purchaser as *Roise.* I haven't gotten a last name yet." Jin referred to his journal. "Charlie lives in an opulent condo in Bal Harbour, drives a collector Karmann Ghia, wears vintage Hawaiian-print shirts, and rents or uses an expensive luxury boat. Yet, he was working part-time at a French bakery. This doesn't make sense. It doesn't fit."

"Contradictions and inconsistencies usually indicate lying or deception," Claire said. "Have you checked on the car and condo ownership?"

"Those are next on my list," Jin said.

"Good. And I believe you should continue watching the man for a time," Claire said. "Let's see what else might surface."

"I agree," Guy said. "Something's definitely up with Charlie, or Richard—whatever his real name is. And his relationship with Estee sounds a little too perfect to be true. Stay on it, Jin."

"You'll find the truth in the details," Claire said. "Look closely."

She went on to inform Jin about the curious findings at the site of Charlotte's crash.

TWO DAYS HAD passed since Claire dropped off the specimens at the crime lab. She decided to give them another call, despite being told they would contact her once the analysis was completed. She couldn't stand the suspense.

"Ms. Caswell, we have conducted only the very basic preliminary testing at this point," the tech informed her. "Many more tests are required before we can tell you with certainty just what it is you discovered at the crash site. Again, we'll call you as soon as we have something definite."

Claire exhaled loudly. "Thank you."

She detested the waiting game. It was the one of the worst parts about being a private investigator. Biding one's time. Being delayed. Standing by. Sitting tight. Being on hold. Postponing her opportunity to check out a potential clue. Treading water when she wanted to swim.

SHE WENT on her computer and decided to do research on Stephen Fox. She spent time looking on many of the social media sites. He definitely kept a low profile. There was no doubt about it. However, she did find a mention of a Stephen and Carli Fox in the Miami area. She searched for any information she could find on Carli Fox and came up with an address.

Claire jumped into her car and drove to the address. It was an apartment complex. She sat outside for a time and then walked to the lobby. She found the name *C. Fox* on the list of residents and pushed the buzzer. It was afternoon when most people were at work, and although she didn't expect an answer, the sleepy voice of a female responded.

"Hello?" she asked. "Who is it?"

"Hi. I'm wondering if you can help me. I'm a private investigator, Claire Caswell, and I have some questions about Stephen Fox. I would appreciate it if you would give me a few minutes of your time."

There was silence for a long minute, and then Carli spoke. "Apartment 307."

Claire heard the click of the security door and pushed it open. She took the elevator up to the third floor and walked down the hallway until she found number 307. She knocked.

The door opened a crack. "Your ID, please," Carli said.

"Certainly," Claire said. She held her identification badge close to the opening so that Carli could see it clearly.

"Come in," she said.

Claire walked inside the apartment. It was small, furnished in shades of teals and beiges, and tidily kept. She turned to get a good look at Carli.

"I was asleep," she said. "I work nights, and I sleep during the day."

Her hair was tousled, and she wore a daffodil-yellow robe. Her close-set eyes were topaz in color and fringed with long lashes. Her skin was translucent, and she had angular cheekbones.

"I apologize for disturbing you," Claire said.

"What is this about?" Carli asked. "You said something about my ex-husband, Stephen?"

"Yes," Claire said. "What can you tell me about him?"

"What do you want to know? And why?" she asked. "What exactly are you investigating?" She furrowed her brow, suddenly suspicious of the questioning.

"Well, a good friend of mine was killed in a horrific car crash a short time ago."

"I'm sorry, but I'd like to know what that has to do with me or with Steve. How could that possibly have something to do with us?" She was definitely on the defensive.

"It seems Stephen, or *Steve*, was dating my friend at the time. Some evidence has surfaced that appears to indicate the crash was not an accident. We're checking out all leads."

"I see," Carli said. She suddenly appeared reflective, and her tone changed. She became more open and helpful.

"How long were you married to Stephen?" Claire asked.

"It was a short marriage. Less than a year. But I kept his last name. I liked it better than my own. Steve was not the marrying kind, if you know what I mean. He was never satisfied with one woman. Always kept more on the string. Not very conducive to a happy marriage, as you can imagine. I loved him, but I couldn't stay married to him."

"Do you still talk to him or see him?" Claire asked.

"Almost never. He moved on after we divorced."

"What can you tell me about the man?" Claire asked.

"He's arrogant. Egotistical. Always right. Impossible. A bona fide bastard, really. He left me with a ton of debt. All in my name. And he walked away free. Need I say more?"

"Have you gone after him for some of the money?" Claire asked.

"There's no point. He never has any. Spends it as quickly as he makes it."

"Ooh. Bad story. I'm sorry."

"Yeah, well, live and learn. I'll be a lot more careful next time around . . . if there is a next time."

"What attracted you to him in the first place?" Claire asked.

"I've asked myself that question many times," she said. "I'm a stripper. He came to my club. Paid a lot of attention to me. Tipped me with big bills. I guess I fell for him after a time. And his looks didn't hurt. He's a good-looking man."

Claire looked deep in thought. "My friend who was killed, Charlotte, had been dating him for a short time. She said she was in love with him."

"Well, she might have been in love with him, but I can assure you he wasn't in love with her. He doesn't know the meaning of the word. He hasn't a clue what real love involves. And he really doesn't know what commitment is either. In my opinion, he's bad all around. You know the saying: 'If there were a sunny side of the street and a shady side of the street, he'd walk on the shady side'? That's Steve. He'd do almost anything to make a buck. He always needs money. Wish I'd never met the man." She pulled out a cigarette and lit it up. She inhaled deeply before exhaling. "Just thinking about him gets me worked up."

"Is there anyone else I could talk to who might also know something about him?" Claire asked.

"Maybe his son, Eric, if he'll talk to you. He's disgusted with him too." She jotted down a phone number and address and handed it to Claire. "Nice kid, but you'll have to catch him on a good day. He suffers from depression. He has his up days and his down days."

"I have a final question," Claire said, "and it's a tough one. Think about your answer before you give it." She looked Carli squarely in the eye. "In your opinion, is Stephen capable of murder?"

CLAIRE DROVE back to the office preoccupied with her conversation with Carli. When she arrived, she filled Guy in.

"Want to come and interview Eric with me?" she asked.

"Thought you'd never ask. There's no time like the present. Let's go."

The two drove in Guy's car to Eric's address.

It was a small house in a marginal area of Miami. They approached the front door and rang the bell. It was the end of the workday, and they hoped he would be home. There was no answer. They would try again later.

JIN'S MISSION to follow Charlie had been exhausting. Mainly because it did not appear that Charlie was doing anything worthy of being followed. Aside from the strange inconsistencies of the names he used, Jin had not witnessed the subject doing anything nefarious.

Today seemed similar to every other day. Charlie picked up Ester, the two went out for a late lunch, and Charlie spent time with Ester at her home. It was after his time with Ester that things unexpectedly became more interesting. Jin trailed behind Charlie, but this afternoon, instead of him going to his showy condo, he drove to a house located miles away but still within the Miami area. Charlie walked toward the house, looked quickly in both directions, and entered through the front door. Several other cars were parked on the street.

Jin called Guy to check in. He gave him the address.

"Be careful out there, Jin. We really don't know who or what you're dealing with. Always err on the side of caution."

"Of course."

Jin wanted to get a look inside. He parked down the street and concocted a plan on the spot. He waited a few minutes. He pulled his shirt out, unbuttoned a couple of buttons, and rolled up the sleeves. He removed his tie and took his straight hair out of the neat ponytail he always wore to let it hang loose. He threw on a baseball cap and sunglasses. He grabbed a notebook and pen. He walked to the front door of the house and rang the doorbell. A man answered.

"Hello, sir. My name's Eugene. I'm a window washer. A really good one. I'm canvassing your area to set up dates to clean windows. I do the outside and the inside or whichever you'd prefer. My rates are reasonable. Can I sign you up?"

As Jin talked, he let his eyes meander past the side of the man's head, scouring the living room behind him. He spotted a game table with several men sitting around it, including Charlie, all holding hands of cards. Bottles of beer and blue smoke were abundant.

"Not interested," the man said.

"Well, thank you for your time."

"Do you have a business card in case I change my mind?" the man asked.

Jin patted his shirt pocket, pretending to feel for a card. "Sorry, man. I just gave the last one away. Would you like me to check back with you in about a month?"

"Sure. Why not?" the man said. He closed the door.

Jin walked around the neighborhood for a few minutes, just in case the guys at the house might be watching. He returned to his car, satisfied that the group was merely having a guys' night of poker and drinking. Again, no criminal element.

CLAIRE AND Guy waited until 7:30 p.m. before returning to Eric's house. This time the lights were on, and Eric answered the door. The investigators introduced themselves, and he invited them in.

Eric was a young man in his twenties. He looked and acted fatigued. Claire wondered about his mental health, because his demeanor exuded melancholy.

"Eric, thank you for talking with us today," Guy said. "We're here because your father was dating a woman named Charlotte Truman."

"She was my friend," Claire said. "There was a terrible car crash, and Charlotte was killed."

"Was she the driver?" Eric asked.

"She was," Claire said.

"Why do you ask?" Guy asked.

"Well," Eric said, "a couple of his other girlfriends, actually three, have died the same way over the last few years. A run of bad luck, I'd say."

Claire shot a quick look at Guy. Her face tried to mask her disbelief. "Tell us more. What were their names? Were these longtime relationships?"

"Longtime?" Eric asked. "If you consider a month each a *long* time. I met them all only once. Their names? Let me think." He paused as if trying to remember. "Cindy Bane was one. And there was a Catherine Hanker. And the third was another name starting with *C*." He closed his eyes. "Her name was Camille. Camille Sullivan, I think. They all seemed like nice people."

"Were these women from the Miami area?" Guy asked.

"I believe so," Eric said. "Executive types. That's the only kind of women Steve dates. Those who are successful. With money. And all with names starting with *C*. It's funny, but it's like he won't date a woman unless her first name starts with *C*. Really strange if you ask me."

"And in each case, these women died in car crashes?" Claire asked.

"Yep. Each time, the women were driving their own vehicles and they collided into something," Eric said. "There were no other cars involved in any of the accidents."

"Over how many years did you say this has been happening?" Guy asked.

"I'd guess maybe three or four." He scratched his head. "And now there's another one? Sounds like anyone dating Steve should be mighty careful."

"Did you meet Charlotte Truman?" Claire asked.

"Another C name. No, I didn't."

"Did you know Carli, your dad's ex-wife?" Claire asked.

"Sure, I knew her. Yet another C name. That didn't last long either," Eric said. "She was too good for him."

"Meaning?" Guy asked.

"Meaning, she was devoted to him. But he could never reciprocate. I wanted to warn her when they were dating. It was her first marriage and his second."

"Describe your relationship with your father, will you, please?" Guy asked.

"Relationship? Now that would entail a connection of some kind. All we have is a family tie. Nothing else. I don't even call him Father—just Steve. We rarely talk, and when we do, I initiate it."

"I'm sorry," Claire said. "That must be painful."

"Not really," Eric said. "It's the way it is. It's been that way since my mom died." He grabbed his forehead.

"Headache?" Claire asked.

"Yeah."

"Tell us about your mom," Claire said.

"She died several years ago. I guess five."

"What took her life?" Guy asked. "She must have been young."

"They never determined her cause of death," Eric said. His eyes started to blink rapidly.

"What was her name?" Claire asked.

"Christine," Eric said. He looked off into the distance.

"Again, we're sorry for your loss," Claire said. "You've had a lot to deal with."

Eric held his head down for a couple of long minutes before looking up.

"How long were your parents married?" Guy asked.

"Eighteen years, I think. I do believe they really loved each other. I miss my mother. The two of us fought a lot, and now that makes me feel really bad. Life has not been happy since she left."

"Can you tell us more about her death?" Claire asked. "The circumstances surrounding it?"

Eric looked at her with incredulity. He seemed startled, yet he also appeared to want to explore her question. "What are you implying? Do you think Steve had something to do with my mom's death? Is that why you're really here? You think Steve had something to do with your friend's death too? And the deaths of those other women?" He shook his head.

"Whoa. Slow down," Guy said. "We're saying no such thing. Right now, we're just collecting information. Nothing else."

"My mother was sick for a couple of days before she died. The medical examiner's office was unable to pinpoint what took her life. Even in the autopsy, no immediate cause of death showed up. I remember they called it a negative autopsy, meaning they couldn't find a specific cause. Not much help, were they?" He again dropped his head. "I really don't want to talk about my mother anymore," Eric said.

He looked irritated.

Unexpectedly, he then made a bold, loud statement. "Get the sonofabitch if he was responsible for your friend's death. And the deaths of those other women he dated. Hang him high." A feral look appeared in his eyes.

"We won't take up any more of your time today, Eric," Claire said, handing him a business card. "If you need to talk, give us a call."

ON THE drive home, Claire was the first to speak. "Most children protect their parents no matter how much they dislike them. Eric did not." She paused. "And did you catch when he talked about Stephen and said if he was responsible for Charlotte's death and the deaths of the other women he dated to hang him high? Makes me wonder if Eric knows more about his mother's demise than he's telling us."

"Also, how very odd that all the women's names begin with the letter *C*," Guy said. "This couldn't get any stranger."

"Yeah. Christine, Carli, Cindy, Catherine, Camille, and Charlotte? And all of them, except for Christine and Carli, died in horrific car crashes. And we don't know what caused Christine's death."

"The name thing could be sheer coincidence," Guy said. "You know that."

"Could be," Claire said. "But I think not."

10

THE FOLLOWING MORNING, Claire and Guy sat at their desks reviewing everything they had learned from Eric.

"I think we need to check out the information he gave us to determine its validity," Claire said. "Let's split up the names and see what we can find. And let's see if there's any connections with the letter C. This is getting very intriguing."

"Keep in mind, if the man *is* guilty, and if he's after women whose names begin with C, you need to have your guard up also, *Claire*," Guy said. "I mean it." His forehead crinkled. "Don't disregard potential danger."

"The thought did cross my mind more than once, I have to admit," Claire said. She gave Guy a serious look. "Now let's get to work."

The two investigators sat at their desks for the next few hours, checking every source at their disposal. Their computers and phones were busy the entire time.

CLAIRE TOOK a breather only once. It was when the office phone rang.

"Caswell & Lombard, Private Investigation. Claire Caswell speaking," she said.

"Ms. Caswell, it's Gloria Adams, assistant administrator at the police crime lab. I'm calling you with an update. We're still working on those samples you dropped off. We're narrowing the field, but I must tell you the specimens have degraded to a level that makes our job more difficult."

"Do you ever get items you are unable to identify?"

"I'd have to say almost never. We stay on it until we usually are able to make a definitive determination. Sometimes it just takes longer for the analysis. Hang in there. We hope to have some information for you before too long."

Claire thanked Ms. Adams.

She hung up and shared the call with Guy.

"Strange, huh?" he said. "I wonder what you found?"

JIN WALKED into the office yawning. He had been at law school a good part of the day and seemed particularly exhausted.

"Jin, my man, you're burning the candle at both ends. Are you getting any sleep?" Guy asked.

"I grab a couple of hours whenever I can," the law student said. "But life is exciting right now. I don't want to give up any part of it." He forced a half smile.

"Will you do us a favor, Jin?" Claire asked.

"Of course. Anything," he said.

"Take the rest of today off. Go home, get something to eat, and get some real sleep. You'll be better off tomorrow."

"But—" he started.

"We insist," Guy said. "End of discussion."

Jin had learned that when Guy used the words *end of discussion*, that was exactly what he meant. Jin had witnessed Guy's temper on rare occasions, and he didn't want to ignite it.

"Okay. I'll do it." He did his best to contain another yawn. "See you both tomorrow." He gathered some items from his desk and left.

"Maybe I'll take a break and drive over to surprise Estee with another visit," Claire said. "I'll pick up some cookies on the way. Besides, I need to see my parents. I've been neglecting them. Want to come along?"

"Thanks, but I think I'll stay here and keep working on the Stephen Fox case."

"Okay." She grabbed her purse and left.

ESTEE ANSWERED the front door immediately when Claire knocked.

"Claire, so nice to see you again," she said. "And so soon. Please come in. Can I fix you a cup of hot tea?"

"I would love that," the investigator said. "And I brought some cookies."

She extended a bakery box to Estee.

"Oh," she said. "How thoughtful. We'll have them with the tea. It will be only a few minutes." She ambled toward the kitchen and stopped. She turned around. "And before I forget, congratulations on your marriage. I always knew the two of you belonged together. I forgot to mention it the last time you stopped by." She offered an adorable smile.

Claire took a seat in the living room. On the coffee table, she noticed several folded note cards. She took the liberty of opening one and scanning its contents. It was a love note signed by Charlie. The penmanship was scruffy, and the words flowery. She picked up another. This one read:

My dear Estee,

You are not just my girl
You are my pearl.

This strand of natural black Tahitian pearls
Is as rare as our eternal love.

It is my gift to you.

Your soul mate, Charlie

This man was wooing Estee to the hilt.

Claire heard a sound and quickly replaced the note to the table.

Just then, Ester reentered the room carrying a tray. It held two lovely English china cups filled with steaming tea, a plate of the cookies, and cloth napkins.

"What a treat!" Claire said.

"You should make time for tea every day," Estee said. "You work too hard. Your parents always talk about it."

"Well, I plan on popping next door to see them next," Claire said.

"It's lovely to see you again, Claire, but what brings you here?" Estee asked. "Did Abbey ask you to check up on me?"

"Actually, I wanted to drop off some cookies for you," the female investigator said. "And to see how everything is going."

"Fine," Ester said. "In fact, I'm more than fine. Things in my life are really good."

"And Charlie is still in the picture?" she asked.

"Oh my, yes. He's a real gentleman. I'm not sure how I'd be doing without him. He came into my life when I needed him most, and he's around all the time. I have no opportunity to feel lonely. He keeps me busy. He's younger than I am, but I don't care a speck and neither does he. We have a connection." She paused. "I talked to you about him the last time you visited me."

"I remember," Claire said.

"Charlie has a good heart," Ester said. She turned up the corners of her mouth. "We enjoy each other's company. We just have fun."

"What kind of fun things do you two do?" Claire asked. She bit into a cookie and took a sip of the hot beverage.

"Well, a lot of times we just sit together, right here, and talk. We have tea. I cherish those times. And sometimes we go out on his boat. It's a marvelous boat called a Picnic Boat. Some days we bring a full lunch with us. Other times Charlie brings these delicious chocolate croissants he picks up at a bakery. We even swim. It's the most fun I think I've ever had." She stopped to pick up her teacup, sip, and taste a cookie. "These are wonderful, Claire! Thank you again for bringing them."

Claire observed Estee and absorbed her words. She seemed trusting and unworldly.

"You told me Charlie knew your husband, William, if I recall correctly?" Claire asked.

"Yes, he told me that immediately. And it gave me great comfort. It still does."

"But you don't recall ever meeting him while your husband was alive?"

"No, but then my husband was a businessman out in the world. He worked with a lot of people I didn't know." She sipped her tea. "Charlie worked with William. He told me so."

Claire did not tell Estee she had checked with Donegale, Inc. and discovered that Charlie had never worked there. Not yet. She would when the timing was right. Her eyes fell to the pricy full strand of pearls hanging around Estee's neck.

"Estee, those pearls are amazing!" Claire said.

"Thank you, dear," she said. "They were a gift from Charlie."

"Wow. What a *nice* gift," Claire said.

"Well, I tried to tell him I couldn't accept them, but he wouldn't hear of it. He insisted I keep them, wear them, and enjoy them. He wore me down until I finally said yes. I know the necklace is a material thing, but I do love it. Because it's from Charlie."

Claire touched the single pearl hanging from her neck chain. It was from Guy. She understood.

"Tell me about the pearls," Claire said.

"All I know is that they're rare. And lavish. They're black Tahitian pearls."

"The colors are stunning, Estee."

"Tell me what colors you see, Claire."

"Well, I see grays, silvers, bronzes, a purplish green blue, and a green with pink overtones to it."

"Notice you didn't say black," Estee said. She smiled. "Black pearls are not actually black. They're all those luscious colors you mentioned. Charlie explained that to me."

"Please wear them in good health. They are extraordinary."

Estee thanked Claire for noticing.

"Have you ever been to Charlie's house?" Claire asked.

"He lives in a condo," Estee said. "Charlie told me it's under renovation, so no, I haven't seen it yet. He wants me to wait until the reconstruction is finished."

"Does Charlie have children?" Claire asked, sipping her cooling tea.

"No. His wife died. He has no children and no relatives. Poor thing," Estee said. "He tells me I'm his only family. And William and I could never have children. So it's Charlie and me against the world. Thank goodness for Charlie. I shudder to think of life alone."

Claire finished her tea and cookie.

"Well, it was very nice to see you again, Estee," Claire said. "I need to stop and visit my parents now and then get back to my office."

"Say hello to Don and Abbey for me, please. And stop over more often for tea. It's important that you take some time away from your hectic lifestyle to relax. Trust me. Life passes all too quickly. Work will always be there, but people won't."

She gave Claire a hug and waved good-bye from the door as Claire walked across the yard to her parent's house.

BACK AT the office, Guy remained hard at work. His research seemed to be meeting one dead end after another. He was checking out Stephen's ex-girlfriends: Cindy, Catherine, and Camille. He found death records on all three. And just as Eric had said, all the women had died in grisly car crashes. There was no mention of anything suspicious in any of the cases. Why was Eric intentionally or unintentionally trying to lead the investigators down a path pointing to his father? Was he so angry with his father that he would do so out of revenge?

Claire walked in, and the two reported in to each other.

"I need that police lab report," Claire said. "Maybe it will shed some light on all of this."

"I certainly hope so," Guy said.

They ordered dinner delivered to the office and kept working. Claire found information on Christine Fox, Eric's mother. She had died five years earlier. The cause of death was uncertain but presumed to be natural causes. Claire picked up her phone and dialed Captain Massey at the Miami-Dade Police Department.

"Glad you caught me, Ms. Caswell," the captain said. "I was just about to leave for the day. What can I help you with?"

"I'd like you to check on the death records of a Christine, C-h-r-i-s-t-i-n-e, Fox. She died approximately five years ago. She was married to Stephen Fox, and they had a son, Eric—with a *c*. I desperately need to know anything you have on her death. I understand the autopsy resulted in a negative conclusion with no specific cause of death determined. Were there any suspicions about the cause of death? Who conducted the autopsy?"

"Hold on, Ms. Caswell. Let me pull it up on my computer," the captain said.

Claire waited as she heard him tapping on his keyboard.

"Okay, I've got it up on my screen." He started scanning through the information. "Medical examiner Paul Wrigley handled the case. I think you've met him. He's an old pro. There was a case opened because the cause of death was not readily apparent. Neither natural causes nor suicide could be ruled out initially. The case was drawn out for some time. Finally, it concluded with a negative autopsy as you indicated—no cause of death could be definitively determined, so the report concluded her death was most probably due to natural causes."

"So this negative autopsy ruling, between you and me, doesn't necessarily rule out foul play, correct? It just means the coroner couldn't identify the cause, right?"

"Between you and me, Ms. Caswell, you're correct. Perhaps you should talk directly to Wrigley."

"That's my plan, Captain. I'll call him in the morning. As always, thank you."

CLAIRE WOKE up early the following day. She was eager to speak with medical examiner Wrigley. She showered, readied for the day, ate a quick breakfast with Guy, and left for the office. "I'll see you when you get there," she said. They kissed good-bye.

She opened the office and immediately made the call. She wanted to reach the medical examiner before he got tied up with other things.

"Hello. Wrigley, here," he said.

"Paul, it's Claire Caswell—private investigator. We've met a handful of times over the years."

"Sure, Claire Caswell. What can I do for you?" he asked.

She quickly noted the case and told him what she needed.

"Ah, I remember it well. Some cases you can't forget. Most times I feel confident about closing a file, but then there are the few I don't feel so good about. And those cases never stop haunting me. This case was one of them. I had an uneasy gut feeling that we missed the cause of death. That it was there, but we just couldn't find it."

"Did you suspect something specific?" the female investigator asked.

He did not answer at first. Then his answer came.

"I did."

"What was it?"

He hesitated again. "I always suspected . . . poisoning."

"*Poisoning?*" Claire asked.

"Yes, but we checked the usual 150 types of poisoning we routinely test for in this office and found nothing. We even checked for some rarer types of poisoning, including the ones that don't show up in an autopsy—where you have to look closely for other signs—and found nothing. But then, there are thousands more possibilities for poisoning that we don't check out. Sad but true, we simply don't have the funds to test for them all."

"But in your decades of experience, your instincts told you that Christine Fox was poisoned?" Claire asked. She needed to be sure.

"This is off the record, Ms. Caswell. If you say you heard it from me, I'll deny it. But my answer to you is a definitive *yes*. I believe Christine Fox was poisoned."

11

THINGS HAD TAKEN a turn. Medical examiner Wrigley believed Christine Fox had been poisoned. That was all Claire had to hear. She knew him, and she knew his reputation, and she believed his level of experience was unbeatable. She did not doubt his instincts. Not for a second. Christine Fox had been poisoned.

Guy walked into the office carrying two lattes. He handed one to Claire.

"You won't believe what I'm going to tell you," she said. "Better sit."

He listened carefully to all the details she reported before he weighed in.

"I dealt with a lot of suspected poisoning cases as a Miami-Dade state attorney, as you know. Some were easy to prove, others not so easy. And, of course, it's a twofold case. Once poisoning is substantiated as the cause of death, you must then prove who is responsible for the poisoning." He paused. "If poisoning is a possibility in an unexplained death, or is suspected for any reason, the medical examiner will routinely test the blood, stomach contents, liver, kidneys, urine, hair, and lung fluid during an autopsy. They even test the vitreous humor."

"Explain, please," Claire said.

"The vitreous humor is the jellylike tissue located behind the lens. It fills the eyeball. It's a transparent substance. Even that is checked for signs indicating poisoning."

"What about poisons that do not show up in an autopsy?" Claire asked. "If the poison does not show up in routine or other tests, and the victim is cremated, the poisoning would go undetected forever. Right? Someone could literally get away with murder."

"Great mind, Claire. And that has happened," Guy said. "Not all murderers get discovered and punished."

"At least not in this lifetime," she said.

"It's the rare or unusual poisons that would not typically be detected in an autopsy," Guy said. "There are something like eight million chemical compounds on this planet. Can you imagine? And medical examiners—even those using the most sophisticated of methods—only test for a few hundred. Oftentimes deaths are ruled as heart attacks when in fact the victims have been poisoned. Perpetrators know this. And prosecutors know this. Laboratories have limits."

Claire listened spellbound as Guy continued.

"Medical examiners always check for the presence of the common substances in an uncertain death case. They test for alcohol, drugs like amphetamines, barbiturates, cocaine, and quaaludes, and of course strychnine and arsenic. They may also use a gas chromatograph to look for the presence of metals and other more muted compounds. But this test would only cover about half of the other possible compounds. The testing would still be incomplete."

"And then hunting for the actual substance used to do someone in would really begin," Claire said.

"Correct," Guy said. "But you'd be looking at a very expensive and time-consuming ordeal. There are those cases where outside labs and researchers are brought in to consult. But certainly not always."

"Do they consider symptoms displayed prior to death?" Claire asked.

"Yes. Sometimes those are the very best evidence. Vomiting can occur for two or three days prior to death when poisoning is injected into someone's food or drink. But it can also be present with heart problems. Some poisons also leave an odor that is detectable when the body is opened during an autopsy. So much of the detection relies on the skills and intuition of the medical examiner—to follow suspicions and perform the tests that should be performed. It's more of an art than a science."

She jotted notes as Guy spoke. He had been an expert prosecutor for an entire career prior to opening the private investigation firm with Claire, and she valued his knowledge and judgment without pause.

"Are any poisons completely untraceable?" Claire asked.

"I would say no. But some are very, *very* difficult to detect," Guy said.

"So I think that's what we're looking at in the case of Christine Fox. Remember Eric said she was sick for a couple of days before she died?" The female investigator stared straight ahead, deep in thought. "How long does a medical examiner keep blood samples from an autopsy?"

"Five years, Claire. Then they're disposed of."

"We're coming up to the five-year mark with Christine. Will you please contact the medical examiner's office and tell them to hold up? To wait until we contact them again? Tell them we're investigating her possible murder."

"I know the medical examiner. Consider it done." He walked to his desk to make the call.

Jin walked into the office.

"You're early," Claire said, glancing at the clock on the wall.

"I had two classes today, and the second one let out early."

"Feeling more rested, Jin?" Claire asked.

"Like a new man," he said. "I slept fourteen hours straight. You both were right. I really needed it."

"Do me a favor, Jin," Claire asked. "Get me a list of all poisons that are nearly undetectable in an autopsy, will you, please?"

"I'm on it," Jin said. He walked to his desk and got to work without asking further questions, although he was more than curious why she needed the list.

Claire walked over to Guy's desk.

"I want to talk to Eric again," she said. "Want to ride along?"

Minutes later, the sleuths were on their way to Eric's house.

"We never asked him what he does for a living," Claire said. "And I need to know the address of the property where he lived with his mother and father.

According to my research, he's twenty-two years old. That would have made him only seventeen when his mom died."

"I think we should visit the property when we learn the address," Guy said.

"You're reading my mind."

When they arrived at the house, Eric was in the front yard puttering on an older-model aqua-pearl Harley-Davidson Sportster motorcycle. He looked up when they arrived. Claire noticed a good amount of dirt on the knees of his jeans.

"Like it?" he asked. "It's a 1994. Got a real steal on it. It has a sports seat—custom made—and these wraparound saddlebags." He pointed to them. "New tires and battery too. I always wanted this exact bike. Since I was a kid. Now I have it. Needs some work, but that's no problem."

"It's nice," Guy said. "I, too, am a fan of Harley-Davidsons. Old and new."

"We need to ask you a couple of more questions, Eric," Claire said. "Where did you live with your parents before your mom passed?"

"We had a house in Coral Gables. I miss that house. I loved it there. When Mom died, Steve sold it immediately, and we moved into Miami. When I turned eighteen, I bought this place with the money Mom left me. I needed to be on my own. I didn't get along with Steve."

"What was the address of that house?" Guy asked.

Eric told them the address, and Claire jotted it down.

"Why the interest in my old home?" Eric asked.

"We're just doing our due diligence," Claire said. "We need to check out everything."

"Oh," Eric said.

"Where do you work, Eric?" Guy asked.

"Where do I work?" Eric looked stunned. "Why would you need to know that?"

"Again, we thoroughly check out everyone and everything in an investigation," Claire said.

"I'm not employed at the moment," he said. "I do some gardening for folks on an as-needed basis. Mom was a superb gardener. The best. She taught me a lot about it growing up. But I don't really need to work. Mom left me enough to survive the rest of my life if I live conservatively. I inherited the money when I turned eighteen. I think I told you that."

"Soon after your mom died, then," Claire said.

Eric looked at her for some time but said nothing.

"Did you father inherit money too?" Guy asked.

"Yeah. You should talk to him about that. I think I got more than him."

"Did you ever suspect what it was that killed your mom?" Claire asked.

"You should ask Steve that question too," Eric said.

"Right now, I'm asking you," she said.

Again, Eric stared at the female investigator.

"She was really sick a couple of days before she died. Vomited a lot. So they thought it might have been her heart, but they weren't sure."

"What do *you* think caused her death, Eric?" Claire persisted.

"It doesn't matter what I think. Steve was cooking all the meals before she got sick. Maybe *he* knows."

Eric suddenly looked indifferent. Distant. Cold. Unfriendly.

"That's all we need today, Eric," Guy said. "Again, thank you."

The investigators got into Guy's car and drove off. Claire looked into the side mirror and saw Eric watching them until they were out of sight.

"Okay. There's an odd side to that young man," Claire said.

"I agree," Guy said. "My gut instinct was to get out of there when we did. And I don't want you returning unless I'm with you."

"He's still not leveling with us about the death of his mother. He knows something he's not telling us," Claire said.

"Coral Gables is a half hour away, give or take the traffic we run into. I think we should check out the house where the Fox family lived right now."

"I agree. I'm eager to see it." A curious sensation came over her.

Once the sleuths arrived in the heart of Coral Gables, Guy stopped and entered the address of the property into his car's GPS.

They followed the directions and soon pulled onto the avenue in front of a pleasant-in-appearance, Spanish-style rambler. Giant banyan trees lined the broad road. The house had a small front yard and a larger backyard.

"Let's do this," Claire said.

They approached and rang the bell. A middle-aged woman opened the door.

"Yes?" she asked.

The investigators introduced themselves and showed her identification.

"Come in," she said. "My husband's not home. He had an errand to run."

They sat on comfortable chairs in the living room.

"Now what is this about?" the woman asked.

Claire told her about the death of Charlotte and explained she and Guy were investigating the matter, and the trail led them to her house.

"This sounds serious," she said. "My husband and I have owned this place a bit under five years. I remember one of the prior owners, the wife, died before we bought it. We were never told anything more about her death, and quite frankly, I guess we didn't want to know the specific circumstances. We've enjoyed the house immensely."

"I can see why. It's a lovely home," Claire said. "Could you show us around?"

"I see no harm in that," the woman said.

She walked the sleuths through the entire home.

"Which room was the boy's?" Claire asked.

"The boy's?" the woman repeated.

"Yes. The owners had a son named Eric. Do you know which room was his?"

"Oh, now that was another part of the story. We never saw the boy, but his room was a mess. Filled with half unpacked boxes. The agent told us he had been sent away to some kind of place to help him with his problems. I guess he returned before his mother died."

"Interesting," Claire said. Her inner voice nudged her to keep asking questions. "Do you know why he was sent away?"

"Well, the agent was kind of a gossip, and I do recall her saying he apparently did a lot of acting out. He had threatened the mom, and she was afraid of him." She shuddered. "Imagine having a child like that."

"Do you recall anything else you were told on the subject by your agent?" Claire asked.

"Well, she did say the parents fought all the time about how to handle this child. The mom was the one who sent him away. They were divorcing. That was the reason they were selling the house."

"Can we please take a look at the backyard?" Claire asked.

"Sure. There's not much out there, but certainly you can take a look," the owner said. She walked to the back door, and they followed her outside.

Claire's eyes immediately fell upon a fenced area in a back corner of the property. The fence was old and high and comprised of wooden slats and posts. It had been mended in certain areas and was struggling to maintain its original green paint.

"What's on the other side of that fence?" she asked.

"It was a garden at one time. Apparently a beautiful garden. We were told the son and his mother created it. It was something they shared. Neither my husband nor I are gardeners, though, and I'm afraid we let it go completely."

"Can we take a look inside?" Claire asked. Her little voice deep inside screamed, *Yes! Yes!*

"There's nothing to look at, really. Just a lot of dead plants and weeds," the owner said. "I'll have to look for the key to the padlock.

It's been almost five years since we've been in there."

She ambled to the house and disappeared inside. Minutes passed.

"I can't find the key!" she yelled out to them. "Oh, wait another minute. There is one other place I can look."

Waiting was driving Claire crazy. Her instincts told her something was on the other side of that fence, and she was dying to get a look.

Additional minutes passed. The woman reappeared.

"Got it," she said, waving her hand high in the air.

She approached the padlock securing the gate and tried the key. It didn't turn. "This key hasn't been used in a long time. I'm afraid it doesn't work."

Claire could barely contain her suspense a moment longer. She made a face of frustration.

"May I?" Guy asked. "I can sometimes get these old keys and locks to work."

But as hard as he tried, he could not get the key to work in the lock.

"Do you have silicone spray, by any chance?" he asked.

"My husband probably does in the garage. But you'll have to come with me to find it."

Guy shadowed the woman to the garage. She entered the combination on the keypad, and the door opened. They walked inside.

"Take a look over there." The woman pointed. "If we have it, it's in that cabinet."

To calm her nerves, Claire examined the ground abutting the fence. At one end, she spotted two indents in the ground. *Looks like marks a ladder would make*, she thought. She made a mental note.

Guy located a small can of silicone spray and the tube needed to direct the spray. It was just what he needed. The two returned to the gated fence. Guy placed the end of the tube into the lock's keyhole and sprayed. He waited a minute and went through the process again. He also sprayed both sides of the key.

"It's now or never," he announced. "Keep your fingers crossed."

He pushed the key into the keyhole. It turned effortlessly. The lock opened.

Guy removed the padlock and stepped aside.

The woman pulled open the gate.

The three walked inside.

It was a sight to behold.

12

JIN LEFT A list of poisons that are nearly undetectable in an autopsy on Claire's desk, along with a note indicating he was back out on surveillance. Minutes later, he parked and waited down the street from Estee's house. Charlie had gone in thirty minutes earlier. Turning the matter of the Charlie McDermott investigation over to him spoke volumes of Claire's and Guy's trust levels, and on some days the intern felt daunted by the responsibility. What if he missed something? The investigators had warned him that conducting surveillance could be a grueling task. And now he knew it firsthand.

He picked up his journal and skimmed the entries he had recorded each day of his mission. Next he reviewed all photos he had taken using his smartphone. He took out his pen and summarized his findings about Charlie on a separate page.

Charlie used different names—Charlie McDermott and Richard Connors; lived in a ritzy condo, but until recently worked in a bakery part-time; spent a lot of hours wooing Estee, often taking her onto the Hinckley Picnic Boat—*Black Pearl*—owned by a man named Roise; played cards and gambled occasionally with other men; dressed casually in Hawaiian shirts and Bermuda shorts; drove a classic green Karmann Ghia; and looked disheveled much of the time.

The student noted that Claire had discovered Charlie gave Estee an expensive strand of rare black Tahitian pearls. She had also learned Charlie never worked at Estee's husband's company as he'd said he did.

What was Jin missing? He scrutinized his writings. Suddenly, it hit him. He had never verified the ownership of Charlie's car or of the condo where he lived. He had forgotten. It was a mistake of a rookie sleuth.

He called Claire at the office.

"Can you do me a favor?" he asked.

"What do you need, Jin?" she asked.

"Would you call your friend Captain Massey and ask him to check on the ownership of the condo where Charlie lives? This could be important."

"Give me the address."

After reciting the street address, he asked Claire to clarify with the captain that Charlie McDermott might also be using the name Richard Connors.

"I'll call him now," Claire said. "If he's in, I'll call you right back with the information."

She hung up and dialed the Miami-Dade Police Department.

"Captain Massey, please. Let him know it's Claire Caswell calling."

The receptionist informed her he was just getting out of a meeting and asked if she could hold.

"Of course," she said. "Thank you."

After two minutes, the captain came on the line.

"Hello, Ms. Caswell. What can I do for you?" he asked.

"I need to know if a man we're investigating owns a condo at the address I'm about to give you. He goes by two names that we're aware of, so I'll give you both." She gave him the information he needed.

"I'll call you back as soon as I have something."

Fifteen minutes later, Claire received the call.

"Well, this is interesting," the captain started. "Neither name shows up as an owner at that condo building. But there's more. I called the building manager, told her we were looking into some confidential matters, and asked if she knew either Charlie McDermott or Richard Connors. The answer I received might surprise you. The manager told me that Charlie McDermott is a personal caregiver to an elderly man who owns a condo unit in the building. Charlie actually lives there in a spare bedroom. He spends some time every day helping the man get set up with his meals, bath, and so forth. He grocery shops for the owner, as needed, and does his laundry, as well."

"Things are often not as they seem," Claire said. "Charlie is all illusion. He's not what he purports to be. The closer you get, the more clearly you see."

"Run that by me again," the captain said. "I missed it."

"Oh, it wasn't important," Claire said. "Did she give you the name of the owner?"

"She did. It's Roise, R-o-i-s-e. Last name Fox."

"Did you say *Fox*?"

"Yes. You sound surprised," the captain said.

"Well, we're looking at *Stephen* Fox as a possible suspect in Charlotte's death," the female investigator said. "What are the odds?"

"Any connection?" Captain Massey asked.

"We'll find out," she said. "Did they tell you how long Mr. Fox has lived there?"

"The manager said four years."

"Thank you! You can't know how helpful you've been. Keep me posted on any new developments in your investigation into Charlotte's murder."

Claire hung up and immediately called Jin to report the information.

"*What?*" Jin exclaimed. He thought for a moment and jotted the information down in his journal. "This is an interesting twist. So Charlie or Richard or whatever his real name is was working two jobs until recently—caretaker for Mr. Roise Fox and part-time baker at the French bakery. And a man named Roise purchased the Hinckley Picnic Boat. That has to be Roise Fox."

"And what about that surname *Fox*?" she asked. "We're looking at Stephen Fox as a person of interest in the death of Charlotte. Could these cases be connected? Somehow related? If not, what a strange coincidence with the names."

"I need to process this," Jin said.

Just then, Charlie and Estee appeared outside her house and walked to Charlie's car.

"I have to end this call, but can you check on one additional thing, Claire? See who Charlie's Karmann Ghia is registered to, will you, please? I forgot to do this." He gave her the license number from his journal. "I assumed it was Charlie's car, but then I assumed he owned the luxury condo too. You and Guy have always taught me never to assume anything until I independently verify it—no matter how apparent it seems. I get that now."

"I need to review this new information too, Jin. I'll call Captain Massey back and ask him to check on the ownership of the car

Charlie is driving. Let me get back to you. In the meanwhile, I think it's time to organize all this information from both cases on a board in the office. Maybe it will help us pull it all together."

The female investigator called the captain.

"Sorry to bother you again so soon, but I need something else. Can you tell me the ownership of a Karmann Ghia with Florida license plates?" She gave him the plate number.

"That's an easy request, Ms. Caswell. Hold on," Captain Massey said.

He returned to the phone minutes later with the information. "The name will be familiar to you, Ms. Caswell. It's *Roise Fox*."

"Roise Fox again?" Claire asked. "Most helpful. Thank you!"

She texted Jin to report the findings.

Claire hung up and reflected. The more information they obtained in a matter, the more the nature of the investigation seemed to evolve. The more questions they asked, the more answers they received. The more answers they received, the more the cases took on new shapes and directions. She thought back to her years of experience as an investigator for the State of Florida. She and Guy had each brought with them unique and exceptional skills and knowledge when they opened their private investigative firm only a few years ago.

The female investigator wheeled a large three-paneled bulletin board from the back room and set it up in a corner of the office. She asked Guy for his help. The duo began the job of posting photos and other information obtained to date on both cases. Claire drew arrows to show any connection between the parties they were presently aware of. They would add further information as it came in. Claire and Guy decided to reserve one side for the Ester Rollings case and the other side for Charlotte's murder case. Would the two cases intersect? Time would tell.

Estee's side showed a photo of her supplied by Claire's parents, as well as photos Jin had snapped of Charlie McDermott. Attached to his picture, Claire wrote, *Alias Richard Connors*. They also posted photos of the Hinckley Picnic Boat, *Black Pearl*, Estee and Charlie swimming, Estee's house, the condo building where Charlie lived and worked, the house where Charlie went to gamble, and the French bakery where Charlie had worked until recently. And they posted a note about Roise Fox, confirming he owned the condo where Charlie lived, the boat Charlie used, and the car Charlie drove.

On Charlotte's side, the investigators posted and identified by label photos of Charlotte, the crash site, the SUV remains, Stephen Fox (which Claire had managed to take when he walked into the car dealership), Eric Fox (which Claire had snapped from the car when he was outside working on the Harley-Davidson), the house where Eric had lived with his parents, the green fence with the padlocked gate, a sweeping view of the fenced-in area, the Porsche dealership, and Stephen Fox and Natalie, the receptionist, entering the dealership together after a lunch break.

Claire also tacked up the checklist of nearly undetectable poisons prepared by Jin, and finally a record of the other women who had died under similar circumstances in the Miami area within the last four years.

All panels of the board were nearly filled to capacity when they finished the task.

JIN DILIGENTLY followed Charlie and Ester. This day they did not go to the boat. Rather, they drove to a small insurance company and entered the building.

Over an hour passed before they reappeared, walking hand in hand.

When they drove off, Jin walked inside.

"Perhaps you can help me," Jin said to the gentleman sitting behind the only desk in the office. He made note that there was no receptionist. He thought on his feet. "I need to check on the cost of insurance."

"Have a seat, sir," the agent said. "What type of insurance are you seeking?" Jin started gag coughing. He held his chest. "Could I have a glass of water, please?"

"Of course," the agent said. He walked off to the back room.

Jin seized the opportunity to eyeball the paperwork still sitting on the man's desk. In a flash, he scanned the application. It was a policy insuring the "strand of natural, perfectly matched, black Tahitian pearls" Charlie had given Estee. Photos stapled to the application displayed the multiple colors, overtones, generous size, and lustrous sheen of the near-perfect exotic piece. The value stated was $5,000 per pearl, or $230,000 for the strand of forty-six, with an added value tacked on for the platinum clasp. The beneficiary named: Charlie McDermott.

The insurance agent returned with a full glass of cold water.

Jin was gone.

He ran to his car and took off. He phoned Claire.

"Jin? Is that you? I think we have a bad connection," she said.

"Hold on. I have important information to tell you. Don't hang up. Let me drive out of this area."

Close to a minute passed.

"Better?" he asked.

"Much. What's up?" Claire asked.

Jin quickly explained what he had just learned at the insurance agency.

"That's nearly a quarter of a million dollars. I don't like this, Claire," Jin said.

"Neither do I."

She hung up, called her mother, and explained the situation. "This is strictly confidential at this point, Mom, but please keep an even closer watch on Estee. Potentially, this is a very scary development. Who knows what Charlie might have in the works? If he is planning something criminal, he won't make his move immediately, but soon. Too soon would raise questions with the insurance company. If you see anything suspicious, call me."

"You have my word, Claire," Abbey said. "Maybe I'll invite Estee over for coffee and see if she'll reveal anything."

"Mom—"

"I know, I know. I'll be careful. I won't let on that I know a thing."

"Promise?"

"Promise!"

JIN CONTINUED his surveillance. He drove to Estee's house, and sure enough, Charlie's car was parked out front. Before long, the two walked to Charlie's car and drove away. Jin followed a reasonable distance behind. The couple traveled to an outdoor restaurant and sat down at a table. Jin parked down the street and used his binoculars to watch them. They ate and shared a bottle of wine. Estee seemed totally taken in by Charlie, acting like a schoolgirl in love for the very first time. He flirted with her shamelessly, and she flirted back. The overly sweet, syrupy scene was almost too much to watch. Jin had no remaining doubt that Estee had fallen head over heels for Charlie.

The law student's eyes gravitated to the stately pearls hanging around Estee's neck.

WHILE JIN was out on surveillance, Guy decided to spend the remainder of the day watching Stephen. He drove close to the dealership and found a spot to park where he could remain out of sight. The showroom was busy that afternoon with potential customers coming and going on a regular basis. It was toward the end of the workday that Guy observed Stephen slip out through the front doors. He walked to his car. Minutes later, the receptionist appeared. She looked all around before walking to Stephen's car. The two drove off. Guy followed.

Stephen drove to an apartment complex and parked outside. The two exited the vehicle and walked into the building. Natalie pulled a key from her purse and opened the security door. They disappeared inside for about forty-five minutes before reappearing. Stephen sped back to the dealership, and Natalie walked in first.

He waited a short time before entering the building.

Guy now seriously questioned whether Stephen and Natalie were entangled in a love affair. Claire had mentioned a similar scenario occurring when she was trailing Stephen. But could it be something else? He wondered. Claire had reminded him so many times never to presume anything until solid evidence confirmed it. On the surface, the relationship appeared secretive, clandestine, and sneaky, to be sure. But what were they really concealing?

He drove back to the office.

"Claire, I followed Stephen and Natalie. They went to her apartment. Stayed inside for three-quarters of an hour. Wonder what's up with the two of them?"

"Not sure."

He placed an arrow with a question mark between Stephen and Natalie on the evidence board.

Claire had worked all afternoon, continuing to do research on the parties involved in both matters. She looked beat.

"Honey," Guy said. "I think we should go out for dinner. We've been at this a long time without letting up."

She exhaled. "That sounds nice. I've been skipping meals, and I am starving. Besides, we can review these cases while we eat."

The two locked up the office and drove to a quaint neighborhood restaurant not far from where they lived. It was a secluded spot down a side street—small and unpretentious—that served amazingly authentic Italian food.

Over dinner, the investigators reviewed all aspects of the two cases that had swallowed them up since Charlotte's death.

Guy excused himself to visit the men's room. When he came back to the table, he whispered to Claire.

"We're being followed."

13

CLAIRE KICKED INTO high alert.

"Talk to me," she said.

"You won't believe it," Guy said. "I saw Stephen Fox sitting at one end of the bar. It's dark in there, and when he saw me, he turned his head fast, but not in time. I saw his face. It was definitely Stephen. And it was clear he didn't want me to see him."

"Interesting," Claire said. "The person we're following is now following us. How very clever."

"The chances of him just happening to be here—a neighborhood restaurant a couple of blocks from where we live—are beyond remote."

"I'd say nearly impossible," she said. "I'm going to confront him."

Claire jumped up and dashed toward the bar.

"Wait!" Guy commanded. But she was gone. He ran after her.

When they arrived at the bar, there was no sign of Stephen.

Claire questioned the bartender.

"Hey, did the man sitting at the far end of the bar just leave?"

"Yeah. I've never seen the likes of him before. He bolted. Left a full drink sitting in front of him. Don't get many of that ilk."

"We're private investigators," Claire said, flashing her identification. "Did the man use a credit card?"

"Nope. Threw down a large bill. Didn't even wait for his change. Best tip of the night." He grinned. "I'm not complaining."

"Did he ask you any questions?" Claire asked.

"Nope."

"Did he talk to anyone at the bar?"

"Nope."

"Did it appear he was waiting for someone to join him?"

"Nope."

"Can you tell us anything at all about the customer?"

"Nope. Not really."

"Well, thank you for your help," she said.

The investigators returned to their table. They ordered a dessert to share and two coffees.

"Well, so much for a peaceful dinner together," Guy said. "Seems to me things are heating up."

"Why on earth is Stephen following us?"

"I think it's *you* he's following, Claire. Remember, we're presuming he doesn't know what I look like. But then he probably does, as of tonight. He certainly knows you, and he knows you're investigating Charlotte's death. He also knows he's probably a suspect. You need to be careful. People around him keep dying. Especially women with names starting with the letter *C.*"

"I understand. I'll be careful."

"I mean it, Claire. We finally got married. I don't want to lose you now." He winked, grabbed her hand, and squeezed it. "Be *more* than careful. Promise me."

"I will. I get it."

THE TWO drove home and climbed into bed. Claire pulled the down comforter up around her chin as her head descended into her favorite pillow. She felt safe lying next to the love of her life and soon nodded off. But sleep was not peaceful for her that night. She woke periodically in fits of anxiety.

The next morning, she felt exhausted.

"Claire, you look tired," Guy said. He poured two cups of fresh-brewed coffee.

"Tough night. There's a lot going through my mind," she said. "I dreamed about Charlotte and the car accident. I relived it. I envisioned her losing control of her car and passing out just before the impact. It was actually a paralyzingly bad dream."

"Have you had this nightmare before?" Guy asked.

"Yes. And it's always the same," Claire said. "Charlotte is driving along, becomes violently ill, and the accelerator sticks. She can't slow down or stop. In fact, the speed only accelerates. At that moment, she realizes she locked in by her seat belt. She wiggles out of part of it. She passes out, and the collision takes her life. She never has a chance. She doesn't live through the terrifying seconds just before the crash because she's not conscious." Claire paused. "My dreams seem so real."

"Your dreams have always seemed real, honey. They have to be draining," Guy said. "Maybe you should stay home today and rest."

"No can do," she said. "We have two cases to solve. I'll be fine."

WHEN THE investigators arrived at Caswell & Lombard, Private Investigation and unlocked the door, the phone was ringing.

Claire rushed over.

"Caswell & Lombard, Private Investigation," she said. "This is Claire Caswell."

"Ms. Caswell, it's the crime lab calling. We have some results for you."

The female investigator sat at her desk and grabbed a notebook and pen.

"Go ahead. I'm ready."

"Well, the specimens you brought in are taking us some extra time to analyze. I apologize for the delay. They had dried up from being outside in the hot sun, and that makes our job more difficult. But one of our lab scientists had the brilliant idea of taking one of the samples and adding some drops of sterilized water to it. The composition remained the same, but it became more flexible and somewhat easier to work with."

"I see," Claire said. "What did it turn out to be?"

"Still not certain. But it appears to be some part of a plant—perhaps a berry. We found evidence that the specimen contains tropane alkaloids that can produce hallucinations when ingested. Minuscule doses are used for medicinal purposes, but larger doses can kill. Obviously the more ingested, the deadlier. We'll have more specific information for you down the road."

The female investigator thanked her, hung up, and shared the findings with Guy.

He sat and looked at her without speaking.

"We need to go and see Eric again," Claire said.

"Let's go," Guy said. "It's early, and hopefully we'll catch him still at home."

THE DRIVE to Eric's house was quiet. Both investigators were deep in thought. A major piece of the puzzle was starting to fall into place.

They arrived at the house and observed Eric's car parked in the driveway. They rang the doorbell.

No answer.

They rang the bell again.

Still no answer.

The two knocked loudly.

No response.

They walked around the house. No sign of Eric.

"I don't like the looks of this," Claire said.

"Me either," Guy said.

"I'm calling Captain Massey," she said. She grabbed her cell phone from her purse.

"It's early, Ms. Caswell," the captain said when he answered. "What's up?"

"We need your help," Claire said. She quickly explained the situation and gave him the address of the property.

"I'll send some officers and a fire truck right away. Stand by."

MINUTES LATER, Miami-Dade County police officers arrived in two squad cars with flashing lights and sirens blasting. A fire engine pulled in behind them.

The lead officer instructed Claire and Guy to stay outside.

Two bulky firefighters kicked open the back door, and officers rushed in.

Time slowed to a halt as they waited. Minutes passed. And more.

The lead officer reappeared and made an announcement.

"He's dead."

14

THE MIAMI-DADE COUNTY chief medical examiner and an ambulance were summoned to the scene. After close to an hour, Eric's covered body was carried out on a stretcher and loaded into the emergency vehicle to be transported to the medical examiner's office.

Those remaining at the scene gathered to talk.

"What happened?" Claire asked the medical examiner.

"Good question," he said. "We found him lying on his bed. Vomit all around. Hands folded in front of him. Dead. No obvious clue as to what took his life. We'll have to run tests."

"Suicide?" Guy asked.

"Could be. Not sure," the examiner replied. "Too early to tell."

"We didn't see this coming," Claire said.

"You two knew the young man?" the lead officer asked.

"Not well, but we talked to him recently," Guy said. "His name is Eric Fox."

"We'll let you know the results of the autopsy," the officer said. "Captain Massey knows how to reach you two, correct?"

"He does," Claire said. "And you should know, the victim's mother is deceased. His father is Stephen Fox. He works at a Porsche dealership here in Miami." She jotted down the address and handed it to the officer. "Will you be contacting him?"

"We can," the officer said. "But if you know the father, perhaps it would be better coming from the two of you. That kind of news is always better coming from someone other than a police officer."

"We'll do it," Claire said. Although she didn't relish the idea, they would accede to the officer's request.

The scene cleared. Claire and Guy got into Claire's car and drove to the dealership. They sat in the car for a time discussing how best to handle the situation.

"This won't be easy," Claire said. "Although Eric and Stephen were basically estranged, Eric was Stephen's son. His only child, I believe. They still had limited contact. Should we go in together, or should I go in alone?"

"Claire, I'm sure Stephen saw me quite clearly at the restaurant, so he now knows who I am. I'm going in with you. We'll do this together."

The investigators entered through the front doors and asked to see Stephen.

"What is this concerning?" Natalie asked. She acted as if she'd never seen Claire Caswell before.

"Natalie," she said. "We would like to speak directly to Stephen, if you don't mind. It's important."

"Concerning . . ." she persisted. She straightened her name tag.

"This is a personal matter. Let him know we're here," Claire said firmly.

"He's busy right now," Natalie said.

Claire motioned to Guy. The two walked past the controlling receptionist and down the hallway to Stephen's office. His door was ajar. They pushed it open and walked in. Natalie raced in behind them.

"I couldn't stop them," she said. "I tried."

Stephen was playing cards with Jimmy, his fellow salesman. Stephen threw his cards onto the desk.

"We need to speak with you, Mr. Fox. Now," Claire said.

Stephen bolted to his feet and waved off Jimmy and Natalie. "Leave us alone," he commanded. He closed the door behind them.

"We were told you were busy," Claire said. "This seems to be a pattern."

"I instructed our receptionist not to let you in," he said. "I told you I would not answer any more of your persistent questions." He fumed. "Why are you here?"

"I think you should sit down," Guy said. "We have bad news."

Stephen's expression changed from rage to puzzlement.

All three sat.

"What is it?" he asked. "What's the bad news the two of you are here to deliver?"

"It's about Eric, your son," Claire said. Her voice softened.

"*Eric*?" Stephen asked. "What about Eric? How do you even know Eric?"

"Eric was found dead in his home today," Claire said. "I'm very sorry."

Stephen let his head fall to his chest. He turned almost colorless. "What happened?" he choked out. He could hardly speak.

"The medical examiner is not certain at this point. An autopsy will be performed," Guy said.

"Where is his body?" Stephen asked. "Where is my boy?" He

heaved and needed to be sick. He ran from the office.

The investigators waited for him to return.

Minutes later, he reappeared. He looked absolutely green.

"Where is my boy?" he repeated.

"He was taken to the Miami-Dade County chief medical examiner's office. He's there now," Claire said. As detestable as she found Stephen, he had just been told about the death of his child. She felt compassion for him. Yet his strong, real reaction to Eric's death only emphasized to a greater degree the fact that he'd barely even blinked at Charlotte's death. It proved to Claire that Charlotte meant next to nothing to Stephen.

"I want to see him," Stephen said. His voice was subdued.

"Can we drive you there?" Claire asked.

He nodded in silent thanks.

The drive to the medical examiner's office was loud in its quietness.

When they arrived, the investigators waited in the lobby while Stephen was taken to a room to view the body of his son.

A half hour passed.

When Stephen returned to the lobby, he spoke in a hushed tone.

"Take me back to the dealership, please," he said.

The drive back was also silent. There simply were no words.

BACK AT the office, Claire and Guy regrouped. It had been a difficult day.

Claire wrote *Deceased* on a notecard and tacked it to the bottom of Eric's photo on the evidence board.

Guy asked the difficult question.

"Do you think Eric killed his mom and now he killed himself out of guilt?"

"I don't," Claire said. "He may have taken his own life, but I do not believe he killed his mother."

"Tell me your thoughts," Guy said.

"Well, I think he figured out what really did kill his mom, but out of anger toward his dad he wanted people to wonder if his dad had done it. He kept mute on the matter."

"Go on," Guy said.

"I think he was lonely. Depressed. And that is what finally convinced him to call it quits. He had been in treatment, and that didn't help. He didn't see things getting any better. And I'm going to bet he used whatever killed his mom to take his own life."

"I'm anxious to hear how the medical examiner rules," Guy said. "They're still holding the blood sample from Christine Fox, so if we can determine what took Eric's life, they can test her sample for the same substance."

"I think we know what it will be," Claire said. "The same substance Charlotte probably had in her system—a substance the autopsy didn't test for."

JIN WALKED into the office. It was midafternoon. He glanced at the large board as he did each day when he arrived. He eyes immediately fell upon the notation *Deceased* at the bottom of Eric's picture.

He pointed to the card. "Eric is *dead*? What happened?"

Guy revealed the events of the day to Jin.

"I'm blown away by this," the law student said. "Things keep changing so quickly in these cases. I've stopped asking what's next."

"I did that years ago," Guy said.

"We need to have a meeting of the minds to mull over where we're heading on both of the cases," Claire said. "We have many pieces to try to somehow fit together."

The three sat at the meeting table. Claire made three cups of hot tea in the Keurig and delivered them.

"I admit I'm stumped," Jin said. "Charlie is a mystery—a true paradox many times over. He has me flummoxed. Not sure where to go or what to do next."

"Well, you haven't talked to Roise Fox yet," Claire said. "I'd put that on the top of your to-do list. He may give you an interesting perspective on things. Go pay him a visit at the condo building when you know Charlie's not there."

Jin picked up his pen to scribble down notes.

Claire continued. "Buzz his unit. Ask for Charlie. When he informs you Charlie is not in, tell him you're gathering information concerning an upcoming reunion at Charlie's high school. You won't keep him, but you need just a little information for the booklet of the classmates that is being prepared." She paused. "Yes, this should work. Once you're inside the condo, kid around a bit to make him feel comfortable, and then ask him some basic information about Charlie. Like where to send his invitation, his phone number, marital status, does he have any children, work other places, and so on. You get the picture. And see if you can squeeze in some questions about how long Charlie has worked for him, how he found Charlie in the first place, and so on. Find out what Mr. Fox thinks of him. You'll know the questions. You're good at this, Jin. Oh, and if possible, ask him if Stephen is a relative. Say you were looking at cars recently and a Stephen Fox helped you. Something like that."

"Got it," Jin said. He finished his note-taking. "Anything else?"

"Yes," Claire said. "Get out of there as soon as you can. Don't linger. You never know when Charlie might drop back to the condo for some reason."

"Last chance. Anything else?" Jin asked.

"I'd pop your ponytail up under a cap and put on that dark-framed pair of glasses you have," Claire said. "Dress casually. You're too young to be a classmate of Charlie's, so tell Mr. Fox you work in the alumni office and have been assigned the task of locating as many of the students from his class as possible and compiling a list of their contact information. That's believable."

"I think it will work," Jin said. "Tomorrow's a lighter day at school. Only three early classes. I can probably catch Charlie leaving for the day if I drive right over to the condo after my class. I'll keep you posted." He paused. "So much of this investigator stuff seems to be role-playing."

"Yes, *Grasshopper*. You catch on fast." Guy chuckled. "As private investigators, we are forced to lie a bit, stretch the truth on occasions, wear disguises to alter our appearances, and do some playacting whenever necessary. But it's always done for a noble cause. To ferret out the truth. It goes with the job description." He flashed his famous grin.

Jin smiled back. "I like it."

"You're good at it," Claire said. "You're a natural."

"Never underestimate your skills, Jin," Guy said. "Pull from your inner strengths whenever you need to."

THE FOLLOWING morning, after classes, Jin drove to Mr. Fox's condo building. He pulled up along the street, parked, and waited for Charlie to leave. He was moderately nervous about the task he would be undertaking. He could play the part, ask the questions, and make notations about the answers. But it was the possibility of getting caught that scared him silly. What if Charlie forgot something, came back, and found him there? How would he talk his way out of that situation? As much as he tried to put the thought out of his mind, it kept jumping back in. *Pshaw!* he told himself. *It's just me being a nervous Nellie. Nothing will go wrong. Charlie never returns once he leaves—unless it's on Fridays after he grocery shops for Mr. Fox. And today is not Friday. So I have nothing to worry about. Nothing at all.*

He shuddered involuntarily.

"Get it together," Jin said aloud. "Life is a series of tests. And this is one of them. Face your fears head on. It will be over soon. Do your job and get out of there fast. Claire and Guy will be proud." And that meant everything.

He glanced at his watch, took in a deep breath, and let it out slowly. He did this five times. He was ready. Cap, glasses, and casual clothing in place, he grabbed his notebook and pen and waited.

Minutes later, he saw Charlie drive past him in the green sports car.

It was time.

Jin waited a few minutes before he walked to the lobby. He found the panel listing residents' names, located an R. Fox, and pushed the buzzer.

Jin froze. He stopped in his tracks. *I can't do this,* he told himself. *I can't do it! There is no way out if I get trapped!*

Just then, an elderly man's voice came through the speaker. "Who's there?"

"My name's Ernie, Mr. Fox. Is Charlie there?" Jin asked. He swallowed hard.

"No, he's not. Can I tell him who came looking for him?"

"Well, I work for the alumni association at his high school. We're trying to compile an up-to-date list with contact information for him and all his classmates. I have a huge job ahead of me. Maybe you can give me a couple of minutes of your time and I won't have to return."

There was silence for a long minute. Then a reply came.

"I can give you a *couple* of minutes. I'll buzz you in. Condo number 1104. On the eleventh floor, of course."

The sound of the buzzer unlocking the security door snapped Jin back to reality. He'd done it. He'd played the part fabulously, almost robotically, despite his dread and trepidation. But now he had to go up to the *eleventh* floor. He hated that it was up so high. What if he had to make an escape? He swallowed the enormous lump solidifying in his throat and pushed the security door open. He walked to the set of two elevators like he had been there a million times before. As an investigator, he knew to exude confidence at all times, and he performed his job well.

One of the elevators opened, and Jin stepped inside. He pushed the button for the eleventh floor. As the doors closed in front of him, he panicked. *What was the condo number?* He suddenly couldn't remember. It was the eleventh floor, but what was the number of the unit? He hadn't written it down, and he had forgotten. Now what? *Now what?*

The doors opened, and Jin stepped out. He looked from side to side down each of the long hallways. Suddenly, a voice called out to him.

"Young man, I'm down here." Mr. Fox had opened the door, peered out, and saw Jin standing near the elevator looking perplexed.

Jin waved to him and trekked down the hallway.

"Sorry," Jin said. "I got up here and couldn't recall your unit number. I guess I'm on overload with all the information I've been gathering." He briskly moved back into investigator mode. "I won't take up much of your time."

"Very well. Come in, young man," Mr. Fox said.

They sat down at his kitchen table.

"Now, what is it you want?"

Jin again summarized why he needed information on Charlie.

"How wonderful," Mr. Fox said. "I'm glad to hear the high school is including Charlie in the reunion despite the fact he never graduated. Kudos to the school."

At that moment, the buzzer sounded in Mr. Fox's condo. He got up to answer. It was Charlie.

Mr. Fox turned to face Jin.

"Ernie, you're in luck. Charlie is here. He forgot his wallet. You can ask him your questions directly." He smiled.

Jin's blood froze.

15

A WAVE OF panic rolled over Jin, and he felt like he was drowning. Charlie was on his way up. Jin had no way out. He had walked into a trap. His worst fears were playing out, and a silent alarm pounded loudly throughout his body. He couldn't move. His heart raced, and he felt weak. He couldn't breathe.

Suddenly, Guy's words pulsed through his head: *Never underestimate your skills, Jin. Pull from your inner strengths whenever you need to.*

Escape options careened through the student's mind.

He turned slightly and pushed his notebook up underneath his shirt.

"Oh, no. I forgot my list of questions in the car. I'll be right back," he said. "Please ask Charlie to wait. I won't be long."

Jin rushed from the condo and sprinted down the hallway. He hit the elevator button repeatedly, hoping against hope that the elevator

Charlie wasn't on would open first. But luck was not on his side. He heard the loud dinging announcing the elevator had reached the eleventh floor, watched its doors open, and saw Charlie walk out. Jin glanced downward as he faked a gagging coughing spell.

"Hey," Charlie said. "You should see a doctor about that."

Jin did not answer. The second elevator arrived on the eleventh floor at that moment, and its doors opened. Jin scuttled on and pushed the *L* button for the lobby, praying the doors would close like greased lightning. He continued with his sham hacking.

When the doors shut, Jin took air into his lungs and expelled it several times over.

Once he reached the main floor, he dashed out the building's front doors, raced to his car, and pulled away.

I'm not sure I'm cut out for this work after all, he thought as he tried to return to a normal breathing pattern. He needed to feel in control again.

He drove back to the office and filled Claire and Guy in on the escapade.

"Close call, Jin," Guy said.

"But you get an A-plus on how you handled the situation," Claire said.

"Well, I didn't do that well," he said. "I failed to get any of the information I went there for."

"Sometimes that's what happens," Guy said. "Sometimes you get out of a bad situation by the skin of your teeth. And you have to be thankful for that."

"We'll figure out something else, Jin. Please know that you did well today," Claire said reassuringly.

Guy nodded. "It was a tough assignment."

Jin did not seem as convinced as they were. But he did learn a valuable lesson that day: *Always expect the unexpected and you'll rarely be disappointed.* He would never forget. Learning the law in his school classes was one thing. Learning about the real world through experience was quite another.

He took in a deep breath. He needed to get back in the saddle. He would continue following Charlie for the rest of the day.

CLAIRE WALKED to Guy's desk.

"I need to go back to the Coral Gables house where the Fox family lived. I want to take more photos."

"I'll come with you," he said. "The more eyes the better."

The two traveled to the house and rang the bell. The man of the house answered. He was not as amenable to the investigators as his wife had been.

Claire explained who they were and discussed what they needed.

"My wife told me about you two snoops," he growled.

"We're conducting a *murder* investigation, sir," Guy said. "I'd hardly call that snooping. There might be something at this house to aid our investigation."

"Do you have a warrant?" the elderly man barked.

"No, we do not," Claire said. "Your wife cooperated fully with us when we were here before, and we ask that you do the same. We need to take a second look at that fenced-in area in your backyard. Not a big deal. It will only take a few minutes."

The woman of the house appeared.

"What is it now?" she asked. "Didn't you see everything you needed the last time you were here?"

"We just need a few more photos of that fenced-in area in your backyard," Claire said. "I only took one last time. Then we'll be out of your hair once and for all."

"Well, I guess it's okay," the woman said.

The husband emitted a low guttural sound.

The woman grabbed the key and accompanied the investigators to the fenced area. She unlocked the padlock on the gate and opened the door.

Claire and Guy stepped inside. The woman shadowed them.

Using her smartphone, Claire snapped photos of every plant in each row of the garden—*the incredible secret garden*— in beyond-belief shape considering that the current owners hadn't touched it. She paid specific attention to a certain plant in one corner, taking many pictures of it. Then she looked over the perfectly tended garden as a whole. Each flower, plant, and shrub looked to be in ideal condition. She decided the private space was hidden away from others for a reason. That much appeared clear. But what was the reason? And who took care of it? And why? Claire relished her moments in the private place, afraid if she blinked it would disappear.

At that moment, she looked upward and noticed ominous dark clouds gathering in the sky.

"Mind if I pinch off a few leaves and pull a handful of berries from this one?" The female investigator pointed.

"Go ahead," the woman said. "I still can't figure out how a little rain now and then has kept this garden looking like this. It seems nearly impossible. Maybe it's all the Florida sunshine."

Claire pulled a pair of latex gloves and plastic bags from her purse. She slipped the coverings onto her hands. She stooped low and skillfully removed some leaves. She placed the samples in a bag. She then extracted dark berries and filled the other bag partway up. She properly sealed both bags and took out a felt-tip marker to write the date and address obtained on each.

"That's it. That's all we need," Claire said, standing. "Thank you again for your cooperation."

"Is that a blueberry plant?" the woman asked.

"It is not!" Claire said. "These berries are *not* edible. They're poisonous."

"Oh, well, we are properly warned. We'll stay far away."

"Please do. And thank you again for letting us take some samples," Claire said.

"Oh, no problem. Sorry my husband was a little crabby. He's not much for strangers."

"We understand," Guy said. "Thank you."

At that moment, it started to rain. Precipitation had not been in the weather forecast.

Once in the car, Guy turned to Claire. "Why that plant? Why those berries?"

"The berries are the same color as the specimens I found at the crash site. I have a hunch."

The investigators stopped at the police lab on their drive back to the office. Claire asked one of the techs on duty to analyze the samples.

"We just received orders from Captain Massey to always consider your requests top priority—at least on this case, Ms. Caswell," the lab tech said. "We'll get right on it."

BACK AT the office, Claire phoned her mother.

"Any news with Estee?"

"Funny you should call. We've been watching her house, and several men have been arriving and going inside during the last few minutes. One of them is Charlie. I was walking to my phone to call you when it rang."

"Odd, huh?" Claire asked. "Has this ever happened before?"

"We've never seen it until today," Abbey said. "Estee is a quiet neighbor. Keeps to herself mostly. She normally has no visitors. Just this Charlie character. He's all she has . . . except neighbors like us and a handful of friends."

Claire thought quickly.

"How many men, including Charlie, are at her house?" she asked.

"Give me a minute," Abbey said. "I'll count the cars on the street."

Abbey set the phone down and returned shortly.

"Looks like six total," she said.

"Do you have any cookies or cake or anything you could bring her?" Claire asked.

"Well, let me think. Not really. But I picked up some trays of Florida honeybells today. They're in season," Abbey said. "Would that work?"

"Perfectly!" Claire said. "They're the best oranges in the world, if you ask me." She chuckled. "Estee will love them. Why don't you put several in a bag and pay her a visit? See what she tells you when she answers the door. Maybe make a comment about all the cars on the street and let her respond. If possible, look behind her into the house and see what you can see," Claire said. "Take Dad with you."

"We'll do it," Abbey said. "And then I'll call you as soon as we're back home."

"Mom?" Claire said. "Be careful."

Claire waited at her desk for the call. Minutes passed. Soon twenty. Then a half hour.

The phone rang.

Claire answered. "Mom?"

"Yes, it's Mom," Abbey said. "What an experience!"

"Tell me everything," Claire said. "I can't wait to hear all about it."

"Well, I put several honeybells and a couple of ruby-red grape-fruit into a bag for Estee. Your dad and I walked next door and rang her bell."

"And?" Claire said.

"Well, both Estee and Charlie came to the door. Estee was overwhelmed by our gift. She said honeybells were her absolute favorite. Even Charlie seemed touched. She invited us in. Her dining room was filled with all these men sitting at her dining room table playing cards. They were drinking beers, but none of them were smoking. Estee wouldn't allow it."

"Why would Charlie bring his poker-playing buddies to her house? I can't imagine. And why would she go for it?" Claire asked.

"Strangely, Estee seemed to be enjoying it," Abbey said. "She invited us to stay and play a few hands, but we said we had to get home."

"Did you notice anything strange, Mom?" Claire asked.

"Nothing out of the ordinary," she said. "Everyone seemed to be having a good time. They looked like a rough crew, but they were all quite polite. Estee made appetizers for the party, and she couldn't stop smiling. She made us stay and try some."

"This is so . . . unexpected," Claire said.

"You said it," Abbey said.

"Well, good work, Mom. You and Dad outdid yourselves. Not that I'm surprised. Keep watching out for Estee. Let me know of anything else that appears unusual with her."

"Will do, Claire."

Claire and Guy discussed the situation with Estee.

"What are we missing?" Guy asked.

"It's not clear," she said.

CAPTAIN MASSEY phoned Claire.

"We've been investigating the death of your friend Charlotte for a little over three weeks now. As you know, we've changed the cause of death ruling to homicide. So far, evidence-wise, we have nothing other than the partial lab results on the specimens you found at the crash site and the tampered-with seat belt buckle."

"Let's get together and compare all the information we have so far," Claire suggested.

"Good plan, Ms. Caswell. I know you and Mr. Lombard have been hard at work on this matter. Should we say tomorrow morning at 10:00? My office or yours?"

"Well, if you don't mind, why don't you come over here," she said. "We have a board set up showing everything we've collected. I'd like you to see it."

"Good. I'll bring the two main investigators on the case with me. I agree it's time we converged our talents."

"Agreed. See you tomorrow."

Claire and Guy worked up a written summary setting forth all information they had put together on the case to date. It was a multi-paged document. Claire made several copies to use as a handout the next day. That, combined with the evidence board sitting so prominently in their office, would paint a clear picture of the systematic examination and research the private investigation firm had undertaken since the fatal crash. It would be helpful for both sides to put everything on the table and combine their efforts to solve the case.

When Jin came into the office after classes that day, Claire asked him to likewise do a written summary of all actions and information obtained on the Charlie McDermott case. She would distribute that at the scheduled meeting, as well. She wanted Captain Massey and his investigators to be aware of that case too.

AT 10:00 a.m. sharp the following morning, Captain Massey and his investigators arrived at the office of Caswell & Lombard, Private Investigation. The conference table was set up. Everyone took a seat.

Even Jin was there. He had explained to his professors the importance of the meeting, and they had excused him from classes.

Guy delivered a tray to the table—a large thermos of coffee, cups, and a plate of pastries.

Introductions were made all around.

"It's time we got together on this," the captain said.

"Probably overtime," Claire said. "It's a tangled case."

For the next two hours, the private investigators and Jin put on their presentations. They were thorough and impressive. Captain Massey and his police investigators then followed suit, setting forth their findings. The group stood and reviewed the evidence board Claire and Guy had assembled. Looking at all the components of the investigation in one place provided a big-picture glance of the matter at hand. And it showed that major additional pieces were missing.

Massey and his investigators also seemed interested in the Charlie McDermott matter.

"We have more work to do to see if there's a connection between the two cases," Guy said. "The name *Fox* comes up in each. Could just be a remarkable coincidence without a connection. Or not."

Claire stared straight ahead. Suddenly, it hit her.

"We're not seeing the real picture," she said. She looked deep in thought. "I think our focus has been all wrong."

16

ALL EYES FOCUSED on the female investigator.

Guy knew she was onto something.

"Explain your thoughts," the captain said.

"According to Eric Fox, Stephen Fox's son, and to additional research we have undertaken, three other women, in addition to my friend Charlotte Truman, all died under similar circumstances. In fact, not just similar but identical. These women were all in the same age bracket—thirties to forties—single, intelligent, and earning top salaries. Each of the four women purchased a new Porsche Cayenne from the dealership where Stephen Fox works. And all four worked specifically with Stephen Fox to make their purchases. All these women lost control of their vehicles shortly after taking ownership and ended up in deadly crashes. *And* the women were all dating Stephen Fox at the time of the incidents, again according to his son, Eric." She paused. "This hasn't been verified yet."

No one at the table said a word.

"We always hear, *You can't see the forest for the trees*. Well, perhaps our focus has been wrong," Claire continued. "Maybe we've been lining up all the trees without seeing the forest as a whole. What if there's a bigger picture here that we haven't been seeing? A large stratagem or scheme?"

All eyes remained focused on Claire.

"What if we're missing a serial pattern that has occurred over the past four years?" she asked. "Same type of victims; same perpetrator; one every year."

She stopped talking and looked around the table.

"What if we're frustrated because we're too involved in collecting micro details and we're missing the clear big picture? Too many small details might be confusing and overwhelming us. We think we're looking at the big picture, but we're not. There's something more."

A hush penetrated the room as the others absorbed what she'd said.

The captain was the first to speak.

"We can plug in the variables and check our computer records at the department. We'll determine if any other similar incidents have occurred and, if so, how many." He paused. "And we'll review the results of the other three women's autopsies. Let's all meet back here tomorrow morning, same time, and discuss our findings."

CAPTAIN MASSEY arrived back at his office, glanced through his messages, and immediately called Claire.

"Ms. Caswell, I just heard from the medical examiner on the Eric Fox case.

The young man's stomach contents indicated some type of poisoning. It appears to be a plant of some kind. The office is running additional tests. It's nothing common in southern Florida, so it might take a while."

"You know the items I found at Charlotte's crash site were a rare type of plant part. A poisonous variety," Claire said. "So this could get really interesting really fast."

"Okay. Maybe we are getting somewhere," the captain said.

"We'll have to wait for the lab results on Eric," Claire said. "Any way to speed them up? And ask the techs to check for the same substance as was found in the samples I brought in on Charlotte's case, will you, please?"

"Will do," he said. "Oh, and by the way, the medical examiner mentioned Eric had an old, polished key in a leather pouch in his pants pocket. It's bagged as evidence."

"Hmm," Claire said.

"In the meantime, we're checking on other female deaths in Porsche Cayennes over the past five years. If we are looking at a serial killer, we might find more than the four."

"Great. See you tomorrow."

CLAIRE HUNG up. Her mind spun as she absorbed what the captain had told her about Eric. Poison had ended his life. And the withered dark berries she had discovered at Charlotte's crash site? Poison also. And Christine Fox was poisoned. Who did Eric, Charlotte, and Christine know in common? Stephen Fox. But would Stephen poison his own son? And why would he want Charlotte out of the picture? And Christine? There were so many unanswered questions. Was Roise Fox related to Stephen Fox? And Charlie, the man who lived a life of illusion, how did he fit in to all of this? And Natalie? And how did Estee play into the plan?

The female investigator went to work on her computer.

Keep searching for connections, she told herself. Relationships. Links. Associations. Arrangements. Tie-ins. Friends. Acquaintances. Allies. Colleagues. Relatives.

Guy also searched. And he made calls. Someone somewhere knew something.

THE FOLLOWING morning, Captain Massey returned with his two investigators to the office of Caswell & Lombard, Private Investigation. Claire and Guy sat down with them.

"What a difference a day makes," the captain said.

"What do you have?" Guy asked.

Captain Massey reached into his briefcase and lifted out copies of his research. He placed one in front of each person at the table.

"We'll need to examine these findings closely," he said. "This is what my department discovered."

Claire's and Guy's eyes scanned the report.

"It's all here in the official reports," Claire said. "Confirmation of the facts we suspected and new information, as well." She summarized for the group. "Looks like the four single women, including Charlotte, lived in the Miami area and met with fatal car crashes while driving their new Porsche Cayenne SUVs—and in each case within weeks of their purchases." She looked down. She scrutinized the dates of the accidents. "One incident each year for the past four years. And no other similar incidents."

"And in each case, the cause of death was determined to be driver error or natural causes," the captain said. "That would be because no other cause could be determined from the testing the medical examiner performed or was able to perform due to the condition of the victims. Remember, poison can mimic a heart attack. My guess is since no specific cause of death could be established, and after learning the specifics of the crashes, the deaths were ruled in the manner they were."

"If we can go back and prove that a poison was ingested in each case, and also prove who did the poisoning, we call that a serial pattern of murder," Guy said. "We can get the perpetrator locked up for life."

"We know the vehicles were all purchased at the dealership where Stephen Fox works," the captain said. "We checked it out. That might be our best and only lead."

Stillness echoed loudly.

"Keep in mind, Christine Fox died of probable poisoning too," Claire said. "We need to have her blood tested for the poison we now suspect."

"I'm on it," the captain said.

"And she died a year before the first victim of our four," Claire said. "So we might even be looking at a total of five female victims killed at the hands of the same culprit." She paused. "Are we looking at the same type of poison in the cases of all the women drivers? And Christine? And Eric?" Claire asked.

Those at the table did not speak.

"We'll interview the family members or friends of the three other women who died in the crashes," Claire said. "Maybe we can get some good information."

"And my department will interview the medical examiners who made the calls," the captain said. "We need to look at all of this as a whole."

"Let's talk in a day or two and compare notes," one of Massey's investigators said. "I think we're getting somewhere."

JIN DROVE directly from classes and searched for Charlie. His first stop was Estee's house, and the Karmann Ghia was not parked out front. He drove to the marina and found *Black Pearl* firmly tied up in place. Next, he drove to the house where Charlie had gone to play cards. No cars were on the street that day. He even drove past the French bakery, but the green car was nowhere in sight. Perhaps he was on an errand for Roise Fox? Or at an early dinner with Estee? He decided to return to the office.

When he arrived, Claire brought him up to date on the Stephen Fox investigation.

"Things are progressing. The wheels are turning," he said. "I can feel it. They always tell us in law school that 'the wheels of justice turn, but they turn slowly,' and I'm seeing that happen."

"Jin, will you take a quick glance through the mail? I haven't had a chance to look at it in a couple of days. See if there is anything important to deal with. Or any payments that have come in on other cases," she said. "Thank you."

A short time later, Jin appeared at her desk.

"Nothing urgent, except for this one letter." He handed it to her. "It's addressed to C. Caswell. It looks kind of strange, Claire. No return address. And it's printed in large letters. Better take a look."

Guy lifted his head. "What is it?"

Claire slipped on gloves and ripped open the envelope, revealing a handwritten note. She read aloud:

People poking into other people's business often perish
Watch your step, C. Caswell
Watch your step or you might take a deadly fall

"That's a threat!" Guy spewed like a volcanic eruption. "Let me see that!"

He reached for the note.

Claire stopped him cold. "Not until you put gloves on. The lab might be able to pull some prints from it."

He hurriedly found a pair of latex gloves and fitted them onto his hands. He grabbed the note and studied it.

"We're getting close," Claire said. "Someone is running scared."

Jin had looked on without speaking. It was clear he was taken aback. He knew the business of private investigation often brought with it danger and close calls. But this was an actual threat made on the life of Claire Caswell. His eyes looked dazed.

Claire sensed his apprehension.

"Jin, I've been threatened before. Don't let it worry you," she said. "I'll be fine. I know how to protect myself."

She walked to a locked cabinet and placed her index finger on the biometric release. The door opened, and she lifted out her Smith & Wesson .38 Special revolver. She checked to confirm it was fully loaded with five bullets. She placed it under the back side of her belt.

"From now on, until this case is solved, I'm carrying," she announced.

"I was going to suggest it, Claire," Guy said.

Jin swallowed hard. This was real life. Claire had been threatened, and now she was prepared to fight back.

"Call Captain Massey," Guy said. "Let him know of this development. Ask him to send an officer over to write up a complaint. And to retrieve the note to check it for prints."

But Claire didn't answer. She had already picked up the phone to call the captain.

THE REST of the day was spent attempting to find information on the three other female victims. They needed to locate relatives, friends, or associates and obtain contact information. Interviews had to be done and information gathered. The three each took a name to concentrate on.

The team began by seeking a photo of each victim and newspaper articles that covered each tragedy. They also checked the obituaries for all of the cases. The afternoon passed quickly.

At the end of the day, a smattering of information and photos for all of the women had been obtained. They tacked the information onto the evidence board. Tomorrow was another day. And they'd be back at it full-time.

CAPTAIN MASSEY and his investigators summoned the Miami-Dade County medical examiner and his staff of doctors trained in the field of forensic pathology to come to the Miami-Dade Police Department. The captain also invited representatives of both the morgue bureau and the toxicology lab—the entity responsible for assisting the medical examiner in investigations to determine causes and manners of death—to be present.

When calling for the meeting, the captain reported the specific cases to be discussed and asked each invitee to first review his or her records and be prepared to speak intelligently about the examinations.

It was time to get to the bottom of these fatal accidents.

All whose presence was requested by Captain Massey filed into a large interview room at the Miami-Dade Police Department at 9:00 a.m. the following morning. The room was filled with professionals who knew one another and had worked on some of the most difficult cases in the history of Miami-Dade County.

At the last minute, the captain phoned Claire and Guy and requested they attend, as well. Many of the invitees had worked with

Gaston Lombard in his capacity as a Miami-Dade state attorney. The private investigators dropped what they were working on and rushed over.

Captain Massey started the meeting by giving a summary of the matters at hand. He set forth specific details about the tragic vehicle accident that took the life of Claire Caswell's friend Charlotte Truman. He spoke of the steps of the investigation taken to date both by the Miami-Dade Police Department and by the private investigation firm of Caswell & Lombard. He even touched upon the investigation of Charlie McDermott and the potential overlap with the surname *Fox*. Lastly, he talked about the recent finding that three other single women had met with similar, sudden, horrific one-car accidents within the Miami-Dade area in the last four years—all while driving new Porsche Cayennes purchased at the same dealership. He added that each of the women had allegedly been dating the finance manager at the dealership.

"The modus operandi in each case appears to indicate a trend or pattern in the method of deaths that these women faced in the SUVs," the captain said. "That's why you're all here today. You are the experts. No one out there has the combined experience of all of you present in this room today." He paused and looked into the eyes of each professional at the table. "We need answers." His look was somber. "I've asked private investigators Claire Caswell and Gaston Lombard to join us today, as they have already expended much time looking into these matters. You all know who they are. Their reputations precede them."

Captain Massey turned the meeting over to the private investigators.

"Perhaps you can fill us all in on the specific details of your efforts."

Claire and Guy took turns going over their findings in chronological order.

All attendees scribbled down notes on the legal pads sitting before them.

"Most interesting," the chief medical examiner said. "It certainly is worthy of a second look." He pulled a sheet of paper from his briefcase. "In each of these cases, my office made a determination that death came from driver error or natural causes. All the women were relatively young and in good health according to all medical records. These rulings were made in each case because my team could not pinpoint another causation."

"Go on," the captain requested.

"Well, we have limited resources and too many cases," the medical examiner said. "As you all know, violent crime is a big problem here in Miami. We spend as much time on autopsies as we can but find we have to move on to service others that just keep pouring in. At some point, we are forced to make rulings, even when we're not happy doing so. It's a question of time and resources."

"What about in the cases of the women we are looking into?" the captain asked.

"These cases always happened a year apart, roughly speaking. That is a lot of time between each autopsy. We would most likely never have thought to put these cases together," the medical examiner said.

Members of his team nodded in unison.

"We always have to move on to the next corpse," he added. "We did make comprehensive notes in our files, and we were able to save a blood specimen from each of the victims, despite their conditions after the horrific crashes. After your call to organize this meeting, I had my lab test the blood samples from each of the three earlier victims and also from Charlotte Truman." He paused. "We found something."

17

AS CLAIRE SUSPECTED, the lab was unable to lift fingerprints from the threatening note she'd received. The author of the menacing writing had obviously worn gloves to cover the ridges and sweat on his or her fingers that would most certainly have left prints behind. No whorls, loops, or arches were detected. And the envelope was contaminated with far too many fingerprints to even do definitive testing.

The female investigator knew that fingerprints were even more unique than DNA, as even identical twins had different fingerprints despite sharing identical DNA. She had hoped for a fingerprint but knew the chances of finding one were not good. Whoever drafted the deliberately frightening message knew exactly how to protect his or her identity.

She exhaled. They needed a break in this case.

CLAIRE AND Guy continued doing research in an attempt to locate friends, relatives, or associates of Cindy Bane, Catherine Hanker, and Camille Sullivan.

The female investigator's mind flashed to Charlotte and to the three other female crash victims. Then to Stephen's ex-wife, Carli Fox. And to his first wife, Christine Fox. What were the odds of all these women having given names starting with the letter *C*? This had to be significant. But what was the meaning? Carli was the only one on the list who was still alive. If Stephen was the one behind all these deaths, then why had Carli survived? Her mind reeled. There had to be an answer.

She grabbed a large sheet of white paper and wrote the names of the victims across the top. She drew vertical lines to give each one a separate column. As she, Guy, and Jin obtained information on any one of them, Claire filled it in on the sheet. *Look at the big picture,* her small voice reminded her.

Before long, each column contained the age, birth date, and address of the deceased. And with the assistance of Captain Massey, Claire added a photo of each victim taken from their respective driver's licenses.

She laid all the photos on the conference table and studied them. The women could not have varied more in physical appearance. Hair colors, eye colors, heights, and weights all differed considerably. She scanned the sheet she had compiled. The age ranges were in the same ballpark—all midthirties to midforties. The similarities were their single statuses and their financial wherewithal.

She picked up the phone and dialed Captain Massey.

"Can you subpoena the purchase agreements, as well as the finance agreements—if there were any—of the car crash victims from the Porsche dealership where Stephen Fox works?" she asked.

"He's certainly a person of interest right now," the captain said. "So yes. I'll do it. I'll get it issued and served tomorrow."

CLAIRE'S MIND was on overload. She needed to take a rest from the case. She grabbed her purse, walked outside, threw on her sunglasses, and jumped into her car. With no destination in mind, the female investigator drove in the direction of a nearby residential area. She lowered the car windows to soak in the sunshine of the day, the endless blue sky, the majestic royal palms, and the numberless hedges of fuchsia bougainvillea lining the boulevards of the upscale area. She needed an interruption. A pause. A recess. A timeout. She parked her car near a row of shops and spotted an empty bench. She walked over and sat down to take in just how glorious the day was.

Before long, Claire spotted several children walking past her on the sidewalk, each one lapping up an ice cream cone. The day was Miami hot, and the delicious treats were quickly melting down their arms before they could consume them fast enough. Claire laughed. *Oh, to be young again,* she thought. *To be carefree, unworried, and happy-go-lucky.*

She got up, strolled to the nearby ice cream shop, and ordered a double scoop of strawberry ice cream. It was her favorite flavor as a child, and for a few minutes she needed to be a child again. She returned to the bench and enjoyed the frozen treat. When she finished, she closed her eyes to feel the warmth of the sun's rays on her face.

Her thoughts turned to Charlotte. What had happened to her friend? The crash occurred not far from where she lived. Was she driving home? Or trying to get there? If so, why? The crash occurred in the middle of the workday. Why was she not at work? She had a job where she could set her own hours, so maybe it was nothing. She wondered if answers would ever come.

Just then, she felt a thud as someone sat down next to her on the bench.

She opened her eyes with a start.

The action of the stranger plopping down whisked her back to adulthood.

But when she turned to look, it was not a stranger after all. Rather, it was Stephen Fox. She adjusted herself on the bench, creating a greater distance between them.

"I don't bite, Ms. Caswell. I was driving by, and I saw you sitting here in front of an ice cream shop. Are you okay?" he asked.

"Fine," she said. She tried not to look stunned that he showed up out of the blue. She avoided eye contact.

"Did you have ice cream?" he asked.

"I did," she said.

"I'd like some too. Will you wait here and save my place on the bench?"

He was gone before she could respond. It seemed a strange request in an obviously awkward situation.

Stephen reappeared moments later holding a chocolate marsh-mallow cone.

"When was the last time you sat on a bench in the middle of the day and enjoyed ice cream?" he asked. "If you're anything like me, it's been a long time." He began to devour the melting sweet treat.

"It's been a while," she admitted. She got up to leave.

"For me too." He suddenly paused as if deep in thought. "Choc-olate marshmallow was Eric's favorite. I've been eating more of it since he died," he said. "You think you have an entire lifetime to make things right and then—"

"I'm sorry about your son," Claire interrupted. "I need to go."

"Well, we both lost Charlotte, and then I lost Eric. It's been a tough time," he continued.

"It has," Claire said. She glanced at her watch. She turned and walked away.

On the drive back to the office, she couldn't seem to shake the coincidence of Stephen Fox running into her. But then she thought better of the situation and reminded herself she really didn't believe in coincidence.

SITTING AT her desk, she relayed what happened to Guy.

"I've warned you about that man," he said. "He's a suspect in the murder of Charlotte and potentially three or four others. Watch your back. Sounds like he's trying to get personal with you."

"I do. I will," she said. "My guard is always up around him."

"What are the odds of the man happening to drive by at that very time?" Guy asked. "I don't believe it for a minute. He's following you."

"I don't believe it either," Claire said. "I think he is following us, or perhaps me. Maybe he's trying to find out what we know about the case."

"Things can turn ugly really quickly," Guy said. "Especially if all roads lead to him."

"I get it," Claire said. "Really, I do." Her expression turned grim. "You don't have to keep reminding me."

Guy realized he needed to lighten up the conversation. "You didn't happen to bring me a cone, did you? You know butter pecan is my favorite." His famous grin lit up his face, and his eyes twinkled.

Her somber expression turned into a smile, and her eyes twinkled back.

"It would have melted . . ."

Working with the person you loved had its benefits, especially in a career like this. After her brief respite from the case, Claire continued her search to locate people to interview regarding the premature deaths of the other female drivers.

By the end of the day, she and Guy had possibilities on two of the three.

"Let's take a recess from this and interview one of the relatives tomorrow," Claire said.

"I agree."

THE FOLLOWING morning, the investigators visited an aunt of one of the victims: Catherine Hanker. They knocked on the door of a small one-story house in Miami.

With chain in place, the door opened slightly.

"Yes?" a female voice asked.

Claire and Guy introduced themselves and held up identifications for the woman to see.

"What's this about?" she asked.

"It's about Catherine, your niece," Claire said.

"She's no longer with us," the woman said. "Rest her soul."

"We're investigating the death of a good friend of mine, Charlotte Truman," Claire said.

"What does this have to do with my niece?" she questioned.

"There are . . . similarities," Guy said.

"Like?" the woman asked.

"Would you mind if we sat down and talked to you for a short time?" Claire asked. "It will only take a few minutes."

"I guess it's okay," she said. Reluctance was evident in her tone.

The door closed, and the chain was removed. She opened the door and motioned them in.

"Tell us about Catherine and the accident," Guy said. "Will you, please?"

"There's not much to say," the woman said. "She was a vibrant, intelligent young lady. Her career had just taken off, she had received a huge promotion, and then it happened."

"Go on, please," Claire said.

"Well, it just about killed my sister and her husband too. After Catherine's death, they moved away, and no one in the family hears from them anymore. It seems they've lost their love of life. It's very sad."

"Your niece was driving a Porsche SUV, correct?" Claire asked. "A new one?"

"Yes, she had just purchased it. She was so proud of that car. She gave me a ride in it as soon as she got it. And then days later, she was killed when it slammed into a parked bus. It was a horrible, horrible tragedy." She paused and looked off into the distance.

The investigators waited a couple of minutes before going on.

"What do you think caused the accident?" Claire asked.

"They said driver error or natural causes. Driver error? Natural causes? No way. I never understood it. Catherine was an excellent driver. They said she most probably had a heart attack, and that caused her to lose control of her car. It never did seem right to me. They said she was traveling at a high speed. But I never believed it." She looked downward.

"Do you know where she bought the car?" Guy asked.

"Yes." She identified the dealership where Stephen worked.

"You may not be able to answer this question," Claire said, "but do you have any recollection of the name of the person she worked with at the dealership?"

The woman did not respond at first. She thought for a time.

"It was a man. She kind of liked this man. She told me about him," Catherine's aunt said. "If you give me a name, I might be able to tell you if it was him."

"Was it Stephen Fox?" Claire asked.

"Yes. That was the name. Catherine was a career person and had never married. I do remember that she was interested in this Stephen, though." The woman's gaze told the investigators she was remembering. "She thought he was a really nice man."

"Did they ever date?" Guy asked.

"I think so. Right after the purchase, they went out a few times. I remember Catherine talking about it," the aunt said. "I never met him, though."

"Hmm," Claire said.

"You said there were similarities between your friend's death and my niece's," the woman said. "What did you mean?"

Claire talked about Charlotte. About how she had just purchased a new Porsche SUV too, about the tragic crash she had while driving it, and how it had also been ruled driver error. She also added that Charlotte purchased the car from Stephen at the same dealership Catherine had used.

"You don't believe it was driver error, do you?" the woman asked. She looked directly at Claire with piercing eyes. "Tell me the truth."

"We're looking into it," Claire said.

"You wouldn't be here at my house if you believed it," Catherine's aunt said.

"We are investigating the matter," Guy said. "We're looking into all possibilities."

"Did your friend date Stephen too?" the woman asked.

"Yes," Claire said. "She was quite taken with the man."

"Was your friend healthy? Was she a good driver?" the woman persisted.

"Yes, she was the picture of health. And, yes, she was a superb driver," Claire said.

"Did they tell you she was speeding way over the limit?"

Claire nodded.

The woman let her eyes return to the floor. She appeared deep in thought.

"Something's not right here," she said. "Something is not right."

18

NEXT ON THE agenda was to interview a cousin of Cindy Bane: Rolf Esteman. He was the only relative in the Miami area the investigators were able to locate. They drove to his address.

Rolf answered the door when they knocked. He was cooperative from the outset. A life-insurance salesman, he worked out of his home. He explained how his life had drastically changed when Cindy had died so suddenly and unexpectedly.

"She was my baby cousin," he said. "The youngest of all the cousins. She was an only child. Her parents both passed when she was in her twenties. I was her only relative who lived in Miami, so the two of us were close. We talked at least once a week." He took in a deep breath and exhaled. "She was a healthy and successful financial planner. She died just weeks after she had become part owner of the highly respected firm where she worked. She was the youngest owner the company had ever had. I was so proud of her." He choked up. "When she died, I became keenly aware of how life dangles from a delicate thread. I had a heavy heart for close to a year. I was afraid to leave my house. And I still am for the most part. I only go out when I absolutely have to. Her death changed my life."

"We are so sorry for your loss, Mr. Esteman," Claire said. "Can you tell us about the accident?"

"Yes. She had purchased a new vehicle a couple of weeks earlier. She was a car person. She loved to drive." Rolf paused to gather his thoughts. "The Porsche Cayenne was her favorite. It was the vehicle she dreamed about. I was told she lost control of the car when it plunged into a median on I-95. There were no skid marks, and the speed was way over the posted limit. This seemed inconceivable to me. How that ever happened will always mystify me."

"Where did she buy the car?" Guy asked.

Rolf confirmed it was the dealership where Stephen was employed.

"Did she tell you the name of the employee she dealt with?" Claire asked.

"Not that I remember," Rolf said. He looked at the investigators with sudden inquisitiveness. "Why are you looking into this matter *now*? It was ruled a death by natural causes or driver error at the time. What's going on?"

Claire told Rolf about Charlotte Truman.

He looked her squarely in the eyes.

"Are you thinking Charlotte's and Cindy's deaths might not have been driver error? Or caused by a heart attack?" He turned pasty white.

"It's an open investigation, and we can't share more at this time," Guy said.

"If it wasn't natural causes or driver error, are you saying Charlotte and Cindy could have been murdered?" Rolf persisted.

"We're not sure at this time, Rolf," Claire said. "We promise to notify you of our findings at the conclusion of our investigation. We're working jointly with the Miami-Dade Police Department. We won't let this go until we get to the truth."

"The truth," Rolf repeated. "*The truth. The whole truth. And nothing but the truth.* Don't stop until you find it."

"One final question, Rolf," Claire said. "Was Cindy dating anyone at the time of the accident?"

He thought for a while.

"There was a man who worked at that car dealership," he said. "She told me he had flirted with her and she thought he was intriguing. I guess I'm not sure if she dated him or not." He paused. "But the more I think about it now, I believe she said she was." He paused again. "Cindy was serious about her work. It was her life. When her parents died, she became driven to succeed. She knew she had to take care of herself."

BACK AT the office, the private investigators continued their search for living relatives, friends, or associates of the third victim. Jin had already been working on it. It wasn't until the end of the day that Jin found a possibility. He located a business associate of Camille's named Mary Katz. Camille had owned a successful dry-cleaning business, and Mary Katz was her CPA.

Claire and Guy agreed to drive to the address.

Claire knocked at the front door.

"Who is it?" a woman's voice called out.

Guy announced who they were, the purpose of their visit, and asked if they could speak to her for a few minutes.

She let them in.

Mary was a middle-aged woman, heavyset, and good-natured.

Her short hair was dyed a honey-blonde, and her eyes were an intense glacial blue.

"You worked with Camille, correct, Mary?"

"I did," she replied. "I was the CPA for her business for several years. We also became friends. She confided in me quite a bit."

"What kind of business did she own?" Guy asked.

"It was a good-sized dry cleaner," the accountant said. "She bought it when it was small and doubled its size and business the first year. The employees loved her."

"What can you tell us about Camille?" Claire asked.

"Well, she was single, successful, and saucy. Also sad."

"Sad?" Claire asked.

"What I mean by that is that she had made it big in business, but she had no other life to speak of—no social life. She had never married. And I think she was at the point where she really wanted to have children. Forty was not far down the road, and it was now or never. She talked about it more and more."

"You were aware that she purchased a new Porsche Cayenne shortly before the accident?" Guy asked.

"Oh, yes. She loved that car as much as someone could love a car. She had worked hard to develop her business, and she saw the car as a reward for all the long hours she had put in. And, beside the point, she could afford it. Money was no object."

"We'd like to talk about the accident," Guy said. "What do you know about it?"

"I know it was a tragedy, to be sure," the accountant said. "Out of the blue it happened. Without warning. Unexpected. Before her time. Too early. What more can I say? It shocked me."

"Was she a good driver?" Claire asked.

"She never even had a speeding ticket, as far as I know. She was an extremely responsible driver. That's why I just couldn't understand the ruling of driver error as the cause of her death. It was a horrific accident. She drove down a road under construction at top speed and headed straight into a concrete blockade. It didn't make any sense to me. She would have had to be drugged or drunk to do something like that."

"Did she drink alcohol?" Guy asked. "Or do illicit drugs?"

"Absolutely no to the drugs question. She felt strongly about that. And alcohol? Maybe a glass of wine with dinner, but never if she was driving afterward."

"Do you know who she dealt with at the car dealership when she made her purchase?" Guy asked.

"Of course. I even spoke to the man on the phone when we were lining up the payment. I recall his name was Stephen Fox and that he asked a lot of questions. Things I really didn't feel were relevant to an all-cash car purchase."

"What kind of questions did he ask?" Claire asked.

"Oh, for example, he asked for Camille's social security number. I'm careful never to give that out. But he insisted he needed it to process the transaction. I reluctantly gave it to him. He assured me the number would be deleted immediately after the processing went through. He even asked me for the balance in her account—the one the dealership was being paid from. I assured him there were sufficient funds in the account to cover the check and refused to give him the balance. Can you imagine? What kind of a question was that? He already had her full name, address, and marital status too. I even said something about it to Camille. His questions bothered me greatly. I'm very cautious about giving any personal information out these days. Bad people can do bad things if they get their hands on it."

"And did a relationship develop between Mr. Fox and Camille?" Claire asked.

"How did you know?" the accountant asked. She raised her eyebrows in surprise. "Yes, they started dating. She was excited about it. I think Camille saw him as a prospective husband. Maybe even a father to the children she wanted. He was the first prospect she'd had in many years. He paid a lot of attention to her."

"Did you meet Stephen Fox in person?" Claire asked.

"I did. He was an attractive man and nicely dressed," she said. "Polished. Confident. All of that. But he was a little too smooth for my liking. Too slick. I didn't trust him. I even warned Camille. I told her my thoughts."

"One more question, if you don't mind," Guy said. "What happened to Camille's business after she died?"

"She left it to me in her will," the CPA said. "I own it now."

AFTER DINNER that evening, Claire preheated the oven and pulled out bowls, measuring cups, measuring spoons, mixing spoons, and all the ingredients she needed to make chocolate chip cookies. She hadn't made Guy's favorite cookies in a while, and she also needed time to think. Baking always allowed her that alone time to be lost in thought. She found it therapeutic.

Every part of the investigation was streaking back and forth across her mind. Information was being collected from so many sources and coming in from every direction. They had gathered an ever-growing collection of puzzle pieces, but none of them seemed to fit together just yet. She knew this was the path that complicated investigations most always took. And she also realized that all of a sudden, two pieces would start to fit together, and then four, and then more, and suddenly the puzzle would take on shape and form and become a clear picture.

She combined butter, oil, eggs, and vanilla extract. She always splurged on the vanilla extract with a stronger flavor, made from premium beans with high vanillin content and few additives. She stirred in sugar, baking powder, salt, flour, and chocolate chips— admittedly, a handful more chocolate morsels than the recipe called for. She placed generous tablespoonfuls of the thick mixture on two cookie sheets and popped them into the preheated oven.

After turning the oven light on, Claire watched as the dough slowly spread, the edges set, and the mounds started to rise and then settle into their final shape before the heat made its way toward the centers to complete the baking process. All the while she thought about the case.

Before long, a tantalizing aroma permeated the room.

Guy walked in. "Okay. I need one or three of those now." He grinned, revealing deep facial dimples he otherwise kept hidden.

Claire glanced at the timer and then shifted her eyes back to the oven, peering in through the glass window. "I'd say you'll have to wait about two more minutes. Can you do that?" She smiled. "I brewed a fresh pot of coffee."

"How did you know?" he asked.

"Because you always like a cup of very strong hot coffee with your warm chocolate chip cookies."

"Nothing better," he said. He pulled two mugs from the cupboard. "Join me?"

Claire nodded. The timer went off, and she pulled the baking sheets from their racks.

"These need to cool for another couple of minutes," she said.

"I can't wait," Guy said.

"You'll have to. They need to set. It'll be worth the wait."

As Guy placed the two cups of steaming coffee on the table, a thought struck Claire.

Investigations are similar to baking cookies, she pondered. *With cookies, you need to collect all the ingredients necessary to make the dough, mix it all together, bake, and then watch them unfold into the finished product. With investigations, you need to collect all the relevant evidence from witness statements, reviewing documentation, and engaging in surveillance techniques, process all that information together, analyze, and watch a scenario build that makes sense.*

On Charlotte's case and on Estee's case, the investigators were still at the point of collecting, processing, and analyzing. She had total confidence they were well on their way to the finished product.

She shared her thoughts with Guy, but he was too busy gorging himself with the warm chocolate chip cookies to give them much thought.

19

CLAIRE RETRIEVED THE materials she had printed about poisons and studied the articles. The usual suspects were all there—arsenic, strychnine, cyanide, thallium (rat poison), hemlock, morphine, and more. Even the juice of the poppy was mentioned in one article as being poisonous, and the leaves of rhubarb in another. And the bulbs and stems of lily of the valley plants. There was much she didn't know.

She thought about the murder mysteries she had read over the years and the whodunits she had watched on television, and she recalled how the poisons were usually administered. The lethal substance was often dissolved into hot tea, hot chocolate, water, wine, or food. And most often the poisons were readily available to the murderers. The killers using poison were cold-blooded and the acts premeditated. Always premeditated. And most of the perpetrators were careful planners who plotted and executed over a period of time; poisoning was not done on impulse. The toxins were typi-cally found nearby—in a garage, under a kitchen sink, at the killer's place of employment, or growing in the countryside. The levels or doses had to be correct; the more ingested, the quicker the death.

A shudder racked Claire's body.

Poisoning was a game on the part of the killer. A game of strategy. A game the killer tried to win.

Claire began doing additional research on her computer. She read about the various plants and flowers that are or could be lethal given the right circumstances.

There were many. She looked for the botanicals common to southern Florida—concentrating on those grown wild that would withstand little rain and hot sunshine much of the time. And she looked for those containing tropane alkaloids—the substance the crime lab personnel said they found in the specimens Claire discov-ered at the crash site. There were several.

Then she looked at the pictures of the garden she had taken at the Fox family home—at the rows of varying plants and shrubs. In a far corner, on a slope, under the shade of a giant hovering oak, her eyes rested on the deadly culprit. She studied the leaves and the shiny black berries. Pretty to look at. Deadly to consume. She waited impatiently for the lab results of the samples she had collected.

CLAIRE TELEPHONED Captain Massey.

She filled him in on the interviews she and Guy had conducted with the relatives and the CPA of the female crash victims. "The stories of the victims are so similar it's unnerving. The names and faces change, but their backgrounds are stunningly almost indistinguishable."

"And to think all of this had been missed and would never have been brought to light without the investigative efforts of your firm. Thank you."

"Don't thank us yet. Determining that poison was the weapon is the easy part compared to finding evidence of who is behind it." She reflected. "I'm reading up on poisons now. And I'm thinking about who had motive to kill these women. Determining motive is often a difficult thing, as you know. Perpetrators go to great lengths to cover their tracks. They often act friendly and nice as they are plotting and carrying out their ploys behind the curtain, so to speak."

"You're thinking like a cop, Ms. Caswell. Means, motive, and opportunity. Without motive, it's difficult to prove the crimes. You can see why many crimes go unprosecuted. Putting together cases of this nature take time and steadfast perseverance. The deaths were spaced out over periods of time, making this case more than difficult to solve—almost impossible, really. No one would ever have connected the dots without the work of your firm. It just wouldn't have happened."

"Well, we're not there yet," she said. "But with you and our firm working on it simultaneously, I believe we'll figure it out. On another note, I've been thinking. I believe we should subpoena the female victims' bank records. See if any monies are missing from their accounts."

"We'd have to know where the victims banked," the captain said, "in order to get subpoenas issued."

"Well, in the case of Camille Sullivan, we interviewed her CPA, Mary Katz. She kept a close watch over Camille's finances when she was alive. She would be helpful in this regard. I'll call her or go see her. As far as Cindy Bane and Catherine Hanker, we'll contact their relatives again and see if they recall the banks the two women used. I'll let you know."

"Yes, get back to me with that information, Ms. Caswell, and I'll get those subpoenas out."

Claire heard the captain cracking his knuckles just before she hung up.

THAT AFTERNOON, Claire and Guy drove back to Mary Katz's house.

"Back again?" she asked.

"We are," Claire said. "We know you kept a detailed eye on Camille's finances. Did you ever notice funds missing after her death? Monies unaccounted for? Notice questions in her bank statements? Anything of that nature?"

Mary looked at the investigators as if trying to decide if she should release information about her client's finances.

"It's important," Claire said.

"No, I didn't," Mary said.

"Which bank did Camille use?" Claire asked.

"I'll give you the bank and her account numbers, if you need them as part of your investigation," Mary said. She disappeared into another room and returned shortly carrying a thick file.

BACK IN the car, Claire looked at Guy.

"One down," she said.

"Two to go," he said.

Their next stop was to see the cousin of Cindy Bane—Rolf Esteman.

When they arrived at his place, he came to the door.

"Do you have something to report so soon?" he asked.

"Not yet," Claire said, "but we have another question for you."

"Anything," he said.

"Do you know where Cindy did her banking?"

"Sure. I was her personal representative. I have all that information."

He walked over to a file cabinet and rummaged for a file. He couldn't find it. "I think it might be in storage in my garage. Can you wait?"

"Sure," Guy said.

He disappeared for twenty minutes and returned.

"Here it is. I finally found it." He started to go through the mass of paperwork.

"We need the bank's name and her account numbers if you have them. And hopefully you do," Guy said.

"Right here." Rolf offered several sheets of statements to the investigators.

Claire jotted down the information they needed.

"Keep me posted," Rolf said. "I know you'll figure this out. We need to see justice prevail."

THE THIRD stop was the aunt of Catherine Hanker. They drove to her home and rang the doorbell.

"Yes? Who is it?" she called out from behind the closed door.

Once she heard it was the investigators, she pulled the door open and invited them in.

"What happened? Did you find out something about Catherine? I've been thinking of nothing else since your last visit. Please tell me you have good news."

"Not yet," Claire said. "But hopefully soon."

"We need to ask you for additional information, if you have it," Guy said.

"Do you happen to know where Catherine did her banking?"

"I don't," she said. "Why do you need that?"

Guy explained.

"I think I know who settled her estate. She would know. I have her card somewhere. You'll have to wait."

The woman disappeared into her kitchen.

"Here it is," she said as she returned. "Her name's Mary Katz. She's an accountant. She'll have the information."

JIN FINISHED class and went on to continue his mission of surveillance. The day was hot, Miami hot, and getting hotter. He reached for his bottle of water and downed much of it. He tracked Charlie down at Estee's house. The man seemed to be there almost daily, with few exceptions, and it was a good bet to try her place whenever he needed to find him.

The intern parked down the street.

Before long, he heard a light rap on the driver's-side window. He turned his head and saw a woman standing there. He lowered his window an inch.

"It's Claire's mom, Abbey," she said. "I noticed you out here, and I thought I'd bring you a sandwich and a soda."

She saw Jin's eyes dart toward Estee's house.

"Don't worry. They didn't see me," Abbey said. "I took the long way around and came up behind you. They couldn't have seen me."

Jin took the items and thanked her. He was starving, and the gesture was more than appreciated.

"Claire has told us all about you," Abbey said. "What an asset you are to the firm. She told me you'd be watching Estee's house and to give you any assistance you might need."

"Claire and Guy are the best," he said. "They've taught me almost everything I know." He smiled.

"I'll let you get back to work. Nice to meet you."

Abbey stepped away quietly.

Moments later, Estee's front door opened, and she and Charlie stepped out. The two walked to his car, and he drove off.

Jin trailed behind.

Today was a shopping day. The two drove to the famous Bal Harbour Shops and made a day of it. They first had lunch at Carpaccio, dining on pasta and engaging in people-watching. Jin waited nearby in the outdoor mall area. Crowds of people milled about, making it easy for Jin to blend in and not be noticed.

Afterward, Charlie and Estee shopped. They went in and out of several of the high-end stores—Neiman Marcus, Gucci, Prada, Harry Winston, Louis Vuitton, Cartier, and Bulgari, to name a few. Each time they came out toting bags. Jin could only imagine the money being spent.

The pair laughed, held hands, and whispered quietly to each other.

After a long afternoon of shopping, they stopped at a café located on the ground floor of the two-story mall—in the central courtyard. They ordered hot teas.

Jin snapped pictures whenever possible.

Who was the big spender? Jin wondered. Estee or Charlie? He guessed it was Estee.

He followed the lovebirds back to her home. Charlie walked her to the door, and Jin noticed the two carried no bags. That meant the shopping had all been for Charlie. Jin made a note in his journal.

Charlie returned to his car and drove away.

Jin followed.

Charlie drove to the condo and disappeared inside. He reappeared twenty minutes later dressed in new clothes. A designer floral shirt, silk Bermudas, a snakeskin belt, and spendy shoes. He'd done well.

He jumped into his Karmann Ghia and traveled down Collins Avenue. He wove his way through heavy traffic, and Jin followed dutifully behind. Minutes passed. Charlie made a turn.

Where is Charlie going? Jin wondered.

CLAIRE AND Guy returned to the home of Mary Katz. They rang her bell.

"I knew you'd be back," she said. Her nervousness from the last visit had now turned to sheepishness and guilt. She knew that they knew.

"Why didn't you tell us?" Claire asked.

"Because I thought it might somehow look bad for me," she said. "I was the accountant for two young women killed in freak car accidents. And I inherited a successful business from one of them. I didn't want to be a suspect, so I kept my mouth shut. I only answered the questions you asked."

"Not too professional, was it?" Claire asked.

"No, it wasn't. And I'm sorry." She looked mortified.

"It was a waste of our valuable time having to travel back to your place again," Guy said. The anger he was feeling showed on his face.

Mary averted her eyes and refused to look at him further.

"People not wanting to get fully involved," Guy said. "It makes our job that much harder."

Claire stepped in.

"Mary, we need banking information on Catherine Hanker. Bank name and account numbers. Please get them for us."

Mary scooted from the room.

When she returned, her eyes were teary. She passed a file to Claire.

"I knew it was wrong of me not to volunteer the information. I apologize," Mary said. "I'm embarrassed by my actions."

"Well, you're helping us now," Claire said. "Throw that into your tank of consideration."

She jotted down the banking information.

"Did Camille and Catherine know each other?" Claire asked.

"They were business acquaintances. I think Camille referred Catherine to me," Mary said.

"Did you also know Cindy Bane?" Claire asked.

"No. I never met her."

"Charlotte Truman?"

"No, I never met her either."

"Thank you, Mary," Claire said.

Guy did not say good-bye.

20

CHARLIE TRAVELED FOR twenty minutes, turned onto a frontage road, made two additional turns, and pulled into the parking lot of an apartment building. Jin trailed far behind and parked a good distance away. He jotted down the address.

Charlie waited in his car.

Jin called the office.

"Caswell & Lombard, Private Investigation. Gaston Lombard speaking," Guy said.

"I need to know if we're aware of a certain address," Jin said. He gave it to Guy and explained the situation.

"We are," he said. "It's the apartment house where the receptionist from the car dealership lives. Her name is Natalie. What the heck is *Charlie* doing there?"

"No idea," Jin said. "I've never tracked him to this address before."

"Keep me on the phone," Guy said. "Let me know exactly what's happening. Tell me everything you see. And let me know your impressions. Be my eyes."

Minutes passed.

Another car pulled into the lot, and a younger woman got out.

"Describe Natalie to me," Jin said.

"Well, she's on the shorter side. She has shoulder-length curly dark hair and dark eyes."

"What type of car does she drive?"

"An Acura," Guy said. "Silver."

"It's her," Jin said. "She's slowly walking over to Charlie's car. She's looking around to make sure no one is watching. This looks cloak-and-daggerish to me. He's lowering the window. The two are talking. He's handing her something."

"What is it, Jin?"

Jin pulled up his binoculars and focused in.

"Let me see. Let me see. I can't make it out. She's blocking my view. Wait a minute. Hold on. Hold on. She's moving. I can almost see it. Okay, I can see it now. Looks like she's cupping an envelope of some kind in her hand. It's thick. She's putting it into her shoulder bag. Hold on. Looks like she's changing her mind. She's handing the envelope back to Charlie."

"If only we knew its contents," Guy said.

"Wait a minute. He's handing it back to her. They're arguing. She took it. She's walking away from his car. Wait. She's turning back. She handed it back to Charlie again. She looks upset. Charlie is driving off in a hurry. She's approaching her car. She's there. She's getting in. And she's driving off." He paused as he watched. "They're both gone."

"Clearly it was a meeting place for some kind of handoff," Guy said. "Sounds to me like a backstairs deal that had some issues."

"Well, actually it was a *parking-lot* deal that had some issues," Jin said.

"It was a turn of phrase, Jin," Guy said. He thought for a moment. "This seems suspicious. Charlie meeting up with Natalie? What the heck is going on?" He exhaled loudly. "It's a connection we weren't aware of."

"We have the Fox connection between the cases and now this," the law student said. "The cases are linked somehow."

"I'm surprised. And I'm getting impatient to get these cases resolved. I'll let Claire know. In the meantime, stay on Charlie. See what this deceitful rat is up to next."

Guy hung up and filled Claire in on what had just occurred.

"The plot thickens," she said. "This new development confirms what we've suspected."

Guy nodded. "Now we have the supposed Roise Fox connection between Charlie and Stephen and a confirmed connection between Charlie and Natalie—who just happens to work for Stephen."

Claire mused, "There's definitely some kind of relationship between the two cases that we're missing. I'm more convinced than ever we're looking at a scheme, a secret plan, and a calculated series of murders." She stared straight ahead. "We must hone in on the players. We need to figure out the ploy."

THE MAN crept through the backyard and walked to the fence, toting a lightweight ladder underneath one arm. He walked to a far end of the barrier and quietly supported the set of steps against it, making sure it was properly secured in the ground to provide stability.

He glanced upward at the nighttime sky. It was his cover. A blue moon impressively decorated the sea of blackness, providing the only reflection he needed for his task. It was the second full moon of the month. He recalled reading something in the *Farmers' Almanac* about a blue moon meaning "to betray."

The garden was stunning, even in the dim lighting. Tonight, it seemed almost intimidating, but in a spectacular way.

He went to work. He put gardening gloves on and pulled a pair of plastic freezer bags from his pocket—one large and one regular sized. He had done this before, and he knew just what to do. He walked to the corner sloped area of the garden—the location shaded by the breathtaking oak tree. He had to move fast. He knelt by a certain plant.

Much time had already passed, and every minute he was there afforded more risk of being caught. His hands started to shake. Ever so carefully, he pulled seven-inch-long leaves from the plant. Some had yellowed, and he made sure to only select the green ones. He filled the larger bag halfway up. Then he picked off shiny black berries from the same plant and filled the smaller bag. He zipped up both bags and sealed them tightly.

A devilish smile appeared on his face.

He was smart. So smart. The smartest.

He'd pulled these things off and no one was the wiser.

He forced in a satisfied chuckle.

Hopefully it would all be over soon.

It was time to exit the scene. He jumped up, reached the upper arms of the ladder, and hefted it unto his side. He lobbed the plastic bags over the top and climbed up the rungs. Once atop the fence, he carefully jumped to the ground. He pulled the ladder back over and collected the bags, and with stealthy footsteps he prowled away.

He stopped in the yard momentarily to take a quick glance back at the moon.

"Thank you, blue moon."

When he arrived home, he carefully placed the bag of leaves in an empty coffee can he kept in the freezer.

He walked into the garage and set the second bag onto his

wooden worktable. He put on canvas work gloves. Reaching up to a high shelf above the table, he pulled down an old blender and plugged it into the nearby outlet. After lifting off its rubber lid, he heedfully emptied the entire bag of berries into the glass container. He replaced the lid, making certain it was securely affixed. He selected the chop feature momentarily, followed by the puree choice for a flash, and finally the liquefying option for just three seconds. Soon he had the consistency he was looking for.

He pulled the lid off and set it upside down on a sheet of aluminum foil. Slowly, he poured the thick mixture into the plastic bag, making certain not a drop or driblet went anywhere else. He sealed it tightly.

He replaced the top on the blender, unplugged it, and toted it to the sink located adjacent to the worktable. He substituted his canvas gloves for a heavy-duty rubber pair. Using an industrial-strength cleaner, the man proceeded to thoroughly wash and rinse both pieces of the electric mixing machine and also the sheet of aluminum foil. When he finished, he set the blender parts on the bench to dry. He threw away the foil. Being ever on his toes, he scrubbed the sink with a firm brush to assure that no residue of the mixture remained. After carefully washing off both sets of gloves and the brush, he returned the items to another high shelf.

The man took the sealed bag of the thick liquid and placed it inside a second tin coffee can. This one he kept in the garage freezer.

An amused expression appeared on his face, and the corners of his mouth turned upward. He'd done it again. He was so taken by his own cleverness and intellect that he could hardly contain his feelings of exuberance. He had been quick to devise his plan. And he was convinced no one would ever figure it out.

He was ready for his next victim whenever the opportunity should arise.

THE NEW day began. Claire and Guy opened the office.

Claire called Captain Massey. She informed him of the connection between Charlie McDermott and Natalie, the dealership receptionist.

"Uh-huh. Most interesting," he said. "Kudos to Jin for discovering this. I'll add that information to the flowchart I'm putting together over here. The noose is tightening. On another note, how are you coming with getting that banking information together?"

"Actually, that was the second purpose for my call. Guy and I collected the information you need to get those subpoenas issued." She informed him of the bank names and account numbers used by each of the three females in question. "We need to rule in or rule out money as a motivation for the murders."

"Quick work, Ms. Caswell. Well done. I'll get right on it."

"Once you receive the information, sir, I think it's time we all get together again. We have a lot of information to discuss and try to make sense of."

"I'll personally call the banks, let them know to expect the subpoenas, and tell them their responses are urgent. Time is of the essence. We need to zero in on the culprit and make an arrest."

"Culprit or culprits. We don't know yet if we're looking at one or more. We do know there are potentially several individuals who could be involved in all of this."

"I stand corrected, Ms. Caswell," he said. He pulled at his knuckles. "Culprit or culprits."

JIN MADE his way to Estee's house. As was so typical, Charlie's car was parked out front. Seeing Charlie meet up with Natalie that afternoon had been a major breakthrough. It had concretely tied the two cases together, but in a way that was not yet clear. And seeing Charlie pass an envelope to Natalie confirmed something was going on between them. Why had she taken it, given it back, and then accepted it again, only to give it back again? What was in the envelope? He had obtained many videos of the clandestine meeting—the cars, the two people involved, Charlie's passing of the stuffed envelope to Natalie twice, and her accepting the envelope both times only to give it back each time seconds later. There could be no denying it. He had obtained evidence that something was at play between the two.

Charlie and Estee walked from her house to the green sports car. Soon the car disappeared down the road, and Jin pulled out after it. Surprisingly, they drove to the condo where Charlie lived. He left his car with the valet, and the pair entered the building.

Jin parked his car on the street. He walked to the circular drive and began making small talk with the parking attendant.

"My name's Kade," Jin said. "My parents are looking to buy a condo in the Bal Harbour area, and I'm doing some scouting for them. Are there units for sale in this building?"

"There's a real estate agent who deals exclusively with the units for rent and for sale," the attendant said. "You can pick up her business card at the front desk."

"No need for that. At least not at this time. It's too early," Jin said. "They're really just trying to decide which buildings they might want to explore further. They assigned me to give them a report. You know how that goes."

"Oh," the attendant uttered. "Yeah."

"Should I tell them to look into this one?" Jin asked. "Are the owners who live here totally satisfied?"

"As you can imagine, I hear grumblings of all kinds from many of the residents. Some people are never satisfied with anything." He made a funny face.

Jin chuckled. "How long have you worked here?" he asked.

"Three years," the attendant said. "They treat me well, and the tips are good. It's not a bad job, at least for this time in my life."

"My parents have a friend who lives here," Jin said.

"Who is that?"

"His name is Roise. Roise Fox."

"Oh, I know him well," the attendant said. "He's a nice older man. He's one of the good tippers."

"Do you know his son, Stephen, then, also?" Jin asked.

"I do. He comes around a couple of times a month, when he's not busy at the Porsche dealership where he works. Word is he set the whole thing up for his dad. Bought him the condo. Bought him a boat too, although he never uses it. It's all the talk around here."

"I've heard the same things," Jin said. "What about Charlie? Do you like him?"

"Oh, you know him too?" the attendant asked. "He's okay. He's upstairs now showing some lady around the condo. He likes to pretend he owns it. Especially when Roise is out of town—like now." He stopped talking to take a drink of water. "What do you think of Charlie?"

"Well, I like his shirts," Jin said. He laughed. "And I really like his Karmann Ghia. It's a beauty. One of my favorite cars."

"Mine too. I think Stephen bought that car for Roise too. Roise lets Charlie drive it. Roise has another car also. A Cadillac. Charlie gets lots of perks working for the old man, that's for sure. Gets to use his boat too. And he gives him a room to live in. Not a bad gig."

"You can say that again!" Jin said. "How did Charlie manage to snare the job?"

"I think Stephen knows him. All the arrangements were made through Stephen."

Just then, a couple walked from the building.

"Our car, please," they said, looking at the parking attendant.

"Got to run," the employee said. "Enjoyed our talk."

JIN COULDN'T wait to tell Claire and Guy all that he'd discovered. He jogged to his car, drove to a nearby gas station, and pulled off to one side. He dialed the office.

"Caswell & Lombard, Private Investigation. This is Claire Caswell. How may I help you?"

"So glad I caught you," Jin said. "We have more confirmations." The excitement in his voice could not be missed.

"Hold on, Jin, let me put you on speaker so Guy can hear this too."

There was a short delay, and Jin waited in great suspense.

"Okay, Jin, go ahead," Claire said. "We're both listening."

Jin proceeded to tell the investigators about the entire conversation, being sure not to omit a single detail.

"Amazing work," Claire said.

"Ditto," Guy said. "Good job."

Jin went on. "So now we've confirmed that Stephen Fox is the son of Roise Fox. We know Stephen purchased the condo, boat, and at least one car for his dad. And we know Charlie gets to use the boat and the Karmann Ghia as perks of working for the elderly Fox, in addition to getting a room to live in at his condo. We know Roise is currently out of town, and Charlie pretends he owns the condo when Roise is away. Charlie continues his sham."

"That's a ton of great information," Claire said.

"The problem is, the attendant could deny ever saying those things if push comes to shove," Guy said.

"Not really," Jin said. "I recorded it."

There was a pause. "Well, that might be a problem," Guy said.

21

CLAIRE PHONED CAPTAIN Massey to fill him in on the particulars of the latest discoveries.

"This gets curiouser and curiouser," he said. "We are definitely focusing the lens. Let's all meet as soon as the subpoenaed documents come in from the banks. I delivered the subpoenas myself, and I don't expect and won't accept delays. And the subpoenaed applications and finance paperwork from the dealership should be coming in soon too. I'll keep you posted on both, of course."

"We'll schedule a meeting as soon as you have those documents in hand," she said. "It's important to analyze everything together as a group. We have a lot of information to sew together into something recognizable."

"Good. Agreed. Oh, and a final thing, Ms. Caswell," the captain said. He hesitated.

"Yes?"

"Be mighty careful, will you? Take that threatening letter you received seriously. They often mean business."

"Of course," she said. "I'm always watchful."

SHE HUNG up, and the office phone rang immediately. Claire answered. She heard breathing on the other end, but no one said a word.

"Hello?" She said. She waited. "Hello?"

No answer.

She hung up.

The caller identification indicated an unidentified caller.

Two minutes later, it happened again.

"Hello?" she said. "Who is this?"

No answer.

Again, she hung up.

"Who was it?" Guy asked.

"No idea."

"I don't like this, Claire. Not one bit. I'd normally think they were just wrong numbers, but coupled with the warning you received, I'm not so sure. Be on your guard at all times. This is serious business."

It was clear Guy was simmering. And it wouldn't take much more for him to reach the boiling point.

"I'll answer our phone until this case is over. Got it?" he said.

"Yes, sir!" she said. She saluted.

"This is not funny, Claire, and I wish you wouldn't try to make it so."

"I know it's not funny," she said. "But I'm a professional. I've been at this for many years. I know to always watch my back. Always. And I can protect myself if I have to. You don't have to continually worry about me."

"Well, I do. You're my wife. I love you. I couldn't go on if something bad happened to you."

She looked at him for a time. The sincerity in his eyes was honest and true.

"And I love you back. But you have to let go of this. You only have to tell me something once. I truly get it."

He still looked upset.

She walked over to him and threw her arms around his neck. She kissed his cheek. "I love you, too, too much," she said. "I promise I'll be on the lookout."

JIN SAT across the street from Estee's house and halfway down the block. That was the trick about long-term surveillance—not to get caught.

The binoculars, his smartphone, altering of his appearance when necessary, and the HD video camera that he toted along on most days all helped avoid the possibility. But still, he had to be careful. He looked at the HD camera sitting on his passenger seat. He could video his subjects from two hundred yards away if necessary. And he didn't have to move in close to obtain on the doorstep footage. The camera did it all for him.

Furthermore, he drove a regular-looking Kia. Midnight brown, nothing fancy or special, nothing to draw attention to him or to his car. It helped him blend into the environment.

Yet, the thought of being found out did leap into his mind from time to time, and when it did, the notion gnawed away at his core. He would worry about being captured, stress about being constrained, and sweat about not being able to escape. And the more time he had to think about it, the more he would tremble. He knew anxiety was at the base of these feelings, and he was happy they subsided whenever he forced his mind to think about other things.

His thoughts went to what Guy had told him about taping a conversation with another person. He was so proud to have taped his conversation with the parking valet at the Bal Harbour condominium. He was so sure it could be used as evidence, if required. But Guy, the former Miami-Dade state attorney, had set him straight on Florida law pertaining to that situation.

He had learned that Florida was one of eleven states requiring the consent of both or all sides in a phone call or conversation. Without the consent of all parties, the recording would not be lawful and could not be used in court. But at least the information he obtained could be used internally within the boundaries of the Caswell & Lombard, Private Investigation firm.

Just then, Charlie and Estee emerged from Estee's house, and soon thereafter, the two sped away in the green car. Jin waited the suitable amount of time and trailed behind them. They went on a drive that day, and Jin did his best to weave around the heavy traffic on I-95 to keep the couple within his sight. Unexpectedly, traffic began to slow, back up, and in a short time come to a dead stop.

Jin looked far ahead and saw the problem. Road construction. He tried desperately to keep his eye on the Karmann Ghia and did a noble job, until the green car and a few others were allowed to pass through the road project and proceed along the interstate. Jin watched the collector car as it disappeared from sight.

He lost them.

CLAIRE GLANCED at her watch and rushed to leave the office. She jumped into her car, entered an address into her GPS, selected the quickest route, and set off on her mission. Her mind was preoccupied, and she felt a little frantic as she drove toward a plant nursery off Biscayne Boulevard in Miami. She couldn't wait to show the staff pictures of the secret garden and get more information about the one specific plant she was interested in. She wanted to know who would buy these plants for a garden or if they simply grew wild.

She crossed over the Broad Causeway from The Beach to Miami proper and drove toward the desired location. Along the way, the tracking system took her down side streets and into areas she had never traveled.

All of a sudden, she noticed in her rearview mirror a dark Jeep coming up rapidly behind her. It positioned itself way too close to the rear bumper of her car and stayed there. Claire tapped her brakes, but the Jeep refused to relent, slow down, or go around. There were no other vehicles on the street, and she didn't like the situation that was quickly developing. She steered her car partway onto the shoulder to allow the vehicle to pass, but the driver remained rigidly fixed behind her. She sped up and so did the Jeep. She slowed down and so did the Jeep. She started to shake as she realized the gravity of the situation. Fear rocked her. She held tightly to the steering wheel.

Then the worst happened. The Jeep slammed into the back of her car, attaching itself to the rear bumper. She heard a crunch. The mysterious vehicle pushed her car into the deserted yard of an abandoned warehouse. The situation quickly spun out of control, and she was helpless to do a thing about it. She reached for her .38, but in her zeal to leave for the nursery and avoid rush-hour traffic, she had forgotten it at her desk. There was no time to grab for her cell phone.

Both cars simultaneously came to a screeching halt. A second later, she looked out her side window to see the barrel of a gun pointed at her head. Her car doors were locked.

"Get out!" a voice bellowed.

She didn't know what to do.

She saw the form of one man.

She turned her head and looked straight ahead, refusing to answer or acknowledge him.

The next thing she heard was the sound of bullets shattering the backseat window on the driver's side of her car.

The piercing noise from the shots pulsed through her head.

She couldn't hear.

Her vision blurred.

She felt dizzy.

He reached into her car and unlocked the rear door.

She searched with her eyes for anything to use as a weapon. She saw nothing.

Time stood still.

She struggled to regain her sense of balance.

She screamed for help, but no one was around.

Strong hands from the back seat grabbed around her neck and squeezed tightly.

Her breathing became restricted.

She struggled valiantly to be freed from the menacing grip, but to no avail.

Everything went dark.

GUY SAT at his desk making calls to learn more about Stephen Fox. He was convinced that someone had to know something. He just had to find the right person. He decided to drive to the dealership to talk to the man again. He telephoned Claire to let her know.

She did not answer her cell.

He tried again.

Still no answer.

He'd try again later.

He left for the dealership. When he arrived, he parked and went in.

"Looking for Stephen Fox," he said. "Is he in?"

Natalie replied. "No, he's out for the rest of the day."

Guy walked past her and made his way to Stephen's office. No lights were on. The receptionist was telling the truth. He walked back to the lobby.

"Let him know Gaston Lombard stopped by, will you, please? I'll drop by again tomorrow."

She scribbled on a pink message slip.

Guy returned to his car and tried Claire again.

Again, no answer.

A worried look appeared on his face. She had left the office earlier to drive to a nursery, to check on the plants in the Fox family garden. Why was she not answering her phone? He racked his brain to recall the name of the nursery. She had told him. What was it?

He called the office. Jin answered.

"Jin, this is important," Guy said. His voice was grimly serious. "Go over to Claire's desk and see if you can find a note about a plant nursery. I need the name or number. Hurry!"

"You got it," Jin said.

He jumped up from his desk and raced over to Claire's. His eyes scanned everything sitting on its surface. He found nothing.

"I can't find it," he said.

"Look again," Guy demanded. "Hurry!"

Jin was frantic. He sprinted back to her desk and frantically searched for any mention of a nursery.

He saw a number written on a note sheet.

"I see a number here, but I have no idea what's it's for," Jin said quickly.

"Give it to me," Guy demanded.

Jin gave him the number.

Guy hung up.

Jin sat down. His breathing felt hindered. He knew something was terribly wrong with Claire. He could feel the loud pounding of his heart. He broke into a sweat and started to shake. He prayed for her safety.

GUY CALLED the number. It was a nursery on Biscayne Boulevard. He described Claire and asked if she was there. He learned that it had been a quiet afternoon for the business. No one matching her description was there presently or had been there.

THE OFFICE phone rang, and Jin forced himself to answer.

"Caswell & Lombard, Private Investigation. This is Jin Ikeda."

He listened carefully, writing notes the entire time.

"This is awful," he said. "I'll let Mr. Lombard know immediately."

He hung up and called Guy's cell.

"Guy, Claire was taken to the 24-7 emergency room at Jackson Memorial. There was some kind of incident. I'll meet you there."

"How bad is she?" Guy asked.

"Go. I'll see you there."

GUY AND Jin both drove to the facility exceeding the speed limits. Guy arrived first and ran to the emergency room.

"Claire Caswell!" he yelled. "Where is she?"

A doctor stood feet away.

"You are?" he asked.

"I'm her husband, Gaston Lombard. Where is she?"

"I'll take you to her," the doctor said. "We've been waiting for you. Follow me."

They wound their way down a long hallway. The doctor stopped in front of an end room. A heavy white curtain was drawn across its opening.

"She's resting," he said in a low voice. "Don't upset her."

Guy pulled back one side of the curtain and stepped inside.

There she was.

Her eyes were closed, and she appeared to be asleep. Guy noticed red bruise marks on her neck.

His eyes misted as he moved in closer.

"My beauty," he said softly. "I'm here." He leaned down and placed a tender kiss on her forehead. He noticed the pearl necklace hanging around her neck.

He stood for minutes, not moving, just staring at the woman he loved.

The doctor poked his head in. "There's someone in the lobby asking for you. His name is Jin Ikeda."

Guy slowly walked from the room and approached the check-in area.

"How is she?" Jin asked. His eyes revealed the terror he felt.

"I don't know yet," Guy said. "What exactly did the police officer say when he called the office? Tell me his precise words. Don't leave anything out."

"That there was an 'incident,'" Jin said. "Something involving another car and a man. He didn't give me specifics. He did leave his name and number, though." Jin passed a small piece of paper to Guy.

"Thanks for being here, Jin. It helps," Guy said.

"I'm not moving. I'm sitting right here until I hear good news. Whatever you need, you let me know."

Guy returned to the room.

Claire was still sleeping.

"Sleep well, my princess. You're in good hands."

Her eyes opened slightly. She had heard his voice.

"Guy?" She reached for his hand.

22

GUY POURED WATER into the Styrofoam cup sitting on Claire's bedside table. He placed his right arm behind her neck and braced her head while he held the liquid to her lips.

"Take a sip," he said.

She took a tiny swallow.

He gently laid her head back on the pillow.

"What happened?" he asked.

"He tried to kill me," she said. She stared off, deep in thought. "And he almost did."

"Were you able to get a good look at him?"

"No. I didn't get a look at his face, and then he was behind me."

"Can you tell me about it?" Guy asked. "Talk slowly."

A pensive look crept onto her face, and she disappeared into thought.

"The shots damaged my hearing, Guy. The doctor told me I might have some permanent hearing loss. Your voice is more subdued than usual."

"We will get you the best doctors around to see what can be done about that. I'm sorry, Claire."

"I need to tell you what happened. I was driving to the nursery. A car raced up behind me. Out of the blue." She paused. "He tailgated me and then drove right into my car. Attached his vehicle to my bumper. Forced my car into an empty lot." She closed her eyes. "I lost all control. I became a helpless victim."

"Can you describe the car?" Guy asked. "Take your time."

"It was dark. Black, I think. A Jeep."

"What happened next?"

"The driver bolted from his car and held a revolver to my window." She winced. "I thought he was going to shoot me."

Guy fought to temper the anger he felt at that moment.

"I refused to get out of my car. It was locked," she said. "I forgot my gun at the office. I had nothing to defend myself."

She started shaking.

"He fired several shots into the window directly behind me, and it shattered. My world started spinning. I couldn't hear."

Tears filled her beautiful green eyes.

"All I could think about was that I might never see you again," she said. "I thought I was going to die."

He squeezed her hand.

"Take it easy, Claire. You're safe. I'm with you," he said. "I love you. I thank God that you're all right."

She closed her eyes and dozed off.

Guy quietly walked from the room. He went to the lobby to fill Jin in on what Claire had told him so far.

"We could have lost her," Jin said. "This has now turned into a deadly game. Whoever is behind this knows we're close to bringing him, her, or them out of the shadows. They'll do anything to stop us."

"I fear we've awakened a sleeping giant," Guy said.

"Can I see her?" Jin asked.

"Afraid not. The doctor will only allow family in at this point, and of course police and clergy," Guy said. "But I'll let her know you're here."

He pulled his cell phone from his pocket and called Captain Massey.

"Claire was attacked," Guy reported.

"*What*? Where are you?"

"Jackson Memorial." Guy filled the captain in on the details and gave him the name and number of the officer who responded.

"I'm on the way."

CAPTAIN MASSEY arrived in short order. Together, Guy and the police captain walked to Claire's room. Her eyes were open when they arrived.

"Captain Massey," she said. She smiled almost imperceptibly.

"Tell us every detail you can remember, Ms. Caswell. We're going to get this bastard. You have my word," the captain said.

She reiterated what she had told Guy and then continued on from that point.

"After he shattered the rear window, he reached in and unlocked the door.

The next thing I knew, his hands were around my neck. He was strangling me. I couldn't breathe. I struggled to break free and stay alive. He was strong." She paused to catch her breath, and she reached up to caress her neck. "Everything went black."

"Do you know what happened next?" Captain Massey asked.

"I came to in the ambulance," she said. "The police were here when they admitted me. I was told a Good Samaritan rode by on a bicycle, saw what was happening, stopped to snap a photo of the perp with her cell phone, and called the police. She pulled her bike into the nearby brush and disappeared from sight. Apparently, the man caught a glimpse of her taking the picture because he released his strangulation hold. He jumped into his car, and hightailed it out of there. His action must have unhooked our bumpers. He was gone when the police arrived."

"I wonder if the officer got the name of the Good Samaritan?" the captain asked. "I have a call in to him."

"I asked. She didn't leave her name. Probably didn't want to get involved," Claire said. "I wanted to thank her."

"We'll have a record of her call. I'll have a tracer put on her cell number. We'll find out who she is," Captain Massey said. "She might end up being a good witness. I'll let you know when I get the information. In the meantime, Ms. Caswell, you take care of yourself. You've been through a tremendous trauma. Rest." He left to call the officer.

"Jin is in the lobby, Claire. He's very concerned about you," Guy said.

She smiled. "That means a lot. Please thank him."

Guy looked at Claire with deep concern. He inhaled and exhaled deeply.

"We need to be brutally honest with ourselves. These investigations have turned life threatening. We cannot underestimate the danger we now face. All of us who are trying to hone in on the killer or killers are in grave jeopardy. We should probably leave it to the police from this point forward."

"I'm not giving up," Claire said. "Someone killed Charlotte and now tried to kill me. I won't stop investigating until whoever is responsible is behind bars."

There was no point in trying to convince her otherwise. That was clear.

"Well, we're in this together, then," he said. "From now on, we both carry our firearms at all times and we don't go anywhere solo. We do this every step of the way as if we're joined at the hip. Okay?"

Claire did not answer. She had succumbed to the need for additional sleep.

The doctor came in to examine her.

"She's exhausted," he said. "She needs time. We're keeping her here overnight for observation. You can come for her in the morning."

Guy walked to the lobby.

"How is she?" Jin asked.

Guy explained the situation.

"I'm staying here overnight," Guy said.

"I'm not going anywhere either," Jin said.

Guy called Claire's parents to inform them about Claire.

THE NIGHT dragged on infinitely. Every hour or so, Guy looked in on Claire.

She struggled through her fitful sleep, and Guy was quite sure she was reliving the incident. At his request, the nurse on duty woke her and gave her a sleeping pill. Things calmed down.

MORNING ARRIVED. It was a new day filled with hope—hope that Claire would feel better and hope that they could zoom in on the perpetrator or perpetrators.

Captain Massey called Guy's cell.

"How is she this morning?" the captain asked.

"Better. She had a rough night, but she ended up getting some good sleep. She's being released in an hour or two. I'm taking her home to rest."

"Good. You take care of her first," he said. "I have the contact information on the Good Samaritan. I plan on going to see her early this afternoon to take a statement."

"I'd like to go with you, Captain, if that's okay."

"Meet me at her house, then." He gave Guy the address. "One o'clock. Her name is Maude Wakely. But if Ms. Caswell needs you at home, stay with her. I'll do it alone and report back to you."

"I'll do my best to be there."

GUY DROVE Claire home and got her situated.

"I really don't have to stay in bed all day," she said.

"Yes, you do. It's the doctor's order. He made me promise you'd follow his request when he signed your release."

"Okay, okay," she said reluctantly. "I'll be a good patient."

"I need to go away for a couple of hours," he said. "Captain Massey and I are interviewing the woman on the bicycle. The one who probably saved your life."

"Did you find out her name?" Claire asked.

"Yes. Maude Wakely."

"Maude Wakely," Claire repeated. "I'd like to go with you."

"No can do," Guy said. "I'll let you know everything she has to say. But you're staying here. In bed."

"Please tell her how grateful I am that she was riding by at that very moment. And please thank her for calling the police. Thank her for saving my life."

"Will do. Make sure to keep the doors locked when I'm gone. Keep the chains on too. We can take no chances."

"I will. And I'll be anxious to hear what she has to say."

Guy kissed her on both cheeks before leaving.

"Can I pick up something for you on my way home? What are you hungry for? You haven't eaten much."

Claire thought for a moment. "Rice pudding sounds good. The coconut variety."

"I'll bring some home with me." He smiled sweetly.

At that moment, sunlight streaming in through a nearby window settled on Guy's face, intensifying the scars remaining from an earlier case that had also turned dangerous. Life as a private investigator brought with it many perils, including exposure to injury and potentially even death. But Claire was programmed to be a sleuth. She could do nothing else. And she guessed Guy would say the same thing. They both wanted to see justice done. Wrongs righted. Criminals sent to prison. It was a life calling for both of them.

Guy left, and Claire locked and chained the door.

The phone rang. It was Claire's parents.

"You scared us half to death, young lady," Don said. "We love you."

"Let us know if you need anything, and we'll be there," Abbey said. "Rest as much as you can."

Claire followed their instructions, got into bed, and fell fast asleep.

CAPTAIN MASSEY was sitting out front in a squad car when Guy arrived at Maude Wakely's house. He parked his vehicle across the street.

The two men approached the front door and knocked.

A kindly faced woman with gray eyes and hair the color of brown sugar opened the door. Guy guessed she was in her sixties.

"Yes?" she asked.

"Captain Massey, Miami-Dade Police Department, and private investigator Gaston Lombard, ma'am," the captain said. "We'd like to talk to you." They showed her identifications.

"About?" she asked. She stood at the entrance.

"About the call you made to the police yesterday. Concerning what you saw yesterday," the captain said.

"I did my civic duty," she said. "I called 9-1-1. Now, please, I don't want to be involved in this matter any further."

"My wife, Claire Caswell, was the one being attacked," Guy said. "I am forever grateful to you for helping her. And she wanted me to make sure to say thank you for her."

"How is she?" the woman asked. Her concern for Claire showed in her eyes.

"She was in the hospital yesterday, and today she's resting at home. She had quite a scare. She's deeply disturbed by the experience," Guy said. "And the sound of the gunshots in her unprotected ears hurt her hearing."

"I can only imagine. Poor woman," Maude said.

She looked from Captain Massey to Guy.

"Okay. Come in," she said.

The three sat in her living room.

"Ms. Wakely, will you please tell us everything you saw yesterday?" the captain asked.

"If I tell you, I don't want to be involved after today. I don't want to live in fear. Will you agree to that?"

"We'll do our best to keep you out of it," the captain said. "But I can't promise."

"We need to stop that man from coming back to hurt my wife," Guy said. "Or anyone else. Please help us."

The pleading look in his eyes convinced Maude to talk.

"I saw the black car force your wife's car off the road and into that vacant lot. It was clear what was happening."

"Please go on," the captain said.

"I heard a blood-curdling scream. And I heard shots. I thought he'd killed her." She paused. "I stopped to take a picture of the attacker, and I called the police as I peddled away as fast as I could. I pulled off onto the shoulder and pushed my bike into the brushy area to hide. The attacker must have seen me snap a photo because I saw the black car whiz past me a minute or two later." She looked at Guy as she talked. "I heard sirens in the background soon after my call."

Guy and Captain Massey listened to her account with interest.

"Your actions probably saved my wife's life," Guy said.

"Did you get a good look at the black car?" the captain asked.

"Yes," she said.

He pulled several sheets picturing black cars and SUVs from his briefcase.

"Will you please take a look at these?" he asked. "Do you see a vehicle that looks like the one you saw?"

She looked over the sheets carefully.

She pointed to an SUV. "This is it. It looked just like this one."

The captain looked where she indicated. It was a Jeep Wrangler.

"Great. Now, did you get a look at the man driving the Jeep?"

"I got a fleeting glance at him as he ran to her car."

"Do you think you'd recognize him?"

"I'm not sure," she said. "He was not a tall man."

"Can you look at some photos I have with me?"

The captain pulled several photos of different men from his briefcase. Among them were shots of Stephen Fox and Charlie McDermott.

Maude viewed all the pictures.

"Do you see him?"

"No," Maude said. "I don't."

23

GUY STOPPED TO pick up several containers of coconut rice pudding on his way back to Claire. She was up and moving about when he arrived.

"You are supposed to be resting in bed, young lady," he said.

"Tell me everything," she said.

She opened a container of the creamy rice dessert and grabbed a spoon. She settled back into the bed.

"First, how are you feeling?" he asked.

"Better," she said.

"How is your hearing?"

"I think better too."

Guy gave her a detailed report of the entire interview with Maude, making sure not to omit a single detail.

Claire listened intently.

"She's a reluctant witness, to be sure," he said. "But she'll come through if we need her. I'm convinced of it."

"Did you thank her for me?" Claire asked.

"I did. Right away."

"I'll need to get my car fixed," Claire said. "I think they can repair the bumper and also replace the back window."

"I'm on it," Guy said. "I'll get it in right away and arrange for a loaner car."

"What would I do without you?" Claire asked.

"You'll never find out," he said, grinning.

Claire found herself gripping the baroque pearl. She loved this man.

Guy's cell phone rang.

"Mr. Lombard, it's Captain Massey. The ruling just came in on Eric Fox. The coroner pronounced it suicide. Looks like he ingested something lethal with the intent of ending his life. Please let Ms. Caswell know."

"I will. And I'll also let Stephen know," Guy said.

"I don't think that's a good idea considering the fact it could have been Stephen who tried to kill Claire," the captain said. "I'd worry about what might happen between the two of you. Let me take care of it."

"No. I'll do it. I insist," Guy said. "I want to confront the man."

"It's against my better judgment, but I know I can't stop you. Go ahead," Captain Massey said. "Just be damn careful."

LATER THAT afternoon, Guy returned to the Porsche dealership. He had missed Stephen the day before. Now he needed to talk to him. He arrived, parked in the lot, and walked in.

"Mr. Fox, please," Guy said.

"He's in a meeting," Natalie said robotically.

"Is he ever *not* in a meeting? Or actually *in* his office?" Guy asked. "He'll see me." The investigator was in no mood for the receptionist's effrontery.

He walked past Natalie and made his way to Stephen's office. When he got there, he opened the closed door and walked in.

Stephen and Jimmy sat at the desk, engrossed in a card game. Guy noticed twenty-dollar bills piled in front of them both and realized they were playing for money.

"Mr. Fox, we need to talk," Guy said.

Jimmy rolled his eyes.

Guy focused his gaze intently on Stephen.

"We need to talk!" he repeated.

"Isn't it about time you and Claire give it a rest?" Stephen asked.

"Not when we're investigating *murders*."

"Did you say *murders*, as in more than one?" Stephen asked.

"Let's talk in private," Guy said.

Jimmy threw up his hands and headed for the door.

Guy took a seat.

"I received a call from the Miami-Dade Police Department just before I drove here. They made a ruling on Eric's death."

He had Stephen's full attention.

"They pronounced it a suicide. I'm sorry."

"I feared that's what it was from the start," Stephen said. "He was an unhappy young man. Depressed. This makes me very sad. First his mother died, and now him." He shook his head.

"I have to ask you where you were yesterday afternoon," Guy said.

"Yesterday afternoon? Where was I yesterday afternoon?" Stephen asked.

"That's the question. Please answer it."

Guy was not willing to be put off. He needed to know if Stephen was responsible for Claire's attack.

"Let me think," Stephen said. "I believe I was here."

"No, you weren't. I came by yesterday afternoon, and you had left for the day."

"I see," Stephen said. "Well, then, I wasn't here."

"Okay," Guy said. "If you drag your feet again in answering a question, I'll have the Miami-Dade Police Department bring you in for questioning. Would you prefer doing it that way?"

Stephen became stone-faced.

"No, of course not. I'm just having a hard time dealing with everything."

"Then let me ask you again," Guy said. "Where were you yesterday afternoon?"

"I took some time off," Stephen said. "I'm planning a memorial for my son."

"Where did you go to plan this event?" Guy asked.

"To my home. I needed to do some serious thinking in a quiet environment. Can't do it here."

"Was anyone else there with you? Helping you with the planning?"

"No, I was alone."

"So there is no one to verify your story?"

"I guess not."

"What plans did you come up with?"

"Well, I'm going to have a simple service at a church. His mother would have liked that."

"Christine?"

"Yes. Christine," Stephen said.

"Christine died about five years ago, didn't she?" Guy asked.

Stephen looked stunned. "How did you know that?"

"Eric told us. He said he loved his mother very much."

"We both loved her very much. She died an untimely death."

"What did she die from?" Guy asked.

Stephen suddenly looked appalled.

"Why are you bringing this up? It's a painful subject."

"What was the coroner's ruling on her cause of death?" Guy persisted.

"I think they said natural causes. They thought it might have been her heart."

"Did she have heart problems? Did she come from a family with heart problems?"

"No. And no."

"So, didn't you think it a bit strange that she died without warning from a heart problem?" Guy did not stop.

"Yes! Yes!" Stephen cried out. "Of course I did." He got up and paced around the room. "Why are you doing this? Why are you making me relive this? Especially after just hearing that my son took his own life? What do you want from me?"

"The truth," Guy said. "I want the truth. We all want the truth." He slammed his fist onto the table. "We need to know what killed Christine. And how Eric ended his life. And we need to know why Charlotte is dead. And Catherine Hanker, Cindy Bane, and Camille Sullivan. This is not going away. And frankly, Stephen, everything is pointing in your direction."

"I am not responsible for any of it. You have to believe me," Stephen said. "Please just go away." His head reeled after hearing all the names.

"Yesterday, my wife was attacked. When you were not in the office," Guy said. "If you think I'm going away, you'd better think again. Stay tuned."

The investigator got up and stormed from the room.

GUY DROVE home. He filled Claire in on his meeting with Stephen.

"How does Charlie McDermott fit into this picture?" she asked. "And Estee? And Natalie?"

"I'm not sure," Guy said.

"We're meeting again in the next day or two with Captain Massey and his investigators. His department will have more information to share, and I'm hoping when we lay it all out and put our collective minds together we'll come up with the path to finally solving these cases."

"Will you be up for a meeting of this nature, Claire?" Guy asked.

"Try to keep me away," she said.

ROISE FOX felt unsettled. He walked to an oversized living room chair and allowed his body to fall into its plushy arms. Life perplexed him. He had lost his wife, his daughter-in-law, Christine, and now his grandson. Eric always came to visit him once a month, and he would dreadfully miss seeing the young man. Eric had problems. Deep problems. Roise was aware of that. And he had tried to counsel the young man—giving him advice on how to get on with his life, how to live a productive life contributing to society in some meaningful way, and how to be happy. He never knew if he was getting through, but he always kept trying. And now this happened. Eric decided to end it all. Roise was profoundly sad. It was a sadness that would remain with him the rest of his days on earth.

He put his face in his hands and wept.

And Stephen. His son. How would Stephen handle the loss of Eric? He shuddered at the thought. His loss of Christine had been overwhelming. Despite the fact they planned to divorce, he loved his wife beyond words. And now his son too?

How could life be so inequitable?

He reflected. Stephen had not been the same since Christine died. His personality had changed, and not in a good way. Roise didn't like it one bit. Sure, Stephen took care of him monetarily. He had everything he could want or need and more. But they almost never spent quality time together. Stephen was always too busy. Dating women when he wasn't working. Living in the fast lane. He had become shallow. And he rarely, if ever, saw Eric.

Roise stared out the window, deep in thought.

And Stephen had mentioned to him on more than one occasion that women clients of the car dealership had died in horrific car accidents while driving cars that he had sold them. Roise often wondered what that was all about. When he gave his mind permission to really think about possibilities, he secretly mulled over the unthinkable that Stephen might somehow be involved in the deaths. But why? Why would he want these women dead? Roise couldn't imagine. But then there was the money aspect. How did Stephen afford to buy him the condo? The Karmann Ghia? The Hinckley? He enjoyed having everything his son provided him, so he never questioned where the money came from. But in his alone thoughts, he did wonder about Stephen's finances. Where did he get all this money? Was he over his eyeballs in debt? Was Stephen in trouble? Doing bad things? Did he need his father's help?

JIN MANNED the office of Caswell & Lombard, Private Investigation that day. He opened the office directly after finishing classes. Claire was resting at home, and Guy was helping her and also investigating out of the office. The intern was happy to help out.

The day before had impacted him greatly. He thought the world of Claire Caswell, and almost losing her cut deeply into his emotional state. He now understood fully the dangers and risks of being a private investigator. It was not like in the movies. This was real life with real consequences. He respected the work she and Guy did even more than before.

He got up and walked over to the paneled evidence board. He paced back and forth, from one end to the other, taking it all in. Together, they had collected so much data. Yet the cases still weren't solved. The amount of work involved to resolve complicated cases boggled his law student mind. He stared at each document, each photo, and each piece of information collected. He remembered Claire's words: Were they missing the really big picture because of all the small details?

The phone rang. He answered.

It was Maude Wakely calling.

"Is Mr. Lombard in?"

"Not at this time," Jin said. "May I be of assistance? I work with Mr. Lombard and Ms. Caswell."

"Well, I'm not sure if this is important or not," she said, "but please let Mr. Lombard know that I remembered something else after he left today. Something about that man that attacked his wife."

"I'll make a note for him," Jin said. "What did you recall?"

"His cap. He wore a purple skullcap."

"I'll be sure to let him know, Ms. Wakely. Thank you for calling."

"You're welcome, young man."

Jin hung up and dialed Guy's cell phone.

"Jin?" Guy answered. "Is everything all right?"

"I just received a call from Maude Wakely. She remembered that the man who attacked Claire wore a purple skullcap. I wanted you to know right away in case it's important."

Guy thanked Jin for reporting this to him. He hung up and called Captain Massey.

"We're looking for a man who drives a black Jeep Wrangler and also owns a purple skullcap."

24

CLAIRE WOKE UP refreshed the next morning. She took a hot shower, and afterward she let icy-cold water beat down on the small of her back. It felt invigorating. The female investigator dressed for work, combed her hair into a low ponytail, and applied light makeup, finishing up with a touch of coral lipstick.

She glanced at her neck. She had not allowed herself to do so since the attack, but this morning she did. Red marks still showed, but she would not allow the injury to distract her. After all, her firm had two investigations to solve. There was no time for self-pity or to feel unhappiness over her personal troubles. Her friend Charlotte had died in a dreadful car crash, and she had to find out who was behind it. Claire knew they were getting close, and that is why someone tried to kill her.

CLAIRE RODE to the office with Guy. He had promised himself and Captain Massey not to let Claire out of his sight until these cases were resolved. And although she balked at the outset, she eventually consented.

When they arrived, they found the office door ajar. They always locked the door tightly at the close of every workday, so alarm bells immediately sounded in their heads. Guy darted a quick look at Claire before kicking it wide open. He walked in, and Claire followed at his heels. The office looked intact, except for the rolling evidence board they had so painstakingly assembled. Every document, photo, writing, hand-drawn schematic, and each and every piece of research discovered and printed had been ripped from the panels and stolen. The two quickly made their way around the workplace to check for other theft or damages. Nothing else appeared to be missing or out of place.

Claire picked up the phone and called Captain Massey to report the break-in and theft.

"I'll drive over and fill out the burglary report myself. Give me a half hour," he said.

"Whoever is doing this is desperate," Guy said. "And we know desperate people do desperate things." He met Claire's eyes. "You've been threatened, attacked, and now this. What next?"

She avoided his question. "We can't and won't be stopped," she said. She looked at the empty rolling board and sighed. "All our work is gone."

"Yeah, but we have it in our heads. They can't obliterate our memories," Guy said.

"We do remember it all," Claire said.

She made a pot of hot tea and filled two mugs. They waited for the police captain to arrive.

When he did, he brought with him a forensic investigator to check for prints. They walked in through the open door.

"Did either of you touch the outside doorknob when you came in?" the captain asked. "Or the inside knob since you've been here?"

"No. The door was slightly open. I kicked it without touching the knob," Guy said. "And, no, neither of us has touched the inside knob."

"Good. Maybe we'll be able to get a good print," Captain Massey said.

"I doubt it," Claire said. "But it's worth a try. Even the threatening letter sent to me had no prints. Whoever is doing these things is clever and knowledgeable. I'll keep my fingers crossed the thief got sloppy."

"I've arranged to have a squad car sit outside your office for the foreseeable future, until these cases come to resolution," the captain said. "I refuse to let the two of you subject yourselves to more danger. Consider it my office protecting the public."

"Really?" Claire asked. "That's not necessary."

"It's already done," Captain Massey said. "And if you need to go somewhere, one of my officers will either escort or follow you. You're swimming in dangerous waters, and an esurient shark is after you. Remember that."

He looked at the paneled board, photographed it, and wrote up a written report of the break-in and theft.

"Someone wanted those papers destroyed," the captain said. "The thief assumed that without them it would be a mighty blow to the investigation."

The forensic investigator went about trying to lift latent prints from the doorknobs. First, he pointed and shined a flashlight, holding it at an angle to the surface to see where prints were located. Using a soft brush, he sprinkled a fine powder onto the prints in an attempt to better define them. The powder stuck to the skin oils left behind. He cautiously brushed away any excess powder. Fingerprints at once became quite visible. He pulled clear lifting tape from a card and pressed it onto the prints. Carefully, he pulled the tape back up and gently pressed the tape back onto the card. He did this on both the outside and inside knobs.

"I got some good prints," he said. "We'll see."

"My bet is that they're a combination of mine, Guy's, and Jin's," Claire said.

The investigator took prints from Claire and Guy for comparison purposes.

Jin walked in at that moment.

"I had a canceled class, so I came right over. What's going on? I see a squad car sitting outside, and the door is open. Are you both okay?" he asked.

Guy filled him in on the break-in and what was missing.

"I looked at that board yesterday," he said. "I think I can remember everything that was on it. I also took photographs of every panel. I have them on my phone."

Jin had definitely progressed since he'd first come to the firm. He was a self-starter, a bright bulb, and a person who thought quickly on his feet.

"Brilliant, Jin!" Claire said.

The forensic investigator took Jin's prints and then set about lifting prints from the top and side perimeter edging of the evidence board panels.

"You never know where you'll find a useful print," the forensic investigator said. "I'll have an answer for you soon. Cross your fingers that I'll find a print other than one of the three of yours."

"On another note, some of the subpoenaed documents are starting to filter in," the captain said. "I should have them all within the next day or two. As soon as I do, we'll meet with the large group of us."

The captain and the forensic investigator left.

Claire looked out the window and saw a squad car parked on the street in front of the office. The captain had kept his word.

"I have to admit, I do feel safer knowing we have protection," she said.

STEPHEN FOX sat at his desk wringing his hands. He was the person of interest in several murders, and he was running scared. He called a meeting with Natalie and the other salespeople on the floor that day.

They sat around tables in the coffee lounge.

Stephen stood.

"I called you together today because you need to be aware of a situation that has developed." He looked around the room and met the eyes of each person. "I am a suspect in a series of murders of some of our female customers."

Shock and awe swept through the group.

"I'm as stunned as you are," he said. "But the police and private investigators are building a case against me. There's no doubt about it. I'm being railroaded."

"Why you?" a salesperson asked. "What do they have on you?"

"Well, I closed all the transactions for these women who met with fatal car crashes shortly after their purchases. And I dated all of them. It puts me in the loop right away."

Sighs were heard throughout the room.

"I am forced to hire a criminal attorney and will do so shortly. And I'm going to ask each of you not to talk to any police officers or investigators who come here snooping around. I fully expect Claire

Caswell and/or Gaston Lombard—the private investigators on this case—to return to this dealership asking more of their incessant questions. Do not talk to them. Refuse. Respond that you have been directed not to answer any questions. If I need to arrange for an attorney for the dealership, as well, I'll do it."

"*Shit!* This sounds serious," another salesperson said.

"It's deadly serious. I could wind up in prison for the rest of my life," Stephen said.

Stephen felt questioning looks hurled his way.

The meeting ended, and the attendees walked from the room, whispering under their breaths.

IT WAS time to interview Charlie McDermott. Claire and Guy decided to drive to the Bal Harbour condominium. According to Jin's observations of the man, they assumed he'd be there. A marked police car trailed them to the building and escorted them inside.

Claire located the name *R. Fox* on the list of residents on the panel box and pressed the correlating buzzer. An elderly voice answered.

"Hello?" he asked. "Who's there?"

"It's Claire Caswell and Gaston Lombard from the Caswell & Lombard, Private Investigation firm. And we're with the Miami-Dade police," she said.

"What is this about?" he demanded.

"We'd like to talk to Charlie McDermott, your employee," Claire said.

There was a pause.

"What's the matter? Has he done something wrong?" Fox asked.

"We'd like to discuss the matter with him," she said. "Please let us in."

There was another pause. Claire heard the closing of a door in the background.

"I believe he just left," the elderly Fox said.

"Then we'll catch him in the garage," she said. "We need to get past the security door. Do not abet him."

After a delay, the three heard the click of the security door being unlocked. They walked in and took the elevators to the lower level. They waited off to the side.

Soon the man they had come to know as Charlie McDermott surfaced. He gazed at the green Karmann Ghia parked two rows away and began his trek toward it.

The police officer's voice was the first sound Charlie heard. The officer rested a hand on his revolver.

"Mr. McDermott, I am with the Miami-Dade Police Department. There are two private investigators here with me, and they want to talk to you."

Charlie stopped cold in his tracks and turned to face them.

"What's going on?" he asked.

"Is there a room where we can sit down?" Claire asked.

The investigators showed him their identifications.

"I guess the party room. Follow me," he said. He was clearly rattled.

Charlie stopped at the front desk to pick up the room key and led the others to the area. They sat on resin chairs at a long table. Guy pulled a recorder from his briefcase and plugged it into a nearby outlet.

"Yes. Now tell me what this is about. What have I done?" he asked.

"Do you have identification with you?" Claire asked.

"I do."

"We'd like to see it," she said.

He pulled his driver's license from his wallet and set it on the table.

Claire and Guy examined it.

"This says your name is Charlie McDermott," Guy said. "Is that your legal name?"

Charlie hesitated. "Yes."

"Is it the name on your birth certificate?" Claire asked.

Charlie hesitated a longer time.

"Why are you asking me this?" he asked.

"Please answer the question," Claire said.

"I'd like to know why you're asking me this question. I have a right to know," he said. Defiance hummed in his tone.

The police officer stepped in. "Answer the question, or you'll be answering it at the station. Your choice."

"Okay. Okay," Charlie said. "I was given a different name at birth, but I changed it."

"What was your birth name?" Guy asked.

"Richard Connors."

"Why did you change it?" Guy asked.

"I had some problems in my life. I drank a lot. Had many DUIs and arrests. Hung with a bad crowd. Got into lots of trouble. I went through treatment, got clean, and wanted to start over with a fresh slate. Can you blame me? I wanted to erase all the bad years associated with my given name." He paused. "Everyone knows me as Charlie now. And I want to keep it that way."

"Did you apply for a formal name change with the court?" Guy asked.

"No," Charlie said. "I suppose I'll be hung out to dry for that."

"We're here for another purpose today," Claire said. "I'm going to throw out some names, and we'd like you to tell us if and how you know them. Understood?"

"Fire away," Charlie said.

"Roise Fox," she said.

"My employer."

"Stephen Fox."

"A friend. We were in AA together. He's Roise's son."

"Ester Rollings?"

He paused before he answered.

"A friend. A good friend." He smiled. "She's my love."

Claire thought she detected a tinge of true, pure feelings for Estee in his response, but she couldn't be sure.

"Natalie Hart, the receptionist at the Porsche dealership where Stephen works."

His look revealed his disbelief.

"An acquaintance. Nothing more. Why are you asking me about her?"

"Jimmy Kesson, salesman at the Porsche dealership where Stephen works."

"I know who he is. I've met the man at the dealership."

"Christine Fox."

"She was married to Stephen. Met her once or twice."

"Catherine Hanker."

"Don't know her or the name."

"Cindy Bane."

"Don't know her or the name."

"Camille Sullivan."

"Don't know her or the name."

"Charlotte Truman."

"Don't know her or the name."

"Eric Fox."

"Stephen's son. I met him a couple of different times. Very sad about that kid. I heard the bad news."

"Carli Fox."

"Stephen took me to watch her perform onstage one time. He

married her too. It was a short union."

"Mary Katz."

"Don't know her or the name."

The investigators had no reason to believe he had provided anything less than truthful answers to their questions. Claire did note, however, that a curious look appeared on his face and a defensive tone surfaced in his response when she asked him about Natalie Hart.

"That's it on the names, Charlie."

Charlie looked at Claire. "Did I pass?"

"We have other questions for you," she said.

He squirmed in his seat and tugged at his collar.

"What is your cell number, Charlie?"

He recited a number.

"You were recently observed passing Natalie Hart an envelope while you sat in your car in the parking lot of the apartment complex where she lives. What was in the packet?"

Charlie turned a bright shade of scarlet. Sweat instantly collected on his brow. He fumbled for words. "This is unbelievable! You've been *following* me? I want an attorney," he said.

"We'll expect you at our offices tomorrow at 1:00 p.m., then, with your attorney to continue the interview," Guy said. He handed Charlie his business card.

Charlie left without saying another word.

Claire, Guy, and the police officer took the elevator up to the main floor and exited the building.

25

THE MONTH MARKER was approaching since the death of Charlotte. Bills were piling up at the firm and they needed to spend time on paying clients. Claire felt pressure building. And she was getting impatient for an answer to her friend's tragic ending. She hungered for resolution. They were close. She could feel it in her bones. But they weren't there quite yet.

THE FOLLOWING afternoon, 1:00 came and went with no sign of Charlie or his attorney. Claire called the number he had given her at the statement the previous day. A recorded message sounded: "You have reached a number that has been disconnected or is no longer in service. If you feel you have reached this recording in error, please check the number and try your call again."

"He either gave us a bum number or he disconnected his service immediately after we saw him yesterday," Claire said.

"Methinks he's running scared," Guy said. "I'll ask Captain Massey to put out an APB on him. With every police officer in Miami-Dade County having his description and that of his car, they'll pick him up in no time. He thinks he can run and hide. But he'll find out otherwise."

"Yeah. That car he drives is easy to spot. He won't get far," Claire said.

Guy made the call.

CLAIRE LOOKED at Guy. "I think we should interview Natalie now—before Charlie warns her, if he hasn't already."

"Jump in my car. I'll have the officer shadow us."

Minutes later, the private investigators pulled into the parking lot of the dealership. They parked and walked in. The police officer trailed just behind.

Natalie sat at her desk filing her nails.

"Stephen isn't in," she said, quickly glancing up and then looking back down again at her hands.

"Natalie, it's you we'd like to talk to," Claire said. "Can we go to the lounge?"

"I have been instructed not to talk to either of you or to the police," she said. "So my answer is no, there is no place for us to go and talk."

The police officer broke in.

"We can do this this easy way or the hard way," he said. "If you refuse to talk to these investigators, I will ask you to come to the station to give a statement. Or we can issue a subpoena."

Natalie swallowed hard. She unconsciously placed her hands on her stomach. "I'm working right now, so you can't take me to the station to answer questions."

"I'm afraid this matter takes precedence over your work," the officer said.

Her look went between the investigators and the police officer. It was clear she had no wiggle room.

"Let me check with Stephen first," she said.

"No can do," the officer said. He moved in closer to her. "Are you talking now, or are we going to the station?"

"To the station, I guess," Natalie said. "I'd prefer to do it there." She looked around to see if other employees were watching.

"Want to ride with us?" Claire asked.

Natalie nodded. Her large, wide-set eyes showed apprehension.

"Follow me to the station," the officer said to the private investigators.

All parties arrived at the police station within thirty minutes and were led to an interview room in a narrow hallway. The group of four sat on cold chairs that surrounded a small table. The room was gray and unfriendly.

Guy pulled his recording device from his briefcase, set it on the table, plugged it in, and turned it on. He stated the date, time, and place of the interview for the record. And he had all parties present identify themselves.

"Natalie, you're here voluntarily, at our request, is that correct?" Guy asked.

"Yes. But I was told not to talk to you," she said.

"Who told you that?" Claire asked.

She hesitated. "Stephen Fox. He also said you were railroading him."

"We're investigating the probable *murder* of four women in the prime of their lives," Claire said. "These women all dealt with

Stephen when they purchased cars from the dealership where you work. And we know Stephen dated each one of them. We also think you might know something about all of this, and that's why we want to talk to you. It can only help you if you're honest with us."

Claire paused and looked directly into Natalie's eyes. "And then there is Stephen's first wife, Christine, who died under suspicious circumstances too. And now his son, Eric, is dead, as well."

"It's all so tragic," she said. She fiddled with her hands.

"And we have one common denominator in the entire mix," Claire said. "Stephen Fox."

"That doesn't mean he killed them," she said.

"Just for clarification, have you decided to talk to us?" Guy asked.

"Obviously. Yes."

"Let's start from the beginning, then," Guy said. He turned to Natalie. "Please state and spell your full name."

"Natalie Hart. N-a-t-a-l-i-e H-a-r-t."

Guy looked at Claire. Interviewing was her expertise, and his look told her to take over the questioning.

"Please give us your address and phone numbers—both business and home."

Natalie cooperated.

"How long have you worked at the dealership?" Claire asked.

"A little over four years," she said.

"Your age?" Claire asked.

"Thirty-three."

"You look much younger."

"Thank you." She smiled.

"How well do you know Stephen?"

"He hired me. And I consider him my boss."

"Do you date him?"

"No!" She rolled her eyes. "He's much too old for me. He's like a father figure."

"Has Stephen ever been to your apartment?"

She thought for a time. "Yes."

"Why?"

"I'm in charge of setting up the promotions the dealership hosts to bring in potential customers. They do a lot of events, many targeting women," she said. "They assigned the promos and marketing of events to me, as I generally have more free time than the salespeople to work on things like this, and they knew I enjoy this type of work. Stephen came to my apartment a couple of times, I believe, over the lunch hour, to look at the advertising and promotional materials I was proposing for an upcoming event. I had left them all laid out on my dining room table because I was working on the project during evenings at home. He came to view what I'd done and give me his opinions. That was why he came to my place."

"I'm going to call out some names, and I'd like you to tell us if you know the person and, if so, define your relationship with that person. Are you clear on this?" Claire asked.

"Yes."

"Stephen Fox."

"My boss."

"Jimmy Kesson."

"Friend, I guess. He's a salesman at the dealership."

"Christine Fox."

"Stephen's first wife. I never met her."

"Carli Fox."

Natalie laughed. "She is Stephen's second wife. We all knew that one wouldn't last. It was a short marriage. I met her a couple of times when she came into the dealership."

"Catherine Hanker."

"A client of the dealership. She died in a car accident. I knew her."

"Cindy Bane."

"Also a client of the dealership. She died in an auto accident too. I knew her too."

"Camille Sullivan."

"Another client of the dealership. She died in a car crash, as well. I knew her."

"Charlotte Truman."

"Yet another client of the dealership. She also died in a vehicle accident. I knew her."

"You talk very matter-of-factly about these deaths, Natalie. Were you upset hearing about them?"

"Very. We all were. Everyone at the dealership talked about them. It's still a topic of conversation. The first one happened right after I started."

"So what do you know about these women? About these accidents?"

"I know they were all single and they had great careers. They were making a lot of money. And all of them loved their new vehicles. I don't know what went wrong."

"Did you know Stephen dated them all?"

"I guess so. He has a reputation of being an incessant ladies' man. He always goes for the rich ones."

"Did you ever wonder if Stephen had something to do with the deaths?"

"I'm not sure. The thought might have crossed my mind. But that's all it did—maybe a fleeting thought once or twice."

"Did others at the firm think Stephen might have had something to do with the deaths?"

"Oh, I heard comments floating around from time to time."

"From who?"

She thought for a full minute.

"Jimmy, I think. Kesson. He thought something was up with Stephen."

"Do you know Charlie McDermott?"

Natalie looked suddenly ill.

"Are you feeling okay?"

"I'm not sure. I feel light-headed. Like I'm going to—"

The officer left the room to get her a glass of water.

When he returned, he handed it to the witness. She drank the entire glass of the cool liquid straight down.

"Are you feeling better?" Claire asked. "Do you need more water?"

"No, I'm okay. I feel better."

"Good. Then let's continue," the female investigator said. "I had asked you if you know Charlie McDermott."

"Yes. He's a friend of Stephen's. And I believe he works for Stephen's dad. I know his name."

"Have you met Charlie?"

Natalie went silent.

"Will you give me an answer, please?" Claire asked.

"I'm thinking."

"You don't remember? Didn't he come into the firm once in a while to see Stephen?"

"Oh, yes, I think he did. I guess I did meet him."

She shifted back and forth and from side to side in her chair. She rubbed her nose.

Claire was hitting a nerve, so she continued her line of questioning.

"Does Charlie know where you live?"

Natalie turned ashen.

Minutes passed. Natalie looked as if she were a million miles away.

"Natalie?" Claire asked. "Are you in there?"

Her eyes met Claire's.

"What was the question again?"

"I asked you if Charlie knows where you live."

"Not to my knowledge."

Claire looked at her for long minutes without speaking, and Guy locked his eyes on the witness.

"Do you know a middle-aged woman named Ester Rollings?"

"No."

"Have you ever received money or a gift or gifts of any kind from Stephen?"

"Never."

"What about Charlie? Have you ever been offered or have you ever received money or a gift or gifts of any kind from Charlie?"

She felt trapped.

She asked for more water. The officer left to retrieve another glassful. He returned, and again she emptied the glass.

"Now back to my question," Claire said. "Have you ever received money or gifts of any kind from Charlie? Or been offered the same?"

"No, I have never received money or gifts from Charlie."

Claire looked at Natalie with stinging eyes.

"Have you ever been asked to engage in an activity you knew was against the law by either Stephen or Charlie or anyone else at the dealership?"

Natalie fainted.

26

MINUTES LATER, NATALIE came to. She lifted her head from the table and held her stomach. Claire asked her if she wanted to continue the interview.

"Yes," she said.

"Do you feel okay, Natalie?" Claire asked. Her glance fell to the receptionist's bracelet.

Natalie nodded.

"Are you pregnant?"

Natalie stared at her with startled eyes.

"How did you know?"

"I guessed," the female investigator said. "I noticed you were wearing an acupressure bracelet for nausea. Who is the father?"

"Can we stay off the record, please?" Natalie asked.

"We can," Claire said.

Natalie hesitated for some time before answering.

"It's Charlie McDermott," she said. "He came on to me really strong one day, and I agreed to go out with him. We had dinner and drinks. I drank too much, and so did he. We went back to my place. It just happened. One dinner. One night. One time. I truly can say I don't like the man much. I refused to ever see him again."

"So you will raise the baby on your own?" Claire asked.

"That's the plan. No one knows about this except Charlie. Stephen doesn't know, and I don't want him to know."

"Okay. Let's go back on the record," Claire said.

Guy turned the recorder back on and announced, "We are back on the record."

"Natalie, have you ever been asked to engage in an activity you knew was against the law by either Stephen Fox or Charlie McDermott or anyone at the Porsche dealership?"

Natalie didn't answer.

"Natalie? Did you go away again?"

"No, I'm here."

"Will you please answer the question?"

"No, I will not. I plead the Fifth. That is my answer. And from now on, I answer no more questions. I want a lawyer."

The interview came to a sudden end.

CLAIRE HEARD her cell phone ring.

"Claire Caswell," she said.

"It's Captain Massey. A couple of my officers picked up Charlie McDermott. He was attempting to flee. Driving that little Karmann Ghia like he was trying out for the Indy 500. Headed north on his way to Fort Lauderdale. They're bringing him in to the station now. Hang around. You can interview him when he arrives."

"Good work, Captain," Claire said.

She filled him in on the Natalie statement.

"More twists and turns. This case is full of them."

"You can say that again."

"Oh, before I forget, surprisingly, my forensics man got a nice palm print off your evidence board. The print is not in the systems we routinely check, but we'll hang on to it. We can use it for comparison purposes at any time." He cracked his knuckles. "Let me know how McDermott's statement goes, will you, please? Oh, and by the way, he lawyered up."

TWO OFFICERS strong-armed Charlie into the station as he struggled to kick his restrainers and break free. He was under arrest and handcuffed. He was not a happy man.

"What is this about?" he yelled. "I'm being framed!"

The officers delivered him to the interview room. They refused to release him from the handcuffs despite his ongoing pleas.

"They're too tight! They're cutting into my wrists!" he bellowed. "You have no right to pick me up and haul me in here like an animal! I have rights! I'm a US citizen!"

The officers kept silent, allowing Charlie to rant on and on.

Claire and Guy appeared in the room and sat down. Guy pulled out his recorder and set it up.

"I will say nothing until my lawyer gets here!" Charlie wailed.

One officer present read Charlie the full Miranda warning. "Do you understand the rights I have just read to you?"

"My lips are sealed," he said. He made a silent motion from one corner of his mouth to the other, indicating he had zipped his mouth shut.

The group waited in silence for his lawyer to appear. Twenty-five minutes later, attorney Roy D. Keller walked into the room and declared he was representing Charlie McDermott in this matter. He distributed his business cards.

Guy Lombard knew Roy D. Keller and was all too aware of his ethics. He was slimy and slick. Slippery and oily. As dirty as they came. He was an attorney known to take on all the hard-core and often repeat criminals inhabiting the Miami area, including the drug scene. *Why would Charlie McDermott hire a lawyer of this caliber?* Guy wondered. He didn't come cheap.

The former Miami-Dade state attorney stood up and offered his hand to the fellow counselor. "Mr. Keller," Guy said, acknowledging him.

"We meet again, Gaston," Roy said.

Roy D. Keller also knew Gaston Lombard. He had been up against him in court when Guy was a lead Miami-Dade state attorney. He knew him to be a man of integrity and, not unlike a bull, a counselor who rammed his targets head on. He was aware that most attorneys who went up against the infamous Mr. Lombard never even knew what hit them. Roy, on the other hand, was cut from a different cloth. Gaston Lombard didn't ruffle his feathers in the slightest.

The two were on opposite ends of the legal spectrum.

And this was going to be war.

Roy sat down on a chair next to his client.

Claire extended her hand. "I'm Claire Caswell."

"So you're Claire Caswell? The famous Miami private investigator that has solved so many quote unquote *unsolvable cases*?" He looked at her with keen interest. "I'm going to enjoy this."

"I beg your pardon?" she said.

"Let the games begin," he said.

His arrogance spilled over onto his client, and Charlie's demeanor suddenly changed. Before the investigators' eyes, the man impudently transformed into a cocky and arrogant creature filled with his own importance.

"Let's get this thing started," Guy said.

He turned the recorder on. He looked over at the police officer and asked him to read Charlie McDermott the Miranda warning. He wanted it on the record. Roy D. Keller would have no reason to cry foul. After Charlie was given the warning and asked for the required acknowledgment that he understood his rights, the questioning began.

Guy identified the date and time and asked everyone in the room to identify himself or herself, spelling both their first and last names.

"Charlie, please state your address and phone numbers," Guy said.

He stated his address and the same phone number he had given the investigators the first time they sat down with him a day prior.

Guy nodded to Claire.

"I think we all know that the phone number you just recited is a nonworking number," Claire said. "So we'll ask you again to state your current working phone number."

"I don't have a working number at this time," Charlie said.

"You don't have a working number?" she repeated. "Then why did you give us this phone number twice?"

"Asked and answered," Attorney Keller said. "Move on."

"What is your relationship with Stephen Fox?" Claire asked.

"He's a buddy. We went through treatment together. He helped find me a job looking after his father when I got out."

"His father being Roise Fox," Claire said.

"One and the same," Charlie said.

"And what is it you do for Roise Fox?" she asked.

"A variety of tasks. I do his grocery shopping, sometimes I cook, I pay his bills, make sure the housekeeper does her job to keep his condo clean, run errands, those types of things."

"And do you earn a salary for doing these things?" she asked.

"The condo is way too large for him alone. He gives me a room to live in."

"Does he also pay you a salary?"

"Yeah."

"How much does he pay you?"

Charlie laughed. "That is confidential information. How much do you make?"

"I am not the one being questioned here today, Mr. McDermott. You are. And I will ask you again how much you earn as a salary for your job with Roise Fox."

"He answered that his salary is confidential, Ms. Caswell," Attorney Keller said. "Asked and answered. Move on."

"What other perks do you enjoy as a side benefit for being a caregiver to Mr. Roise?" Claire asked.

"Perks?"

"Yes, perks. Goods, products, things you can use, or other benefits you are entitled to as an employee of Roise Fox."

"He lets me use whatever I want to," Charlie said.

"Like his Hinckley boat?" she asked.

"Yeah."

"How about the Karmann Ghia you drive?"

"Yeah. That too."

"So let me confirm. You get to live in his pricy condominium in Bal Harbour, use his prestigious boat, and drive his prized car. Wow. What a job. Lots of amazing perks." She looked at Charlie with a face revealing no emotion.

"Is there a question in that litany, Ms. Caswell?" Keller asked.

"There is not. Just observations."

"Then let's get on with it," he said. "Ask your next question."

"Do you ever do favors for Stephen Fox?" she asked.

"What kind of favors?" Charlie asked.

"Any kind of favors," Claire said.

"Overly broad question," Attorney Keller said. "Please rephrase and be more specific."

"Have you ever engaged in illegal activities as the request of Stephen Fox?"

"Certainly not," Charlie said. His body and face became stiffer.

"Tell us about your friend Ester Rollings," Claire said. "Start with how the two of you met."

"I have to think," he said. "Let's see. I guess I went to her home to check on her after her husband died—to see if she needed anything."

"Did you know her husband?"

"Yeah. We worked at different companies, but we did business together. He always talked about how he was fortunate to have such a wonderful wife. I heard it so often over the years that I guess I wanted to check on her after he passed—to make sure she was okay. I guess she really appreciated it. We became instant friends."

Claire watched Charlie with interest as he answered. She didn't know if he was responding truthfully or not. Something under the surface nudged her to question his genuineness. Yet, whenever he talked about Estee, she noticed something almost innocent and harmless about the man.

"What is the extent of your relationship with Ester, Mr. McDermott?" Claire asked.

"I told you before. We're great friends."

"Have you given her any expensive gifts?" Claire asked.

"I guess that's my business," Charlie said.

"Gifts you might buy an insurance policy on to protect?" Claire went on. "And list yourself as the beneficiary?"

Charlie went silent.

Whispering went on between Keller and his client.

"My client is asserting his Fifth Amendment right against self-incrimination," Attorney Keller said.

"I see," Claire said. She looked at her watch. "I would like to take a fifteen-minute break and then reconvene in this room." She motioned to Guy.

He stated the time on the record and added, "We will be going off the record at this time." He turned the recorder off.

Claire walked from the room, and Guy followed.

"We need to find a place to talk," she said quietly.

"Let's go outside," Guy suggested.

They exited the station and walked nearly a block down the street.

"What do you think about Charlie's attorney?" Claire asked.

"He's a pain in the ass," Guy said. "It's his usual modus operandi. But you're holding up admirably. You show no signs of being annoyed or getting worn down."

"Any suggestions as far as continuing?" she asked.

"We'll get nowhere on the tough questions," Guy said. "Keller will keep objecting or claiming the Fifth on behalf of his client each and every time."

"Then I suggest we take back control," Claire said. "Let's go in there and end the statement without further explanation. Let's keep them guessing. We'll find another way to go after Charlie."

"Good plan. I like it," he said.

Claire and Guy returned to the room. Everyone returned to his or her previous seat.

Guy started up the recorder and stated the time. "We are now back on the record, and it should be known that nothing was said regarding this matter between the parties off the record."

Claire looked from Charlie McDermott to his attorney.

"We will be ending the statement of Charlie McDermott at this time. We have no further questions."

"*What?*" Keller asked. He looked befuddled. "And just when it was getting interesting."

Claire did not respond.

"Thanks. Thanks for ruining my day," Charlie said. He glared at Claire Caswell.

27

ALL PERSONS OF interest seemed to be hiring lawyers. It would definitely make resolution of the cases more difficult, and it was a clear attempt to draw out the process of the investigations. But Claire and Guy were not about to give up. They were too close. They decided to interview Stephen Fox again, this time with his attorney present, and ask him the difficult questions. They would watch for his reactions.

The two investigators drove to the Porsche dealership. The police officer guarding them followed behind in his marked car. Claire, Guy, and the officer walked in through the front doors.

Natalie looked up from her magazine.

"We're here to talk to Stephen," Claire said. "Please let him know. He'll want to call his attorney to be present. We'll wait."

The receptionist got on her phone. She talked in a low tone.

"They're here—the private investigators and a policeman. They want to talk to you. They will wait until your attorney gets here."

Natalie hung up and asked the three to wait in the coffee lounge. "Help yourselves to coffee or a smoothie and pastry," she said in a programmed manner. It was what she said to all visitors to the dealership.

Minutes turned into an hour.

Natalie announced that Stephen's lawyer had arrived but that she first wanted to talk with her client for a few minutes. The receptionist informed them that she would come to get them for the meeting to be held in Stephen's office when the time was right.

They waited fifteen additional minutes.

Natalie reappeared and said, "Follow me."

The investigators and the officer walked down the hallway to Stephen's office. Introductions and business cards were exchanged. Guy retrieved his recorder, plugged it in, and got it ready. When he turned it on, he stated the date, time, and place of the meeting. As in every statement, he asked those present in the room to introduce himself or herself.

"I'm Avery Lopez. I represent Stephen Fox in this matter," Stephen's attorney said.

"Claire Caswell, private investigator."

"Gaston Lombard, private investigator."

"Officer Perez, representing the Miami-Dade County Police Department."

It was time to begin the interview.

"Mr. Fox, we have talked to you before regarding the matter at hand," Claire said. "We have a few additional questions."

Stephen's demeanor was stiff as cardboard. They had never seen him like this before. He acted starchy and austere. He refused to look at Claire Caswell or Gaston Lombard.

"Stephen, it is our understanding that you purchased the pricy condominium in Bal Harbour where your father, Roise, resides as a gift to him. Is this true?" Claire asked.

"Yes."

"Did you also purchase a Hinckley boat for your father?" she asked.

"Yes."

"What about the Karmann Ghia? Did you purchase this vehicle for your father, as well?"

"Yes."

"Have you purchased other large-ticket items for your father, as well?"

"No."

"How did you afford to make the purchases we just discussed?"

"I took out loans. They're all mortgaged. He's been a good father, and I want him to live a good life. It's important to me. I make monthly payments on all of it."

"Does Roise Fox use the Hinckley boat?" she asked.

"No."

"But you purchased it for him anyway?"

"Yes."

"You are a friend or acquaintance of Charlie McDermott, correct?"

"Yes."

"Have you met Ester Rollings—the woman he spends much of his time with? Her nickname is Estee."

"No."

"Do you know about Estee?"

"Yes."

It was clear Attorney Lopez had instructed her client to give only a yes or no answer whenever possible.

"We need to talk about the four female Porsche purchasers who all met with violent deaths in their new vehicles: Catherine Hanker, Cindy Bane, Camille Sullivan, and Charlotte Truman. You were acquainted with all these women, correct?"

"I sold each of them a car. I handled the financing for the purchases. Yeah."

"What did these women share in common?"

"Meaning?"

"Please rephrase so my client understands your question," Attorney Lopez said.

"What did these four women have in common with each other?"

"I guess they were around the same age," Stephen said.

"Anything else?" Claire asked.

"They had all climbed the ladder of success."

"So they were all wealthy?"

"Yes."

"They all purchased Porsche Cayennes, correct?"

"Yes, I believe that is the case."

"You don't remember?" Claire asked.

"Yes. They did."

Stephen stirred uncomfortably and started to rub his eyes.

"At the time of their purchases, did each of the women receive hands-on instructions and training from the dealership on how to operate the vehicle?" Claire continued.

"Yes."

"Who instructed them? Who taught them the ins and outs of the particular vehicle?"

"I did."

"Okay. Has Porsche reported any problems with the Cayenne that could or would cause the driver to lose control of the vehicle when driving it?"

"No."

"So when all four of these women ended up in fatal one-car crashes while driving and operating their new Porsche Cayennes, and the ruling was driver error or natural causes in each case, what were your thoughts?"

"They happened about a year apart each time, if I am recalling correctly. I thought they were tragic accidents, and I was startled." Stephen looked up at the ceiling.

"You were startled," Claire repeated, looking at Stephen until he could feel her gaze.

He refused to return the look.

"Did you date each of the four women in question?"

"Date? I guess you could call it dating."

"What would you call it, Stephen?" the female investigator asked.

"I would say I befriended them."

"Did you have sex with each of these women?" Claire asked.

"Objection," his attorney said. "Improper. Unfairly prejudicial to my client."

"I disagree," Claire said. "Either he had intimate relationships with these women or he did not."

"Ask your question again," Attorney Lopez said.

"When you befriended each of the four women that are the subject of this investigation, did befriending include sleeping with them?"

Stephen hesitated. He whispered to his attorney. She whispered back.

"Yes. It was consensual in each case," he said.

"I want to talk about your first wife, Christine," Claire said. "She died suddenly, I understand. The autopsy was a negative one, meaning no conclusion could be drawn as to her cause of death. Is that your understanding, as well?"

Again, Stephen exchanged whispers with his attorney.

"Yes, that is my understanding."

"What do you suspect caused the death of your wife?"

"I don't know."

"Did you ever think she might have been poisoned?"

Stephen turned pale.

"If she was poisoned, it wasn't me who did it."

"That's a strange response, Stephen. If not you, who would it have been?"

He whispered to his attorney at length.

"My client is claiming his Fifth Amendment rights and refusing to answer that question," Attorney Lopez said.

"Do you know of anyone who owns a used black Jeep Wrangler?"

"No."

"Is it possible the dealership you work for might have a used one in a back lot? Perhaps one traded in on the purchase of a new Porsche?"

"I would have to check our used car inventory list. I can't answer that offhand. None that I know of."

"Does Roise worry about you?"

"Objection. Relevance," Attorney Lopez said.

"With ongoing mortgages on Roise's condo, boat, and vintage car that Stephen is responsible for, in addition to his own mortgage and expenses, I'm wondering how he makes ends meet. The question is relevant because in each case the four women who died prematurely were quite wealthy. He may have borrowed money from them or asked them to help him out."

Stephen gazed straight ahead.

"Rephrase your question, please," Attorney Lopez said.

"Mr. Fox, are you in serious debt?"

"Yes. I'm overly extended. I have several large loans."

"How did you arrange for financing on so many assets?" Claire asked.

"I have connections. I kept getting loans whenever I asked for them. Now I'm in slightly over my head. But I'm sure it will all work out in the end."

"Did any of the women we are talking about today loan or give you money?"

"No."

"Did you ask any of them for money?"

"No."

"Did you love any of these four women?"

Stephen hesitated.

"Objection," his attorney said. "Overly broad question."

"Did you love Charlotte Truman?" Claire asked.

"I liked her very much."

"Before we end today, I'd like to talk a bit about your son, Eric. I again express my condolences on his premature death. This has to be very difficult for you."

Stephen looked catatonic. He did not respond.

"The coroner has ruled that he ingested something to take his own life. Do you know why he would have chosen this route? And do you have any idea what he might have ingested?"

No response was forthcoming. Stephen had slipped into an unresponsive stupor.

"I think that is all for today," Attorney Lopez said. "If you have further questions, call me to set up another meeting."

Stephen closed his eyes as the investigators and officer walked from the room. As they approached the front doors, Natalie Hart and Jimmy Kesson stood looking at them.

"WHAT DID you make of all that?" Guy asked Claire on the drive home.

"I think Stephen was obviously covering for someone when I questioned him about his first wife's death. I have to wonder if that someone was Eric. I also believe his shock and grief over Eric's death is genuine."

"And what about his involvement in the death of Charlotte and the other women?"

"The jury is still out. But he remains the strongest suspect."

BACK AT the office, Jin sat at his desk, looking through the pictures on his smartphone and making notes to re-create what had been stolen from the firm's evidence board.

Claire and Guy greeted him and filled him in on the interviews with Charlie and Stephen.

"What a case this is," Jin said. "Ever changing and ever getting more complicated. So many parties involved. So many possibilities."

"The question is whether there is one culprit or more and who it is or who they are," Guy said.

"We're getting there," Claire said. "Just a little more time."

The office phone rang. Jin picked it up.

"It's for you, Ms. Caswell."

Claire answered.

"Captain Massey here. I've received all the documents now that I subpoenaed from the Porsche dealership and also from the banks. I think we should get together tomorrow to review all of this, if tomorrow works on your end."

"It does. Why don't you and your investigators come to our office again? We can spread everything out on our large meeting room table and collectively give it a hard look."

"Sounds good, Ms. Caswell. Should we say 10:00 a.m.?"

"That's perfect. I'll put on a pot of coffee."

"I'll bring the bagels."

Claire, Guy, and Jin spent the rest of the day reviewing and discussing all aspects of the investigations that the Caswell & Lombard firm had collected in the two investigations. The evidence board having been destroyed, they all took notes. They were anxious to learn if the subpoenaed documents would shed new light on the cases.

In the end, light shines brightest in the dark, Claire thought.

28

GUY DROVE CLAIRE to their office the following morning. On the way, they soaked up the gloriousness of the typical Miami day. Sunshine emblazoned the nearly cloudless sky, royal palms swayed gently in the balmy breeze, and bright flowering hedges appeared almost everywhere, together adorning the entire route. Glimpses of the amazing turquoise waters on either side of The Beach brought smiles to their faces.

Claire's neck had almost completely healed, but she remembered the attack like it had happened only minutes ago. It would take some time for her to emotionally recover, and it played itself out in many of her sleepless nights. Her hearing had miraculously returned to what it used to be, and she was thankful.

But Charlotte had been gone for over a month now. And Claire would continue to spend nearly every waking moment attempting to find her killer.

When they arrived, Claire started brewing a large urn of coffee. Soon the meeting would begin.

The private investigators gathered together all the remaining evidence they had gleaned over the course of the investigations. Subtracting the mass documentation stolen from the rolling evidence board, what remained were photos in their phones and cameras, notes in Jin's journal, and miscellaneous documentation on their respective desks. And of course their memories would serve them, as well. They knew the cases backward and forward.

CAPTAIN MASSEY and his forensic investigators rolled in right on time. The captain carted with him a large box of fresh bagels and several containers of flavored cream cheese. He set them down at the center of the table, along with plastic knives and napkins.

Today's meeting was a significant one with skilled individuals coming together to merge and share their brainpower to come up with some answers and plans moving forward. Or at least come up with the remaining questions that had to be answered.

The chief medical examiner, a member of the investigations bureau, two members the Miami-Dade medical examiner's toxicology lab, and an employee of the morgue arrived within the next few minutes.

Jin walked through the door and joined the group.

Captain Massey, accompanied by his investigators, addressed those gathered, summarizing the two cases for those who weren't at the last meeting. The captain introduced everyone present.

"We've put in tremendous time and effort to solve these cases. And this private investigation firm has gone above and beyond. Much information has been gathered." He passed around photos of the persons of interest and suspects from his file. He went on to inform the group of the recent burglary and theft of the private investigators' evidence board documents.

"My forensics man lifted a clear palm print from the edge of the board," he reported. "It matches nothing we have in our system, and it's not in the federal database either. But we have the print. We're holding on to it. If we zero in on a suspect, or suspects, we'll compare the prints."

He went on to inform the group of Claire's attack and told them of the threatening letter and hang-up calls she had received.

"We're not sure if we're looking at one perpetrator or more. Whoever is responsible for the deaths of these women is a cold-blooded killer, capable of anything." He stopped to sip some coffee. "We may review some items we're already discussed, but it is my desire today to look at the entirety of the cases with fresh sets of eyes—from the beginning of our efforts up to today—as though we've never heard any of this before. Maybe we have missed a detail or two along the way. Listen with alertness. Oh, and by the way, my team has thoroughly reviewed the documentation received under subpoenas from the Porsche dealership and from the banks of the victims. We found absolutely nothing out of the ordinary to report. The dealership documents only confirm that Stephen Fox worked with all four of the females when they purchased their cars, and the information from the banks confirmed no missing monies, so we can rule out money as a motive."

He turned the meeting over to the private investigators. Together, with input from Jin, the three took the time needed to paint the entire chronology of the investigations from day one to present. They defined the breadth of the persons of interest and possible suspects. They included a specific listing of each piece of evidence they had found along the way and included a summarization of each and every statement they had taken. They also talked about the mysterious death of Stephen Fox's first wife, Christine Fox, and the recent death of his son, Eric Fox—ruled to be at his own hand.

The astute group members listened carefully, taking thorough notes and asking numerous questions.

The representative from the toxicology lab went next. The man with hazel eyes, bushy brows, pockmarked skin, and a high forehead explained how the scientists on his staff assisted the medical examiner in investigating deaths appearing unnatural in nature. He described in vivid and explicit detail the rigorous process his team goes through on each and every case to examine blood, fluid, and tissue samples of the deceased.

The entire group got a clear visual image in their minds as the man talked.

"We look for any evidence of toxins, drugs, or poisons, and we pay extreme attention to all details," he said. "Our routine is intense and exhaustive. We leave no stone unturned in our efforts to search for both the cause and manner of death, to provide the families of the victims with closure—with the confirmed cause of death.

"Now, as far as the four female victims we are here to discuss today, I personally have reviewed each of their files many times over." He paused and poured a cup of coffee. "I have noted the similar variables between all the victims, and we have retested the blood samples we maintained on each. I believe my colleague may have talked about this at the last meeting. We did reach a conclusion."

Those at the table waited with bated breath to hear the next words out of his mouth.

"We have no doubts whatsoever that each of these women was poisoned with the same substance. We would never have caught the similarities unless we were asked to review these specific cases all together at the same time, looking for the same substance in their blood samples. The time spread between the incidents was too great to possibly tie together a pattern. So I give great praise for those here today who put this all together."

He sipped his hot beverage.

Just then, the office phone rang. Jin excused himself and walked from the room to answer it.

He reappeared moments later.

"Claire, I think you'd better take this call," he said.

"If we can take a short break, I'll be right back," Claire said. She left to take the call.

"Ms. Caswell, it's the police crime lab. Sorry it's taken us so long, but we finally have a definitive answer for you regarding the samples you brought in for analysis—both from the crash site and from the bags you brought in later collected from a garden in Coral Gables. First of all, the samples are all from the same type of plant. We knew the crash site samples were from a poisonous plant—we told you that earlier—but we still needed to conduct elaborate testing to further define the specimens due to their deteriorated condition. We have determined they are all from the belladonna plant. The full name is the *Atropa belladonna*. Its leaves are poisonous. Its berries are even more poisonous than its leaves. And its roots are the most poisonous. The first samples you brought us were the berries. The right quantities, if ingested, can easily kill a person. Effects would usually kick in within a couple of hours. Of course, if a large quantity is ingested, the effects could be rapid."

Claire scribbled notes.

"If I e-mail you a photo, would you take a quick look and tell me if it is a belladonna plant? I need the information pronto, please," she said.

"Of course."

Claire e-mailed the photo of the plant in the shaded area of the secret garden.

In less than a minute, a response came back.

"That's it," the lab tech said. "That's a belladonna plant."

Claire thanked him profusely and returned to the meeting.

Before she could say a word, the man from the toxicology lab started to finish what he had to say.

"Now, each death was officially determined to be driver error, as we could not confirm anything else. We did our routine testing and nothing showed up. In each case, if viewed alone, no red flag was raised. It's just when we looked at all the cases together that a pattern began to surface. The poison ingested in each case was from the *Atropa belladonna*, or simply the belladonna plant."

Claire broke in.

"I just received confirmation from the police crime lab that the samples I found at Charlotte Truman's crash site were berries from the belladonna plant. Now we just heard confirmation that the three other female victims had the same poison in their systems."

A police investigator asked the representative from the toxicology lab to explain more about the deadly plant.

"It's a plant that actually resembles a shrub," the lab representative said. "A single leaf, if ingested, is fatal. And the berries are even more dangerous. Consumption of ten berries would be lethal. Children have died from eating only two." He paused to catch his breath. "Actually, there are medical reports that indicate ingestion of two to five of the berries is sufficient to kill an adult. It kicks in within a couple of hours to days depending on the dose—the greater the quantity, the quicker, of course." He took a bite of the bagel sitting in front of him.

All present scratched notes furiously. Finally, a major breakthrough in the murder cases.

"The plant was used to make poison-tipped arrows far back in history due to its deadly nature," the lab representative continued.

Another investigator from the police department asked, "Does this plant go by any other names?"

"Great question. It does. It is also known as deadly nightshade, death cherries, and devil's berries. There might even be a few more. It's more common in northern Florida. We seldom see it here in southern Florida."

"What are the symptoms one experiences if he or she is poisoned with this plant?" Claire asked. She had to know what Charlotte had experienced before her death.

"It's a bad scenario, I'm afraid," he said. "The list is long." He pulled a sheet from his file to make sure he covered them all. "Confusion. Convulsions. Hallucinations. Sensitivity to light. Loss of balance. Staggering." He went on. "Headache, dry mouth, dry throat, and rash. Also, blurred vision, delirium, slurred speech, and dilated pupils. Ingestion of this deadly substance disrupts the person's breathing and heart rate. It causes tachycardia—a rapid heart rate." He passed around a picture of the plant. "As you can see, the berries of the plant actually resemble blueberries—although they're black, not blue."

Claire finished jotting down notes. She got up and walked from the room.

Captain Massey called for a fifteen-minute break.

Claire's head was spinning as she pictured what Charlotte had gone through before she'd lost control of her vehicle and slammed into the restaurant's plate glass window. And to make matters worse, Charlotte's seat belt had been tampered with, and she was locked into it. It was clear she had slipped out of the cross strap, but the belt across her waist was securely locked into place. She had no chance of surviving.

The female investigator felt sick. She dashed to the restroom and vomited. She splashed cold water on her face as tears flowed from her eyes. "I'm sorry, Charlotte," she said out loud.

She heard a knock on the door.

"It's me," Guy said. "Are you okay in there?"

"Yes," she said.

"I'm sorry you had to hear that. I can only imagine . . ."

After a few minutes, the private investigators returned to the table.

"Have a bagel, Ms. Caswell," Captain Massey said. "It might calm your stomach." Without him saying more, Claire knew he was aware of what she was going through.

She took a plain bagel and poured herself a cup of hot coffee. She forced herself to eat and drink. It did help her feel better.

The meeting resumed.

One by one, all in attendance took a turn at adding thoughts, impressions, and conclusions drawn after hearing all the information.

The man from the toxicology lab added a final point.

"We found this same substance in the blood of Christine Fox and Eric Fox."

Claire grabbed the photos she had printed of the plants in the secret garden located on the former Fox family property in Coral Gables.

"Look. Here it is—belladonna." She pointed it out to the group.

The man from the lab confirmed it to be the case.

"I think it's time we arrested Stephen Fox," Captain Massey said. He left the room to make the call and then returned. "My officers are off to find him. He'll be locked up within the hour."

TWO SQUAD cars with lights flashing and sirens blasting made their way to the Porsche dealership.

Four uniformed police officers burst through the front doors.

"We're here to arrest Stephen Fox. Where is he?" one asked the shaking receptionist. "Take us to his office."

Natalie could barely walk. She felt like she would collapse. She led the four officers to Stephen's office, pointed, stepped aside, and listened just outside the door.

The officers charged in. Two lifted Stephen from his chair. They grabbed his arms and forced them behind his back. He was handcuffed.

"You are under arrest for the murders of Catherine Hanker, Cindy Bane, Camille Sullivan, and Charlotte Truman. More charges might be added at a later time," one officer said. He read Stephen the Miranda warning and confirmed he understood his rights.

Minutes later, Stephen Fox was led away, wrists cuffed and feet shackled.

Employees of the dealership stood with shocked expressions on their faces, none of them knowing what to think of it all.

Jimmy walked over to stand by Natalie. They knew Stephen better than the others.

"Hard to believe Stephen is capable of doing what they say he did. Didn't he think he'd eventually get caught?" Jimmy said. "You work side by side with people for years, and you don't know who they really are."

Natalie couldn't respond. She was choking back tears.

STEPHEN FOX was fingerprinted and photographed at the station. He emptied his pockets of his personal belongings. From one pocket of his suit jacket, he pulled out a folded thin purple skullcap.

"That's not mine," he said. "I don't know how it got in there."

The intake officer merely said, "Uh-huh."

All Stephen's personal effects were carefully recorded in writing on a sheet of paper and then placed into individual small plastic bags. A label identifying his name and assigned intake number was affixed to each one.

Stephen was given an orange jumpsuit to change into, and the intake officer stood by him as he put it on.

"You have the right to make one phone call. Use that phone over there. Make it quick."

Stephen called his attorney.

"Help me!" he said. "I don't want to be in here."

He was led down the hallway to a barred jail cell and forced to walk in. The door slammed shut behind him.

He was alone with his thoughts. How did things go so wrong in his life? He had lost his first wife and his son—the two people he loved most, if truth were told. He felt isolated in the world. By himself. Single. Partnerless. Companionless. Deserted. Forsaken. And these other women who died, he had tried to date them all, and none of them had met the standards of Christine. He had even sought out women whose names started with the letter *C* in an attempt to replace Christine. But none of them had worked out, and he'd had to end each clingy relationship. He thought about Carli. He had even tried marriage again, but that ended in disaster.

He was in a fine mess. And he saw no way out.

A tray of food was delivered to him, and he ordered it away. He had no appetite.

He waited for his attorney to arrive.

He estimated forty-five minutes passed. They had taken his watch, so he couldn't be sure. Each minute seemed like an eternity. He couldn't leave, and he hated the feeling of being captured in a cell behind bars. His breathing became difficult, and he forced in air. He exhaled and forced in air again. He couldn't take this. He had to get out. He was being treated like a convicted felon without a trial.

At last Avery Lopez, his attorney, stood by his cell.

"Let me in, please," she ordered the guard.

She walked in and the door closed tightly behind her. She sat next to Stephen on the hard concrete bench.

"Talk to me," she said. "What have you done?"

29

IN BED THAT night, Guy and Claire faced each other.

"This has been an exhausting few weeks," he said. "But at last the bastard is getting his comeuppance. Justice does prevail!"

"There are still loose ends here," she said. "Things we don't have answers to. And these things bother me."

"Can we talk about them in the morning?" Guy asked. "I'm drained. And I know you have to be too."

Claire leaned over and kissed Guy.

"Sleep well, my beautiful bride."

"You too, my prince."

Guy was out like a light, but Claire spent the entire night wriggling. Something about the arrest of Stephen Fox didn't sit well with her. She couldn't turn off her mind, and she couldn't sleep. The way Maude Wakely had described Claire's attacker kept coming back to her. "He was not a tall man," she had said. But Stephen Fox was tall—over six feet. No one would describe Stephen in the words chosen by Maude. Something didn't fit. And what about Charlie? And Charlie and Estee together? And Natalie? Or someone who had escaped their scrutiny altogether? And did Captain Massey now assume Stephen Fox also killed his first wife, Christine? Pinning this all on Stephen Fox was a nice, neat package. Too nice and too neat for her liking. She needed more answers.

MORNING ARRIVED. Claire seemed troubled. Over breakfast, she shared her doubts with Guy.

"You might be reading too much into this, Claire," he said. "I think we have our perp."

"I don't think so."

They finished breakfast in silence.

Their strong personalities didn't always agree on things, and tension was building.

CAPTAIN MASSEY phoned Claire as soon as they walked into the office. He explained Stephen had been arrested and charged with the murders of the four women, including Charlotte. He told her additional charges might follow. And he informed he had called off the police guard at Caswell & Lombard, Private Investigation.

"I'm not sure arresting Stephen Fox was the right move, Captain," she said. "It may turn out to be, but there remain unanswered questions." She reviewed her thoughts with the captain.

JIN HAD three classes that morning, and he came to the office afterward, anxious to hear what had transpired following the meeting the day before. He listened carefully as Claire and Guy filled him in.

"Other charges might be added, as well," Guy said.

"Hmm," Jin said. "The puzzle is finally solved. Or is it?"

"What do you mean, Jin?" Guy asked.

"I don't know why I said that. Just an instinct, I guess. You both are always telling me that things are seldom as they seem. I'm just wondering if something is yet lingering right around the corner. Something we've missed while being swept away in the entangled details of these two cases."

He walked to his desk and sat down in his office chair. He was a student intern. Who was he to doubt an arrest decision? He would leave that to the professionals.

When Jin sorted through the day's mail, he found another letter, this one in handwriting, addressed to Claire Caswell. But it looked different from the first. He walked it over to her.

"Ms. Caswell, better take a look at this." He handed it to her.

"What is it, Claire?" Guy asked. He joined the two at her desk.

"Another mailing. This one is handwritten versus hand-printed. No return address again," she said. "And it's on tan, lined paper."

She slid on a pair of gloves and pulled out its contents. It was a one-page note. She read it aloud:

Look around! Pay attention! Refocus!

"Strange. What do you make of it?" Guy asked.

"I think someone is telling us that Stephen Fox is not the murderer," Claire said. "And I have a hunch I know who wrote this." She got up from her chair. "I'll be back."

Claire drove to the Porsche dealership. She parked and walked in. Natalie sat at the welcoming desk.

"Can we talk?" Claire asked.

Natalie looked around.

"Not here. Meet me at my apartment at noon." She scribbled her address on a notepaper for Claire's convenience. "Now go."

Claire immediately recognized the paper. It was the same paper the note she'd received in that day's mail was written on. Her suspicion was confirmed.

Claire returned to the office and waited.

At the appropriate time, she left to drive to Natalie's apartment. She entered the lot and parked. She walked into the entrance of the building and looked for the receptionist's name on the list of tenants. There it was: N. Hart. She buzzed. There was no answer.

The female investigator looked at her watch. It was exactly noon. She decided to wait in her car until Natalie arrived. Ten minutes passed. Then twenty. And thirty. Had something gone wrong? Was Natalie delayed and couldn't leave for some reason? Suddenly, Claire's inner voice pressed the alarm button. *Natalie needs help!*

Claire called Captain Massey as she sped back to the dealership.

"Send an officer to the Porsche dealership now! I'm on my way. Natalie Hart is in trouble!"

"You be careful, Ms. Caswell. I mean it," the captain pleaded. "Wait to go inside until my officer arrives. I want confirmation on that."

But Claire didn't answer. She had already hung up.

Minutes later, Claire arrived at the dealership. She parked and raced in through the double doors. Natalie was not sitting at the front desk. She looked around. The dealership was quiet, and she saw no one. She ran from office to office until she spotted a salesman in one talking to a client.

"Where is everyone?" she demanded. "Where is Natalie?"

"They're all in a staff meeting," the salesman said. "Everyone is in it, except for me. I'm with a client, as you can see. What's going on?"

"Where is the meeting?"

"At the end of the hall. Past Stephen Fox's office. Turn the corner. Past Jimmy Kesson's office. At the far, far end."

Claire didn't take time to thank the salesman. Instead she bolted down the hallway. Her instincts had become louder and louder. Natalie needed help. She found the meeting room at the far end of the dealership, ripped the door open, and barged into the room.

The sales staff members were seated in chairs around a long rectangular table. Jimmy Kesson was standing at the front of the room conducting the meeting. Claire's eyes scanned the attendees. Natalie was not there.

"I'm looking for Natalie," Claire said loudly. "Where is she?"

"I believe she went home sick," a salesperson said.

"When?" Claire asked.

"Around eleven this morning."

Claire fled from the room.

When she got to the lobby, a police officer from the Miami-Dade County Police Department had just arrived.

"Claire Caswell. Thanks for coming," she said. "We need to find Natalie Hart."

Claire ripped open one drawer after another at Natalie's desk until the investigator located a sheet listing cell and home numbers for all the staff. She found Natalie's cell and called it. No answer. She tried the home number listed for the receptionist. No answer. She frantically searched the top of the desk. There, near the telephone, she noticed a small folded note with the initials *CC* written on it. *Claire Caswell.* She grabbed it and opened it. The message was short, and it was in the same handwriting as on the note she had received in the mail earlier in the day. It simply said:

Ask Jimmy Kesson.

"Come with me," Claire said to the officer. "We need to find Jimmy Kesson. Now!"

She couldn't turn her mind off, and it began to spin frantically as she stepped up her pace. Details of the investigations galloped through her head as she walked. Suddenly, she realized she needed to rethink everything! That they'd been looking at it all wrong!

"We've got it all wrong!" she declared loudly. "All wrong!"

It was imperative to break through the entangled web they'd all been caught up in—the intertwining and complicated details that led them all astray. It was time to clear the slate and look at it all again.

The officer dutifully trailed behind Claire to the meeting room. When they arrived, the meeting was breaking up and the staff exiting the room. Claire frantically looked over the crowd for Jimmy. He wasn't there.

"Where's Jimmy?" she shouted.

"He just left through the back door," someone said.

"What kind of car does he drive?" she demanded.

"A Porsche Panamera—dark blue metallic."

She turned and spotted the rear exit door.

"Come with me," she implored the officer. "We must find him!"

The two ran out the door searching for Jimmy Kesson.

He was nowhere to be seen.

Claire darted back to the front entrance, the officer at her heels.

She looked outside in time to see Jimmy's car careening out of the lot.

"We have to stop him," Claire said.

"You ride with me," the officer said.

The two loaded into the squad car. Lights flashing and sirens blaring, the officer took off after the sporty dark blue car.

"I need backup," he said.

He made the call. He told the dispatcher where he was traveling and described the car he was chasing.

"We need to cut him off," he said.

"I'm on it, Officer. Sending backup as we speak."

FIFTEEN ADDITIONAL minutes passed before squad cars converged on the speeding sports car. Jimmy was forced to pull over.

He was yanked from his car at gunpoint.

"Where is she?" Claire demanded.

"Who? Where is who?" Jimmy asked.

"You know who. Natalie Hart."

"She went home sick."

"She's not at home. And I'll ask you one more time. Where is she?"

He refused to say another word.

"Arrest this man, officers," Claire said. "Bring him in."

Jimmy was cuffed and read his rights.

He was driven to the station and would be placed in a holding cell.

The officer returned Claire to her car at the dealership and handed her his card.

"I'll meet you at the station," she said.

Claire called Captain Massey and Guy on her drive there. She filled them both in, and they agreed to meet her.

Where was Natalie?

What had Jimmy done with her?

But he was at the dealership that morning.

Where could he have hidden her?

Claire knew Natalie would be terrified.

She had to find her fast.

Claire's instinct told her to look close. Jimmy would not have had the time to take Natalie anywhere. He had a staff meeting to conduct. If he was responsible for her going missing, then he had to make that happen at the dealership.

Then it hit her.

His car!

The trunk!

She got on her phone and called the officer who had assisted in his arrest.

"Where was Jimmy Kesson's car towed?"

"Where they're always towed, Ms. Caswell," the officer said. He gave her the address of the impound lot.

"I'm going there first. Please tell Captain Massey and Gaston Lombard when they arrive."

Claire sped to the towing facility and made it there in record time.

She held her breath and prayed that if Natalie were in the trunk she would be okay.

She burst through the front door and explained to the man on duty what she needed. She flashed her identification.

"Follow me," he said. "That car just came in." He grabbed the keys.

The man led Claire to the Porsche.

"Nice car," he said.

"Open the trunk," she said.

The man pressed the open-trunk feature on the key remote.

The trunk popped open. Claire lifted it up and looked inside.

She saw a black blanket covering something and knew what might be under it. She yanked it off.

There was Natalie.

On her side and crunched tightly into a fetal position.

Her wrists and ankles had been bound and her mouth gagged.

Terror showed in her chocolate-brown eyes.

"Natalie, you're safe," Claire said. "We're here. You're going to be okay."

Claire and the lot employee removed her bindings and gag and carefully helped her from the trunk.

Natalie started to cry. And she couldn't stop.

"I was out back, doing my weekly inventory. Someone hit me . . . on the back of my head . . . and the next thing I knew, I was waking up in darkness, all tied up and with a rag in my mouth."

She could hardly talk.

"Yesterday I saw Jimmy mixing a smoothie for a client, and it struck me—he was the one who made a smoothie for Charlotte Truman on the day she died. This morning, I got the courage to confront him. I asked him if he thought that these deaths might have something to do with the smoothies, and he denied it. He got very angry. Claire, I just know it was him who attacked me . . ."

30

THINGS WERE ABOUT to move at top speed. As Claire drove to the police station, her mind rapidly sorted through all the variables and evidence to get a clear picture. The puzzle parts were fitting together at last. When she arrived, she asked to see Stephen Fox. She signed in as a visitor for the inmate and flashed her identification. She was his only visitor for the day and was allowed in without question.

She approached his cell and asked the guard to let her in.

"What are *you* doing here?" he asked. "You're the one who put me in this cage!"

"Talk to me, Stephen," Claire said. "I need answers."

He looked at her in disbelief.

"My attorney is not present. You know I won't talk to you unless my attorney is here."

"I know, but I need answers now. I believe it will help your case and maybe even get you out of here. You can talk to me if you agree to without the presence of your attorney. Do you agree to that?"

"Okay," he said. "Yes."

The guard standing outside the cell acknowledged that he heard Stephen's consent.

"Tell me about the secret garden," she said. "Tell me everything."

"It was a special place for Christine and Eric," he said. "The two bonded there. She taught him about the different plants, and he loved to watch them grow. It was something they did together. It was hidden away from the rest of the world. They kept it in beautiful condition—free of weeds, watered. Eric had behavioral problems that seemed to get worse and worse as he aged, but in the garden, he was better."

"Go on," she said.

"When they were not in the garden, the two argued incessantly. She didn't understand Eric's problems, and neither did I, for that matter. Eventually, we sent him away for a time to a place we thought could help him. He hated us for doing that, but he specifically blamed Christine."

"Tell me about her death," Claire said. "Was Eric back home when she died?"

"Yes. He had been home a couple of weeks. Christine got sick. Confused. She said she couldn't see well, and her speech slurred. She had headaches. And her balance seemed off. She thought she had a bad case of the flu. She stayed in bed for two full days."

"And then what happened?" Claire asked.

"She died." He hung his head. "If only I could turn back time, I'd have rushed her to the hospital or called an ambulance. But we all thought it was a case of the flu that would pass."

"I'm sorry," Claire said. "I can't imagine."

"The medical examiner never did pinpoint the cause of her

death," he said. "I always thought Eric had poisoned her. I never suggested it to the police because he was my son. I had to protect him. I lived with that thought for months, hating Eric for what I thought he'd done. I kept him an arm's length away, refusing to get close. I regret that now."

"Are you familiar with the belladonna plant?" Claire asked.

"It's in the secret garden. I learned about it from Eric. It's highly poisonous."

"The garden is in perfect shape to this day. Do you know how that can be? The present owners of the property never go behind the fence. They abandoned the garden completely after moving in."

"I have the answer. After we sold the house and moved out, Eric told me one day that he would sneak onto the property during the dead of night, unlock the padlock, and go inside the fenced area. You see, he kept one key to the padlock and the new owners were given the other. He refused to give it up. In fact, I think he polished it every day. The purchasers never knew there were two. He said he honored his mother by continuing to take care of it. It was all that remained to remind him of her. He loved that garden."

Stephen dropped his head and wept.

"He had his key to the padlock in a leather pouch in his pocket when he died," Claire said.

"Yes. He always had it with him."

"When did Eric find out about the belladonna plant? That is was poisonous?"

"A few months after Christine's death," Stephen said. "Eric called me one day at work, out of the blue, to let me know that he thought he'd figured out what killed his mother. He thought she had eaten some berries from the plant, thinking they were blueberries. He had done research on the plant. He told me about the symptoms. It made sense and explained her sickness the days before she died. I knew in my heart he was right. The berries had poisoned her. I felt a huge burden lifted because for the first time I knew Eric had not killed her. I finally admitted to him why I had been so angry with him since her death. Do you know what he said?"

"What?"

"He told me he thought *I* had killed her. Christine and I had been fighting and had agreed to divorce. He thought I was responsible for her death. That's why he was so angry with me. We thought each other had intentionally caused her death. We wasted time hating each other. What a horrible misunderstanding on both our parts. Eric was damaged beyond repair. The relationship between us had been so strained that even after the revelation it never healed." Stephen paused. "I'm convinced he took his life the same way his mother had died—by eating berries from the belladonna plant. In some strange way, that none of us could ever understand, I think his self-induced poisoning gave him the peace he was seeking."

Tears rolled down Stephen's cheeks, and he wiped them away.

"Did you ever go to the secret garden again after you sold the house?"

"No."

"Did you tell anyone else about it? Think hard. This is important," Claire said.

"Not that I recall."

"Did you ever mention that conversation you had with Eric to anyone else?"

He let his memory take him back. Two long minutes passed.

"I think I did. Jim Kesson was in my office when that call came in. I think I told him about it."

"Did you tell Jimmy Kesson the name of the poisonous plant in the secret garden?"

"Yes, I believe I did. And I recall the two of us even looked it up on the Internet—on my office computer—to see what the plant looked like." Stephen stared at Claire without blinking. "It's all coming back to me now."

"Does Jimmy Kesson like you?"

"What?"

"Do you get along well with Jimmy Kesson?"

"In truth, I think he hates me. But he comes and sits with me in my office much of the time. He likes to shoot the breeze and play cards. Actually, I always thought he was spying on me. Trying to study me and be like me."

"Why does he hate you?"

"Because I have received each and every promotion he thought belonged to him. He is always passed over. He has a personality problem, and the higher-ups know that. He sells cars, all right, but they would never promote him beyond that."

"A final question, Stephen. Why were you following me?"

"I needed to know how the investigation was progressing. I apologize if my actions scared you."

Claire thanked Stephen and left his cell.

"Hold tight," she said, walking away. "I know what happened."

CLAIRE FOUND Captain Massey.

"Go out to the dealership, will you? Bring a search warrant and take a look through Jimmy Kesson's desk." Together they reviewed what he should look for.

She walked to the interview room.

Guy, a police officer, and Jimmy Kesson were seated around the table. The statement was being recorded, and the interview was newly under way.

Claire entered the room and sat down.

Guy announced for the record that private investigator Claire Caswell had just entered the room. The interview continued.

"Ms. Caswell, do you have any questions for the subject?" Guy asked.

"I do. Mr. Kesson, describe your relationship with Stephen Fox."

"My relationship with Stephen Fox?"

"Yes. How do the two of you get along?"

"Okay, I guess. We work together."

"Let's go beyond that," she said. "Do you like the man? What do you think of his work skills?"

"I think he's a tall, good-looking man. He gets his way through charm and manipulation."

"You started working at the dealership long before Stephen came on board, correct?"

"Yeah. Years before he ever got there."

"And he's been promoted several times over you? Isn't that the case?"

"Dammit. Yes. I deserved those promotions and the raises. Not him. But he always got them."

Claire continued pushing his buttons.

"I'd be mad if that happened to me," she said. "I'd hate him. I'd hate him so much I'd—"

"I was mad. I was furious! I do hate him! I deserved what he got. I taught him everything he knows when it comes to cars—specifically Porsches. He came to me with all his questions. He still does. I'm the one with the knowledge and the know-how. Not him."

"And he was the one the ladies liked, right?"

"You're making my blood boil!" Jimmy said. "He went after everyone in a skirt. Especially the rich clients."

Claire looked raptly at Jimmy without saying a word. Sweat dripped from his brow. She continued her piercing gaze.

"I think I know how you did it," she said. "I think I know exactly how you pulled it off."

"Did what?"

"I'm guessing you retrieved the poisonous berries from the fenced area of Stephen's former yard when you heard about their deadly qualities from Stephen. Then you concocted smoothies for the female victims using the deadly berries. Am I right? After all, they're sweet. You may have even added sugar to the mixture. You gave the smoothies to the women when they were visiting Stephen at the dealership."

Jimmy stared at the female investigator with a strange look on his face.

"In each case, you bided your time until the opportunity was absolutely perfect."

His eyes widened.

"And I'm going to guess the smoothies were so thick with the poisonous berries that they acted very quickly on the women. I think that is why Charlotte Truman started to drive home in the middle of the day instead of going back to work. She started to feel horribly ill after sipping down the drink." Claire paused. "She never made it home."

Silence filled the room.

Claire pushed herself up from the table and began to pace several feet away from Jimmy, hands on her hips, before jolting back around to face him head on. She walked to his chair and lowered her face to within inches of his, staring him squarely in the eyes. "Charlotte Truman was my friend, you bastard! You killed her!"

He refused to look at Claire.

"And you tinkered with the driver's seat belt in each case, too, so that it would lock in place the next time it was used," she said. "You played with the accelerator pedal. And you disabled the driver's side airbag. After all, you would know just how to do these things quickly. You told us yourself; you're the one with all the knowledge about cars, specifically Porsches. How am I doing, Jimmy?"

He did not respond.

"And I'm guessing you're the one who sent me the threatening note."

Jimmy looked pasty and drained.

"I have two final questions," Claire said. "First, do you own a purple skullcap? And second, do you own a ladder?"

His face turned a pale shade of gray.

"I want an attorney," he muttered.

JIMMY WAS booked, fingerprinted, and photographed. Before he was locked in a cell, Claire requested they take his palm prints.

CAPTAIN MASSEY phoned Claire.

"I'm out at the dealership," he said. "I searched Jimmy Kesson's desk. I found something, Ms. Caswell. In the back of a file cabinet drawer, I found a color picture of the belladonna plant. I bagged it as evidence. I'm going to guess Jimmy Kesson's prints are all over it. I'm bringing it in. Oh, and we located a used black Jeep Wrangler on a far back lot. It has a damaged front bumper. My man is lifting prints from the door handle and the steering wheel as we speak."

"Good work, Captain," Claire said. She filled him in on her talk with Stephen and on the interview with Jimmy Kesson.

In no time, the captain appeared carrying a sealed plastic bag containing the evidence he found in Kesson's desk and also another bag holding the fingerprints his forensic investigator lifted from the Jeep Wrangler.

"Take some prints off this paper," he ordered a crime lab tech. "Compare them to Kesson's. And compare his palm print to what was lifted from the board at the Caswell & Lombard firm. Also compare the prints just lifted from the door handle and the steering wheel to Kesson's. Do it stat."

Claire and Guy waited impatiently for the results. Guy called Jin to let him know where they were, and minutes later he appeared at the station. The investigators brought him up to date on all that had happened.

The captain came to deliver the announcement an hour later.

"We have a match on all four! Kesson's fingerprints are on the paper, on the door handle and the steering wheel of the black Jeep, and his palm print is a perfect match to the one lifted from your evidence board. I'd say we finally have our killer. The right one."

"And all because of jealousy," Claire said. "Jealousy that turned to envy and envy that turned to resentment. The resentment grew in Jimmy by stages—until it turned to outright hatred. Stephen told Jimmy about the secret garden and the poisonous plant one day after receiving a call from Eric. And that was all Jimmy needed to hear. He devised an elaborate ploy to finger Stephen for the deaths of women customers at the dealership, and he acted on his plan. He brought a ladder to the Coral Gables property and collected the poisonous berries and leaves from the plant. I recall seeing marks from a ladder in the lawn adjacent to the fence. He spaced out the murders to make it look like the perpetrator was trying to avoid being caught. I'm guessing Jimmy made drinks using the deadly berries for each of the victims. In his mind, Jimmy believed he'd get rid of Stephen once and for all. Jimmy would frame Stephen for the murders of the female clients using poison obtained from Stephen's former property. Eventually, he'd get caught and end up behind bars. Then, at last, Jimmy could take his proper place at the dealership. The one he so deserved."

"Unbelievable!" Captain Massey said.

"Unbelievable!" Guy parroted.

"Oh, and, Captain, if you send some officers to Jimmy's house with a warrant, my guess is you'll find more of the poisonous mixture he concocted—probably in the freezer," Claire said. "No doubt in preparation for the next victim."

"I'll do it now."

"And look in his garage for a ladder."

"But then what about Charlie McDermott?" Jin asked. "Doesn't he fit into this somehow?"

"It was pure coincidence that Charlie happened to be involved with Stephen, Roise, and Natalie. He had absolutely nothing to do with the death of Charlotte or the other female victims," Claire said. "I realize now that we overlooked the simplest answer because we all became entangled in the sea of other details. It was never as complicated as we thought."

"So Charlie is a sincere man with good intentions?" Jin asked.

"Looks that way," Guy said.

"And he really loves Estee?" Jin asked.

"I believe he does," Claire said.

STEPHEN FOX was released from his cell. His belongings and clothing were returned to him after each item was carefully matched to the list of items taken from him at the time he was booked. He was asked to sign a document confirming his receipt, and then he quickly changed out of his orange jumpsuit. Attorney Lopez arrived to drive him home.

In an adjacent room, Jimmy Kesson was changing into an orange jumpsuit. He would be tried for the murders of Catherine Hanker,

Cindy Bane, Camille Sullivan, and Charlotte Truman, as well as for the assault, battery, and attempted murder of Claire Caswell. Also for the kidnapping of Natalie Hart with intent to do harm. He faced a long future in prison.

Stephen walked over to Claire on his way out.

"Thank you," he said.

She nodded.

BACK AT the office, Claire phoned Mary Katz, Rolf Esteman, and the aunt of Catherine Hanker to fill them in on the latest developments. At last, at long last, they could have some closure to the deaths of the three women.

CAPTAIN MASSEY called later in the day to inform the investigators that his officers had found both leaves and berries—in individually sealed plastic bags, both hidden in separate tin cans, in two separate freezers—on Kesson's property. "They will be tested, of course, but we know what they are. We also found an old blender in his garage. Probably used to blend up the berries. We're testing that too."

CLAIRE DROVE to Estee's house the following day. When she arrived, she observed Charlie's green Karmann Ghia parked out front. She walked to the front door and knocked. Estee answered the door and invited her in.

"Charlie is here," Estee said. "Come talk to us. I'll make tea." She hesitated at the doorway and looked Claire squarely in the eyes. "Claire, I'm not angry with you. I understand how both your parents and you thought things looked somewhat suspicious with Charlie. I know you were all concerned for me and that you were just being cautious. You were looking out for me, and I appreciate it. I really do. But I love him. You have nothing to worry about." She smiled sweetly and gave Claire a hug.

Estee disappeared into the kitchen to prepare hot tea, and Claire took a seat in the living room.

Claire was alone with Charlie.

"We love each other," Charlie said. "I hope you realize that now. She brings a light to my life that I've never experienced before."

"I have some remaining questions, Charlie," Claire said.

"Let me give you the answers. I tried to hightail it from Miami because I thought I was being targeted for those murders due to my past record," he said. "And the pearls I gave Estee, I inherited from my mother when she died. Estee insisted I list my name as the beneficiary on the insurance policy in case they were ever stolen. It was something the two of us discussed beforehand." He thought for a moment. "What else? Roise let me name his boat, and I selected the *Black Pearl* to honor my mother, as she loved her pearls. And the card playing I do with my buddies is just for fun. Nothing else." He hesitated.

"What about Natalie?" Claire asked.

"I was about to get to Natalie. I came clean with Estee about the one-night stand I had with Natalie and the resulting pregnancy. It happened before I met Estee. The envelope I offered Natalie in her parking lot that day was a packet of money to help with the baby. She wouldn't accept it, though. She wants to raise this child on her own. I told her I'd be there for whatever the child needs. We have a lot of things to still work out, and Estee wants to be part of it all."

Estee appeared with a tray holding cups of steaming tea. The three sipped and talked, and any remaining bad feelings melted away.

THE LAB investigators soon concluded that the dark fragments Claire found at the scene of Charlotte's car crash—that tested as belladonna—were actually partial bits of whole belladonna berries not totally pulverized by Jimmy's blender.

Claire knew that without her tireless sleuthing, and without finding those bits of the deadly berries at Charlotte's crash site, the series of murders would never have come to light, and Charlotte's death may have remained a mystery forever.

CLAIRE DROVE to the cemetery where Charlotte was buried.

"We know what happened to you, my friend. Jimmy Kesson, not Stephen Fox, was responsible for taking your life. He'll spend the rest of his days locked away in prison."

She placed a handful of white daisies on the headstone.

Rest in peace, dear Charlotte. I will always miss you.

31

CLAIRE AND GUY sat at a white cloth-covered table at the famous Joe's Stone Crab restaurant in south Miami Beach. It was a favorite of both the investigators. And after closing the cases, a great seafood dinner was just what they craved. It had been some time since either of them had been there.

The place was packed, as always, and the happy chatter of diners all around them filled the air. But neither investigator noticed the hubbub. They only saw each other. Everything else seemed to fade into the background.

They ordered Manhattan clam chowder to start and an à la carte platter of jumbo stone crab claws—served chilled and cracked, with a mustard sauce for dipping—to share. They also ordered sides of Lyonnaise potatoes and grilled asparagus. A bread basket was delivered to the table.

"Yum, yum, and yum!" Claire exclaimed, diving in.

"We deserve this," Guy said.

They didn't want the evening to come to an end, so they ordered coffees and a piece of Joe's famous key lime pie for dessert.

After they finished, Guy reached over to hold Claire's hands.

"You know, we never did go on a honeymoon. We didn't have the luxury of getting away when we got married. Work didn't allow it."

"And?" She guessed where this was going.

"And I think we should do it now before we get embroiled in our next big case. I'm thinking two glorious weeks away at any place of your liking."

"Actually, that sounds heavenly."

"Where would you like to go, my beauty?"

"Hmm. Let me think."

For jealousy makes a man furious,
and he will not spare when he takes revenge.

Proverbs 6:34 ESV

Ploy:

A ruse, tactic, move, device, stratagem, scheme, trick, gambit, maneuver, dodge, subterfuge, wile, or cunning. A calculated and clever plan or action designed to turn a situation to one's own advantage.